Mary Higgins Clark

Silent Night

All Through the Night

Simon & Schuster

New York   London   Toronto   Sydney   Singapore

SIMON & SCHUSTER
Rockefeller Center
1230 Avenue of the Americas
New York, NY 10020

These titles were previously published individually.

SIMON & SCHUSTER and colophon are registered trademarks
of Simon & Schuster, Inc.

For information regarding special discounts for bulk purchases,
please contact Simon & Schuster Special Sales at
1-800-456-6798 or business@simonandschuster.com

Manufactured in the United States of America

1   3   5   7   9   10   8   6   4   2

Library of Congress Cataloging-in-Publication Data is available.

ISBN 0-7432-4691-8

Contents

Silent Night

Acknowledgments

This story began when my editors, Michael V. Korda and Chuck Adams, over dinner started musing about the possibility of a suspense story set on Christmas Eve in Manhattan. I became intrigued.

Many thanks for that initial discussion and all the wonderful help along the way, Michael and Chuck.

My agent, Eugene Winick, and my publicist, Lisl Cade, offered constant support and help. *Merci* and *grazie,* Gene and Lisl.

And finally many thanks to the readers who are kind enough to look forward to my books. I wish all of you a blessed, happy, and safe holiday season.

For Joan Murchison Broad,
and in memory of Col. Richard L. Broad,
with love and thanks for all the
marvelous times we shared.

St. Christopher, patron of travelers,
pray for us, and protect us from evil.

1

It was Christmas Eve in New York City. The cab slowly made its way down Fifth Avenue. It was nearly five o'clock. The traffic was heavy, and the sidewalks were jammed with last-minute Christmas shoppers, homebound office workers, and tourists anxious to glimpse the elaborately trimmed store windows and the fabled Rockefeller Center Christmas tree.

It was already dark, and the sky was becoming heavy with clouds, an apparent confirmation of the forecast for a white Christmas. But the blinking lights, the sounds of carols, the ringing bells of sidewalk Santas, and the generally jolly mood of the crowd gave an appropriately festive Christmas Eve atmosphere to the famous thoroughfare.

Catherine Dornan sat bolt upright in the back of the cab, her arms around the shoulders of her two small sons. By the rigidity she felt in their bodies, she knew her mother had been right. Ten-year-old Michael's surliness and seven-year-old Brian's silence were sure signs that both boys were intensely worried about their dad.

Earlier that afternoon when she had called her mother from the hospital, still sobbing despite the fact that Spence Crowley, her husband's old friend and doctor, assured her that Tom had come through the operation better than expected, and even suggested that the boys visit him at seven o'clock that night, her mother had spoken to her firmly: "Catherine, you've got to pull yourself together," she had said. "The boys are so upset, and you're not helping. I think it would be a good idea if you tried to divert them for a little while. Take them down to Rockefeller Center to see the tree, then out to dinner. Seeing you so worried has practically convinced them that Tom will die."

This isn't supposed to be happening, Catherine thought. With every fiber of her being she wanted to undo the last ten days, starting with that terrible moment when the phone rang and the call came from St. Mary's Hospital. "Catherine, can you come right over? Tom collapsed while he was making his rounds."

Her immediate impression had been that there had to be a mistake. Lean, athletic, thirty-eight-year-old men don't collapse. And Tom always joked that pediatricians had birthright immunization to all the viruses and germs that arrived with their patients.

But Tom didn't have immunization from the leukemia that necessitated immediate removal of his grossly enlarged spleen. At the hospital they told her that he must have been ignoring warning signs for months. And I was too stupid to notice, Catherine thought as she tried to keep her lip from quivering.

She glanced out the window and saw that they were passing the Plaza Hotel. Eleven years ago, on her twenty-third birthday, they'd had their wedding reception at the Plaza. Brides are supposed to be nervous, she thought. I wasn't. I practically ran up the aisle.

Ten days later they'd celebrated little Christmas in Omaha, where Tom had accepted an appointment in the prestigious pediatrics unit of the hospital. We bought that crazy artificial tree in the clearance sale, she thought, remembering how Tom had held it up and said, "Attention Kmart shoppers . . ."

This year, the tree they'd selected so carefully was still in the garage, its branches roped together. They'd decided to come to New York for the surgery. Tom's best friend, Spence Crowley, was now a prominent surgeon at Sloan-Kettering.

Catherine winced at the thought of how upset she'd been when she was finally allowed to see Tom.

The cab pulled over to the curb. "Okay, here, lady?"

"Yes, fine," Catherine said, forcing herself to sound cheerful as she pulled out her wallet. "Dad and I brought you guys down here on Christmas Eve five years ago. Brian, I know you were too small, but Michael, do you remember?"

"Yes," Michael said shortly as he tugged at the handle on the door. He watched as Catherine peeled a five from the wad of bills in her wallet. "How come you have so much money, Mom?"

"When Dad was admitted to the hospital yesterday, they made me take everything he had in his billfold except a few dollars. I should have sorted it out when I got back to Gran's."

She followed Michael out onto the sidewalk and held the door open for Brian. They were in front of Saks, near the corner of Forty-ninth Street and Fifth Avenue. Orderly lines of spectators were patiently waiting to get a close-up look at the Christmas window display. Catherine steered her sons to the back of the line. "Let's see the windows, then we'll go across the street and get a better look at the tree."

Brian sighed heavily. This was some Christmas! He hated standing in line—for anything. He decided to play the game he always played when he wanted time to pass quickly. He would pretend he was already where he wanted to be, and tonight that was in his dad's room in the hospital. He could hardly wait to see his dad, to give him the present his grandmother had said would make him get well.

Brian was so intent on getting on with the evening that when it was finally their turn to get up close to the windows, he moved quickly, barely noticing the scenes of whirling snowflakes and dolls and elves and animals dancing and singing. He was glad when they finally were off the line.

Then, as they started to make their way to the corner to cross the avenue, he saw that a guy with a violin was about to start playing and people were gathering around him. The air suddenly was filled with the sound of "Silent Night," and people began singing.

Catherine turned back from the curb. "Wait, let's listen for a few minutes," she said to the boys.

Brian could hear the catch in her throat and knew that she was trying not to cry. He'd hardly ever seen Mom cry until that morning last week when someone phoned from the hospital and said Dad was real sick.

·   ·   ·

Cally walked slowly down Fifth Avenue. It was a little after five, and she was surrounded by crowds of last-minute shoppers, their arms filled with packages. There was a time when she might have shared their excitement, but today all she felt was achingly tired. Work had been so difficult. During the Christmas holidays people wanted to be home, so most of the patients in the hospital had been either depressed or difficult. Their bleak expressions reminded her vividly of her own depression over the last two Christmases, both of them spent in the Bedford correctional facility for women.

She passed St. Patrick's Cathedral, hesitating only a moment as a memory came back to her of her grandmother taking her and her brother Jimmy there to see the crèche. But that was twenty years ago; she had been ten, and he was six. She wished fleetingly she could go back to that time, change things, keep the bad things from happening, keep Jimmy from becoming what he was now.

Even to *think* his name was enough to send waves of fear coursing through her body. Dear God, make him leave me alone, she prayed. Early this morning, with Gigi clinging to her, she had answered the angry pounding on her door to find Detective Shore and another officer who said he was Detective Levy standing in the dingy hallway of her apartment building on East Tenth Street and Avenue B.

"Cally, you putting up your brother again?" Shore's eyes had searched the room behind her for signs of his presence.

The question was Cally's first indication that Jimmy had managed to escape from Riker's Island prison.

"The charge is attempted murder of a prison guard," the detective told her, bitterness filling his voice. "The guard is in critical condition. Your brother shot him and took his uniform. This time you'll spend a lot more than fifteen months in prison if you help Jimmy to escape. Accessory after the fact the second time around, when you're talking attempted murder—or murder—of a law officer. Cally, they'll throw the book at you."

"I've never forgiven myself for giving Jimmy money last time," Cally had said quietly.

"Sure. And the keys to your car," he reminded her. "Cally, I warn you. Don't help him *this* time."

"I won't. You can be sure of that. And I did not know what he had done before." She'd watched as their eyes again shifted past her. "Go ahead," she had cried. "Look around. He isn't here. And if you want to put a tap on my phone, do that, too. I want you to hear me tell Jimmy to turn himself in. Because that's all I'd have to say to him."

But surely Jimmy *won't* find me, she prayed as she threaded her way through the crowd of shoppers and sightseers. Not this time. After she had served her prison sentence, she took Gigi from the foster home. The social worker had located the tiny apartment on East Tenth Street and gotten her the job as a nurse's aide at St. Luke's–Roosevelt Hospital. This would be her first Christmas with Gigi in two years! If only she had been able to afford a few decent presents for her, she thought. A four-year-old kid should have her own new doll's carriage, not the battered hand-me-down Cally'd been forced to get for her. The coverlet and pillow she had bought wouldn't hide the shabbiness of the carriage. But maybe she could find the guy who was selling dolls on the street around here last week. They were only eight dollars, and she remembered that there was even one that looked like Gigi.

She hadn't had enough money with her that day, but the

guy said he'd be on Fifth Avenue between Fifty-seventh and Forty-seventh Streets on Christmas Eve, so she had to find him. O God, she prayed, let them arrest Jimmy before he hurts anyone else. There's something wrong with him. There always has been.

Ahead of her, people were singing "Silent Night." As she got closer, though, she realized that they weren't actually carolers, just a crowd around a street violinist who was playing Christmas tunes.

". . . Holy infant, so tender and mild . . ."
Brian did not join in the singing, even though "Silent Night" was his favorite and at home in Omaha he was a member of his church's children's choir. He wished he was there now, not in New York, and that they were getting ready to trim the Christmas tree in their own living room, and everything was the way it had been.

He liked New York and always looked forward to the summer visits with his grandmother. He had fun then. But he didn't like this kind of visit. Not on Christmas Eve, with Dad in the hospital and Mom so sad and his brother bossing him around, even though Michael was only three years older.

Brian stuck his hands in the pockets of his jacket. They felt cold even though he had on his mittens. He looked impatiently at the giant Christmas tree across the street, on the other side of the skating rink. He knew that in a minute his mother was going to say, "All right. Now let's get a good look at the tree."

It was so tall, and the lights on it were so bright, and there was a big star on top of it. But Brian didn't care about that now, or about the windows they had just seen. He didn't want to listen to the guy playing the violin, either, and he didn't feel like standing here.

They were wasting time. He wanted to get to the hospital and watch Mom give Dad the big St. Christopher medal that had saved Grandpa's life when he was a soldier in World War II. Grandpa had worn it all through the war, and it even had a dent in it where a bullet had hit it.

Gran had asked Mom to give it to Dad, and even though she had almost laughed, Mom had promised but said, "Oh, Mother, Christopher was only a myth. He's not considered a saint anymore, and the only people he helped were the ones who sold the medals everybody used to stick on dashboards."

Gran had said, "Catherine, your father believed it helped him get through some terrible battles, and that is all that matters. He believed and so do I. Please give it to Tom and have faith."

Brian felt impatient with his mother. If Gran believed that Dad was going to get better if he got the medal, then his mom had to give it to him. He was positive Gran was right.

"*. . . sleep in heavenly peace.*" The violin stopped playing, and a woman who had been leading the singing held out a basket. Brian watched as people began to drop coins and dollar bills into it.

His mother pulled her wallet out of her shoulder bag and took out two one-dollar bills. "Michael, Brian, here. Put these in the basket."

Michael grabbed his dollar and tried to push his way through the crowd. Brian started to follow him, then noticed that his mother's wallet hadn't gone all the way down into her shoulder bag when she had put it back. As he watched, he saw the wallet fall to the ground.

He turned back to retrieve it, but before he could pick it up, a hand reached down and grabbed it. Brian saw that the hand belonged to a thin woman with a dark raincoat and a long ponytail.

"*Mom!*" he said urgently, but everyone was singing again, and she didn't turn her head. The woman who had taken the wallet began to slip through the crowd. Instinctively, Brian began to follow her, afraid to lose sight of her. He turned back to call out to his mother again, but she was singing along now, too, "*God rest you merry, gentlemen . . .*" Everyone was singing so loud he knew she couldn't hear him.

For an instant, Brian hesitated as he glanced over his shoulder at his mother. Should he run back and get her? But he thought again about the medal that would make his father better; it was in the wallet, and he couldn't let it get stolen.

The woman was already turning the corner. He raced to catch up with her.

Why did I pick it up? Cally thought frantically as she rushed east on Forty-eighth Street toward Madison Avenue. She had abandoned her plan of walking down Fifth Avenue to find the peddler with the dolls. Instead, she headed toward the Lexington Avenue subway. She knew it would be quicker to go up to Fifty-first Street for the train, but the wallet felt like a hot brick in her pocket, and it seemed to her that everywhere she turned everyone was looking at her accusingly. Grand Central Station would be mobbed. She would get the train there. It was a safer place to go.

A squad car passed her as she turned right and crossed the street. Despite the cold, she had begun to perspire.

It probably belonged to that woman with the little boys. It was on the ground next to her. In her mind, Cally replayed the moment when she had taken in the slim young woman in the rose-colored all-weather coat that she could see was fur-lined from the turned-back sleeves. The coat obviously was expensive, as were the woman's shoulder bag and boots; the dark hair that came to the collar of her coat was shiny. She didn't look like she could have a care in the world.

Cally had thought, I wish I looked like that. She's about my age and my size and we have almost the same color hair. Well, maybe by next year I can afford pretty clothes for Gigi and me.

Then she'd turned her head to catch a glimpse of the Saks windows. So I didn't see her drop the wallet, she thought. But as she passed the woman, she'd felt her foot kick something and she'd looked down and seen it lying there.

Why didn't I just ask if it was hers? Cally agonized. But in that instant, she'd remembered how years ago, Grandma had come home one day, embarrassed and upset. She'd found a wallet on the street and opened it and saw the name and address of the owner. She'd walked three blocks to return it even though by then her arthritis was so bad that every step hurt.

The woman who owned it had looked through it and said that a twenty-dollar bill was missing.

Grandma had been so upset. "She practically accused me of being a thief."

That memory had flooded Cally the minute she touched the wallet. Suppose it did belong to the lady in the rose coat and she thought Cally had picked her pocket or taken money out of it? Suppose a policeman was called? They'd find out she was on probation. They wouldn't believe her any more than they'd believed her when she lent Jimmy money and her car because he'd told her if he didn't get out of town right away, a guy in another street gang was going to kill him.

Oh God, why didn't I just leave the wallet there? she thought. She considered tossing it in the nearest mailbox. She couldn't risk that. There were too many undercover cops around midtown during the holidays. Suppose one of them saw her and asked what she was doing? No, she'd get home right away. Aika, who minded Gigi along with her own grandchildren after the day-care center closed, would be bringing her home. It was getting late.

I'll put the wallet in an envelope addressed to whoever's name is in it and drop it in the mailbox later, Cally decided. That's all I can do.

Cally reached Grand Central Station. As she had hoped, it was mobbed with people rushing in all directions to trains and subways, hurrying home for Christmas. She shouldered her way across the main terminal, finally making it down the steps to the entrance to the Lexington Avenue subway.

As she dropped a token in the slot and hurried for the express train to Fourteenth Street, she was unaware of the small boy who had slipped under a turnstile and was dogging her footsteps.

2

"God rest you merry, gentlemen, let nothing you dismay . . ." The familiar words seemed to taunt Catherine, reminding her of the forces that threatened the happily complacent life she had assumed would be hers forever. Her husband was in the hospital with leukemia. His enlarged spleen had been removed this morning as a precaution against it rupturing, and while it was too early to tell for sure, he seemed to be doing well. Still, she could not escape the fear that he was not going to live, and the thought of life without him was almost paralyzing.

Why didn't I realize Tom was getting sick? she agonized. She remembered how only two weeks ago, when she'd asked him to take groceries from the car, he'd reached into the trunk for the heaviest bag, hesitated, then winced as he picked it up.

She'd laughed at him. "Play golf yesterday. Act like an old man today. Some athlete."

"Where's Brian?" Michael asked as he returned from dropping the dollar in the singer's basket.

Startled from her thoughts, Catherine looked down at her son. "Brian?" she said blankly. "He's right here." She glanced down at her side, and then her eyes scanned the area. "He had a dollar. Didn't he go with you to give it to the singer?"

"No," Michael said gruffly. "He probably kept it instead. He's a dork."

"Stop it," Catherine said. She looked around, suddenly alarmed. "Brian," she called "Brian." The carol was over, the crowd dispersing. Where was Brian? He wouldn't just walk away, surely. *"Brian,"* she called out again, this time loudly, alarm clear in her voice.

A few people turned and looked at her curiously. "A little boy," she said, becoming frightened. "He's wearing a dark blue ski jacket and a red cap. Did anyone see where he went?"

She watched as heads shook, as eyes looked around, wanting to help. A woman pointed behind them to the lines of people waiting to see the Saks windows. "Maybe he went there?" she said in a heavy accent.

"How about the tree? Would he have crossed the street to get up close to it?" another woman suggested.

"Maybe the cathedral," someone volunteered.

"No. No, Brian wouldn't do that. We're going to visit his father. Brian can't wait to see him." As she said the words, Catherine knew that something was terribly wrong. She felt the tears that now came so easily rising behind her eyes. She fumbled in her bag for a handkerchief and realized something was missing: the familiar bulk of her wallet.

"Oh my God," she said. "My wallet's gone."

"Mom!" And now Michael lost the surly look that had become his way of disguising the worry about his father. He was suddenly a scared ten-year-old. "Mom. Do you think Brian was kidnapped?"

"How could he be? Nobody could just drag him off. That's impossible." Catherine felt her legs were turning to rubber. "Call the police," she cried. "My little boy is missing."

The station was crowded. Hundreds of people were rushing in every direction. There were Christmas decorations all over the place. It was noisy, too. Sounds of all kinds echoed through the big space, bouncing off the ceiling high above him. A man with his arm full of packages bumped a sharp elbow into Brian's ear. "Sorry, kid."

He was having trouble keeping up with the woman who had his mom's wallet. He kept losing sight of her. He struggled to get around a family with a couple of kids who were blocking his way. He got past them, but bumped into a lady who glared down at him. "Be careful," she snapped.

"I'm sorry," Brian said politely, looking up at her. In that second he almost lost the woman he was following, catching up to her again as she went down a staircase and hurried through a long corridor that led to a subway station. When she went through a turnstile, he slipped under the next one and followed her onto a train.

The car was so crowded he could hardly get in. The woman was standing, hanging onto a bar that ran over the seats along the side. Brian stood near her, his hand gripping a pole. They went only one long stop, then she pushed her way to the opening doors. So many people were in Brian's way that he almost didn't get out of the subway car in time, and then he had to hurry to catch up with her. He chased after her as she went up the stairs to another train.

This time the car wasn't as crowded, and Brian stood near an old lady who reminded him of his grandmother. The woman in the dark raincoat got off at the second stop and he followed her, his eyes fixed on her ponytail as she practically ran up the stairs to the street.

They emerged on a busy corner. Buses raced past in both directions, rushing to get across the wide street before the light turned red. Brian glanced behind him. As far as he could see down the block there were nothing but apartment houses. Light streamed from hundreds of windows.

The lady with the wallet stood waiting for the light to turn. The WALK sign flashed on, and he followed his quarry across the street. When she reached the other side she turned left and walked quickly down the now sloping sidewalk. As he followed her, Brian took a quick look at the street sign. When they visited last summer, his mother had made a game of teaching him about street signs in New York. "Gran lives on Eighty-seventh Street," she had said. "We're on Fiftieth. How many blocks away is her apartment?" This sign said Fourteenth Street. He had to remember that, he told himself, as he fell in step behind the woman with his mom's wallet.

He felt snowflakes on his face. It was getting windy, and the cold stung his cheeks. He wished a cop would come along so he could ask for help, but he didn't see one anywhere. He knew what he was going to do anyway—he would follow the lady to where she lived. He still had the dollar his mother had given him for the man who was playing the violin. He would get change and call his grandmother, and she'd send a cop who would get his mom's wallet back.

It's a good plan, he thought to himself. In fact, he was *sure* of it. He had to get the wallet, and the medal that was inside. He thought of how after Mom had said that the medal wouldn't do any good, Gran had put it in her hand and said, *Please give it to Tom and have faith.*

The look on his grandmother's face had been so calm and so sure that Brian knew she was right. Once he got the medal back and they gave it to his dad, he would get well. Brian *knew* it.

The woman with the ponytail started to walk faster. He chased after her as she crossed one street and went to the end of another block. Then she turned right.

The street they were on now wasn't bright with decorated store windows like the one they had just left. Some places were boarded up and there was a lot of writing on the buildings and some of the streetlights were broken. A guy with a beard was sitting on the curb, clutching a bottle. He stretched out his hand to Brian as he passed him.

For the first time, Brian felt scared, but he kept his eyes on the woman. The snow was falling faster now, and the sidewalk was getting slippery. He stumbled once, but managed not to fall. He was out of breath trying to keep up with the lady. How far was she going? he wondered. Four blocks later he had his answer. She stepped into the entranceway to an old building, stuck her key in the lock, and went inside. Brian raced to catch the door before it closed behind her, but he was too late. The door was locked.

Brian didn't know what to do next, but then through the glass he saw a man coming toward him. As the man opened the door and hurried past him, Brian managed to grab it and to duck inside before it closed again.

The hall was dark and dirty, and the smell of stale food hung in the air. Ahead of him he could hear footsteps going up the stairs. Gulping to swallow his fear, and trying to not make noise, Brian slowly began to climb to the first landing. He would see where the lady went; then he would get out of there and find a telephone. Maybe instead of calling Gran, he would dial 911, he thought.

His mom had taught him that that was what he should do when he *really* needed help.

Which so far he didn't.

"All right, Mrs. Dornan. Describe your son to me," the police officer said soothingly.

"He's seven and small for his age," Catherine said. She could hear the shrillness in her voice. They were sitting in a squad car, parked in front of Saks, near the spot where the violinist had been playing.

She felt Michael's hand clutch hers reassuringly.

"What color hair?" the officer asked.

Michael answered, "Like mine. Kind of reddish. His eyes are blue. He's got freckles and one of his front teeth is missing. He has the same kind of pants I'm wearing, and his jacket is like mine 'cept it's blue and mine is green. He's skinny."

The policeman looked approvingly at Michael. "You're a real help, son. Now, ma'am, you say your wallet is missing? Do you think you might have dropped it, or did anyone brush against you? I mean, could it have been a pickpocket?"

"I don't know," Catherine said. "I don't care about the wallet. But when I gave the boys money for the violinist, I probably didn't push it down far enough in my purse. It was quite bulky and might have just fallen out."

"Your son wouldn't have picked it up and decided to go shopping?"

"No, no, no," Catherine said with a flash of anger, shaking her head emphatically. "Please don't waste time even considering that."

"Where do you live, ma'am? What I mean is, do you want to call anyone?" The policeman looked at the rings on Catherine's left hand. "Your husband?"

"My husband is in Sloan-Kettering hospital. He's very ill. He'll be wondering where we are. In fact, we should be with him soon. He's expecting us." Catherine put her hand on the door of the squad car. "I can't just sit here. I've got to look for Brian."

"Mrs. Dornan, I'm going to get Brian's description out right now. In three minutes every cop in Manhattan is going to be on the lookout for him. You know, he may have just wandered away and gotten confused. It happens. Do you come downtown often?"

"We used to live in New York, but we live in Nebraska now," Michael told him. "We visit my grandmother every summer. She lives on Eighty-seventh Street. We came back last week because my dad has leukemia and he needed an operation. He went to medical school with the doctor who operated on him."

Manuel Ortiz had been a policeman only a year, but already he had come in contact with grief and despair many times. He saw both in the eyes of this young woman. She had a husband who was very sick, now a missing kid. It was obvious to him that she could easily go into shock.

"Dad's gonna know something's wrong," Michael said, worried. "Mom, shouldn't you go see him?"

"Mrs. Dornan, how about leaving Michael with us? We'll stay here in case Brian tries to make his way back. We'll have all our guys looking for him. We'll fan out and use bullhorns to get him to contact us in case he's wandering around in the neighborhood somewhere. I'll get another car to take you up to the hospital and wait for you."

"You'll stay right here in case he comes back?"

"Absolutely."

"Michael, will you keep your eyes peeled for Brian?"

"Sure, Mom. I'll watch out for the Dork."

"Don't call him. . . ." Then Catherine saw the look on her son's face. He's trying to get a rise out of me, she thought. He's trying to convince me that Brian is fine. That he'll be fine.

She put her arms around Michael and felt his small, gruff embrace in return.

"Hang in there, Mom," he said.

3

 Jimmy Siddons cursed silently as he walked through the oval near Avenue B in the Stuyvesant Town apartment complex. The uniform he had stripped from the prison guard gave him a respectable look but was much too dangerous to wear on the street. He'd managed to lift a filthy overcoat and knit cap from a homeless guy's shopping cart. They helped some, but he had to find something else to wear, something decent.

He also needed a car. He needed one that wouldn't be missed until morning, something parked for the night, the kind of car that one of these middle-class Stuyvesant Town residents would own: medium-sized, brown or black, looking like every other Honda or Toyota or Ford on the road. Nothing fancy.

So far he hadn't seen the right one. He had watched as some

old geezer got out of a Honda and said to his passenger, "Sure's good to get home," but he was driving one of those shiny red jobs that screamed for attention.

A kid pulled up in an old heap and parked, but from the sound of the engine, Jimmy wanted no part of it. Just what he'd need, he thought; get on the Thruway and have it break down.

He was cold and getting hungry. Ten hours in the car, he told himself. Then I'll be in Canada and Paige will meet me there and we'll disappear again. She was the first real girlfriend he'd ever had, and she'd been a big help to him in Detroit. He knew he never would have been caught last summer if he had cased that gas station in Michigan better. He should have known enough to check the john outside the office instead of letting himself be surprised by an off-duty cop who stepped out of it while he was holding a gun on the attendant.

The next day he was on his way back to New York. To face trial for killing a cop.

An older couple passed him and threw a smile in his direction. "Merry Christmas."

Jimmy responded with a courteous nod of the head. Then he paid close attention as he heard the woman say, "Ed, I can't believe you didn't put the presents for the children in the trunk. Who leaves anything in sight in a car overnight in this day and age?"

Jimmy went around the corner and then stepped into the deep shadows on the grass as he returned to watch the couple stop in front of a dark-colored Toyota. The man opened the door. From the backseat he took a small rocking horse and handed it to the woman, then scooped up a half-dozen brightly wrapped packages. With her help he transferred everything to the trunk, relocked the car, and got back on the sidewalk.

Jimmy listened as the woman said, "I guess the phone's all right in the glove compartment," and her husband answered, "Sure it is. Waste of money, as far as I'm concerned. Can't wait to see Bobby's face tomorrow when he opens everything."

He watched as they turned the corner and disappeared. Which meant from their apartment they wouldn't be able to glance out and notice an empty parking space.

Jimmy waited ten minutes before he walked to the car. A few snowflakes swirled around him. Two minutes later he was driving out of the complex. It was quarter after five. He was headed to Cally's apartment on Tenth and B. He knew she'd be surprised to see him. And none too happy. She probably thought he couldn't find her. Why did she suppose that he didn't have a way to keep track of her even from Riker's Island? he wondered.

Big sister, he thought, as he drove onto Fourteenth Street, you promised Grandma you'd take care of me! "Jimmy needs guidance," Grandma had said. "He's in with a bad crowd. He's too easily led." Well, Cally hadn't come to see him *once* in Riker's. Not once. He hadn't even heard from her.

He'd have to be careful. He was sure the cops would be watching for him around Cally's building. But he had that figured out, too. He used to hang around this neighborhood and knew how to get across the roofs from the other end of the block and into the building. A couple of times he'd even pulled a job there when he was a kid.

Knowing Cally, he was sure she still kept some of Frank's clothes in the closet. She'd been crazy about him, probably still had pictures of him all over the place. You'd never think he'd died even before Gigi was born.

And knowing Cally, she'd have at least a few bucks to get her little brother through the tolls, he figured. He'd find a way to convince her to keep her mouth shut until he was safely in Canada with Paige.

Paige. An image of her floated through his mind. Luscious. Blond. Only twenty-two. Crazy about him. She'd arranged everything, gotten the gun smuggled in to him. She'd never let him down or turn her back on him.

Jimmy's smile was unpleasant. You never tried to help me while I was rotting in Riker's Island, he thought—but once again, sister dear, you're going to help me get away, like it or not.

He parked the car a block from the rear of Cally's building and pretended to be checking a tire as he looked around. No cops in sight. Even if they were watching Cally's place, they probably didn't know you could get to it through the boarded-up dump. As he straightened up he cursed. Damn bumper sticker. Too noticeable. WE'RE SPENDING OUR GRAND-CHILDREN'S INHERITANCE. He managed to pull most of it off.

Fifteen minutes later, Jimmy had picked the flimsy lock of Cally's apartment and was inside. Some dump, he thought, as he took in the cracks in the ceiling and the worn linoleum in the tiny entranceway. But neat. Cally was always neat. A Christmas tree in the corner of what passed for a living room had a couple of small, brightly wrapped packages under it.

Jimmy shrugged and went into the bedroom, where he ransacked the closet to find the clothes he knew would be there. After changing, he went through the place looking for money but found none. He yanked open the doors that separated the stove, refrigerator, and sink from the living room, searched unsuccessfully for a beer, settled for a Pepsi, and made himself a sandwich.

From what his sources had told him, Cally should be home by now from her job in the hospital. He knew that on the way she picked up Gigi from the baby-sitter. He sat on the couch, his eyes riveted on the front door, his nerves jangling. He'd spent most of the few dollars he found in the guard's pockets on food from street vendors. He had to have money for the tolls on the Thruway, as well as enough for another tank of gas. Come on, Cally, he thought, where the hell are you?

At ten to six, he heard the key inserted in the lock. He jumped up and in three long strides was in the entryway, flattened against the wall. He waited until Cally stepped in and closed the door behind her, then put his hand over her mouth.

"Don't scream!" he whispered, as he muffled her terrified moan with his palm. "Understand?"

She nodded, eyes wide open in fear.

"Where's Gigi? Why isn't she with you?"

He released his grip long enough to let her gasp in an almost inaudible voice, "She's at the baby-sitter's. She's keeping her longer today, so I can shop. Jimmy, what are you *doing* here?"

"How much money have you got?"

"Here, take my pocketbook." Cally held it out to him, praying that he would not think to look through her coat pockets. Oh God, she thought, make him go away.

He took the purse and in a low and menacing tone warned, "Cally, I'm going to let go of you. Don't try anything or Gigi won't have a mommy waiting for her. Understand that?"

"Yes. Yes."

Cally waited until he released his grip on her, then slowly turned to face him. She hadn't seen her brother since that terrible night nearly three years ago when, with Gigi in her arms, she had come home from her job at the day-care center to find him waiting in her apartment in the West Village.

He looks about the same, she thought, except that his hair is shorter and his face is thinner. In his eyes there wasn't even a trace of the occasional warmth that at one time made her hope there was a possibility he might someday straighten out. No more. There was nothing left of the frightened six-year-old who had clung to her when their mother dumped them with Grandma and disappeared from their lives.

He opened her purse, rummaged through it, and pulled out her bright green combination change purse and billfold. "Eighteen dollars," he said angrily after a quick count of her money. "Is that all?"

"Jimmy, I get paid the day after tomorrow," Cally pleaded. "Please just take it and get out of here. Please leave me alone."

There's half a tank of gas in the car, Jimmy thought. There's money here for another half tank and the tolls. I might just be able to make Canada. He'd have to shut Cally up, of course, which should be easy enough. He would just warn her that if she put the cops onto him and he got caught, he'd swear that she got someone to smuggle the gun in to him that he'd used on the guard.

Suddenly a sound from outside made him whirl around. He put his eye to the peephole in the door but could see no one there. With a menacing gesture to Cally, indicating that she had better keep quiet, he noiselessly turned the knob and opened the door a fraction, just in time to see a small boy straighten up, turn, and start to tiptoe to the staircase.

In one quick movement, Jimmy flung open the door and scooped up the child, one arm around his waist, the other covering his mouth, and pulled him inside, then roughly set him down.

"Eavesdropping, kid? Who is this, Cally?"

"Jimmy, leave him alone. I don't know who he is," she cried. "I've never seen him before."

Brian was so scared he could hardly talk. But he could tell the man and woman were mad at each other. Maybe the man would help him get his mother's wallet back, he thought. He pointed to Cally. "She has my mom's wallet."

Jimmy released Brian. "Well, now *that's* good news," he said with a grin, turning to his sister. "Isn't it?"

4

A plainclothesman in an unmarked car drove Catherine to the hospital. "I'll wait right here, Mrs. Dornan," he said. "I have the radio on so we'll know the minute they find Brian."

Catherine nodded. *If they find Brian* raced through her mind. She felt her throat close against the terror that thought evoked.

The lobby of the hospital was decorated for the holiday season. A Christmas tree was in the center, garlands of evergreens were hung, and poinsettias were banked against the reception desk.

She got a visitor's pass and learned that Tom was now in room 530. She walked to the bank of elevators and entered a car already half full, mostly with hospital personnel—doctors in white jackets with the telltale pen and notebook in their breast pockets, attendants in green scrub suits, a couple of nurses.

Two weeks ago, Catherine thought, Tom was making his rounds at St. Mary's in Omaha, and I was Christmas shopping. That evening we took the kids out for hamburgers. Life was normal and good and fun, and we were joking about how last year Tom had had so much trouble getting the Christmas tree in the stand, and I promised him I'd buy a new stand before this Christmas Eve. And once again I thought Tom looked so tired, and I did nothing about it.

Three days later he collapsed.

"Didn't you push the fifth floor?" someone asked.

Catherine blinked. "Oh, yes, thank you." She got off the elevator and for a moment stood still, getting her bearings. She found what she was looking for, an arrow on the wall pointing toward rooms 515 to 530.

As she approached the nurses' station, she saw Spence Crowley. Her mouth went dry. Immediately following the operation this morning, he had assured her that it had gone smoothly, and that his assistant would be making the rounds this afternoon. Then why was Spence here now? she worried. Could something be wrong?

He spotted her and smiled. Oh God, he wouldn't smile if Tom were . . . It was another thought she could not finish.

He walked quickly around the desk and came to her. "Catherine, if you could *see* the look on your face! Tom's doing fine. He's pretty groggy, of course, but the vital signs are good."

Catherine looked up at him, wanting to believe the words she heard, wanting to trust the sincerity she saw in the brown eyes behind rimless glasses.

Firmly he took her arm and ushered her into the cubicle behind the nurses' station. "Catherine, I don't want to bully you, but you have to understand that Tom has a good chance of beating this thing. A very good chance. I have patients who've led useful, full lives with leukemia. There are different types of medicine to control it. The one I plan to use with Tom is Interferon. It's worked miracles with some of my patients. It will mean daily injections at first, but after we get the dosage adjusted, he'll be able to give them to himself. When he recuperates fully from the operation, he can go back to work, and I swear to you that's going to happen." Then he added quietly, "But there is a problem."

Now he looked stern. "This afternoon when you saw Tom in ICU, I understand you were pretty upset."

"Yes." She had tried not to cry but couldn't stop. She'd been so worried, and knowing that he had made it through the operation was such a relief that she couldn't help herself.

"Catherine, Tom just asked me to level with him. He thinks I told you it was hopeless. He's starting to not trust me. He's beginning to wonder if maybe I'm hiding something, that maybe things are worse than I'm telling him. Well, Catherine, that is simply not so, and your job is to convince him that you have every expectation that you two will have a long life together. He mustn't get it in his head that he has a very limited time, not only because that would be harmful to him, but equally important because I don't believe that's *true*. In order to get well, Tom needs faith in his chances to get better, and a great deal of that has to come from you."

"Spence, I should have *seen* he was getting sick." Spence put his arms around her shoulders in a brief hug. "Listen," he said, "there's an old adage, 'Physician, heal thyself.' When

Tom is feeling better, I'm going to rake him over the coals for ignoring some of the warnings his body was giving him. But now, go in there with a light step and a happy face. You can do it."

Catherine forced a smile. "Like this?"

"Much better," he nodded. "Just keep smiling. Remember, it's Christmas. Thought you were bringing the kids tonight?"

She could not talk about Brian being missing. Not now. Instead, she practiced what she would tell Tom. "Brian was sneezing, and I want to make sure he's not starting with a cold."

"That was wise. Okay. See you tomorrow, kiddo. Now remember, keep that smile going. You're gorgeous when you smile."

Catherine nodded and started down the hall to room 530. She opened the door quietly. Tom was asleep. An IV unit was dripping fluid into his arm. Oxygen tubes were in his nostrils. His skin was as white as the pillowcase. His lips were ashen.

The private duty nurse stood up. "He's been asking for you, Mrs. Dornan. I'll wait outside."

Catherine pulled up a chair next to the bed. She sat down and placed her hand over the one lying on the coverlet. She studied her husband's face, scrutinizing every detail: the high forehead framed by the reddish brown hair that was exactly the color of Brian's; the thick eyebrows that always looked a bit unruly; the well-shaped nose and the lips that were usually parted in a smile. She thought of his eyes, more blue than gray, and the warmth and understanding they conveyed. He gives confidence to his patients, she thought. Oh, Tom, I want to tell you that our little boy is missing. I want you to be well and with me, looking for him.

Tom Dornan opened his eyes. "Hi, Love," he said weakly.

"Hi, yourself." She bent over and kissed him. "I'm sorry I was such a wimp this afternoon. Call it PMS or just old-fashioned relief. You know what a sentimental slob I am. I even cry at happy endings."

She straightened up and looked directly into his eyes. "You're doing great. You really are, you know."

She could see he did not believe her. *Not yet,* she thought determinedly.

"I thought you were bringing the kids tonight?" His voice was low and halting.

She realized that with Tom it was not possible to utter Brian's name without breaking down. Instead she said quickly, "I was afraid they'd be hanging all over you. I thought it was a good idea to let them wait until tomorrow morning."

"Your mother phoned," Tom said drowsily. "The nurse spoke to her. She said she sent a special present for you to give me. What is it?"

"Not without the boys. They want to be the ones to give it to you."

"Okay. But be sure to bring them in the morning. I want to see them."

"For sure. But since it's just the two of us now, maybe I should climb in the sack with you."

Tom opened his eyes again. "Now you're talking." A smile flickered on his lips. And then he was asleep again.

For a long moment, she laid her head on the bed, then got up as the nurse tiptoed back in. "Doesn't he look fantastic?" Catherine asked brightly as the nurse put her fingers on Tom's pulse.

She knew that even slipping into sleep, Tom might hear her. Then with a last glance at her husband, she hurried from the room, down the corridor and to the elevator, then through the lobby, and into the waiting police car.

The plainclothesman answered her unasked question: "No word so far, Mrs. Dornan."

5

"I said, give it to me," Jimmy Siddons said ominously.

Cally tried to brave it out. "I don't know what this boy is talking about, Jimmy."

"Yes, you do," Brian said. "I saw you pick up my mom's wallet. And I followed you because I have to get it back."

"Aren't you a smart kid?" Siddons sneered. "Always go where the buck is." His expression turned ugly as he faced his sister. "Don't make me take it from you, Cally."

There was no use trying to pretend she didn't have it. Jimmy knew the boy was telling the truth. Cally still had her coat on. She reached into the pocket and took out the handsome Moroccan leather wallet. Silently she handed it to her brother.

"That belongs to my mother," Brian said defiantly. Then

the glance the man gave him made him shiver. He had been about to try to grab the wallet; instead, now suddenly fearful, he dug his hands deep in his pockets.

Jimmy Siddons opened the billfold. "My, my," he said, his tone now admiring. "Cally, you surprise me. You run rings around some of the pickpockets I know."

"I didn't steal it," Cally protested. "Someone dropped it, I found it. I was going to mail it back."

"Well, you can forget that," Jimmy said. "It's mine now, and I need it."

He pulled out a thick wad of bills and began counting. "Three hundred-dollar bills, four fifties, six twenties, four tens, five fives, three ones. Six hundred and eighty-eight dollars. Not bad, in fact, it'll do just fine."

He stuffed the money in the pocket of the suede jacket he had taken from the bedroom closet and began to dig through the compartments in the wallet. "Credit cards. Well, why not? Driver's license—no, two of them: Catherine Dornan and Dr. Thomas Dornan. Who's Dr. Thomas Dornan, kid?"

"My dad. He's in the hospital." Brian watched as the deep compartment in the wallet revealed the medal.

Jimmy Siddons lifted it out, held it up by the chain, then laughed incredulously. "St. Christopher! I haven't been inside a church in years, but even I know they kicked him out long ago. And when I think of all the stories Grandma used to tell us about how he carried the Christ child on his shoulders across the stream or the river or whatever it was! Remember, Cally?" Disdainfully he let the medal clatter to the floor.

Brian swooped to retrieve it. He clutched it in his hand, then slipped it around his neck. "My grandpa carried it all through the war and came home safe. It's going to make my dad get better. I don't care about the wallet. You can have it. This is what I really wanted. I'm going home now." He turned and ran for the door. He had twisted the knob and pulled the door open before Siddons reached him, clapped a hand over his mouth, and yanked him back inside.

"You and St. Christopher are staying right here with me, buddy," he said as he shoved him roughly to the floor.

Brian gasped as his forehead slammed onto the cracked linoleum. He sat up slowly, rubbing his head. He felt like the room was spinning, but he could hear the woman he had followed pleading with the man. "Jimmy, don't hurt him. Please. Leave us alone. Take the money and go. But get out of here."

Brian wrapped his arms around his legs, trying not to cry. He shouldn't have followed the lady. He knew that now. He should have yelled instead of following her so that maybe somebody would stop her. This man was bad. This man wasn't going to let him go home. And nobody knew where he was. Nobody knew where to look for him.

He felt the medal dangling against his chest and closed his fist around it. Please get me back to Mom, he prayed silently, so I can bring you to Dad.

He did not look up to see Jimmy Siddons studying him. He did not know that Jimmy's mind was racing, assessing the situation. This kid followed Cally when she took the wallet, Siddons thought. Did anyone follow him? No. If they had, they'd be here by now. "Where did you get the wallet?" he asked his sister.

"On Fifth Avenue. Across from Rockefeller Center." Cally was terrified now. Jimmy would stop at nothing to get away. Not at killing her. Not at killing this child. "His mother must have dropped it. I picked it up off the sidewalk. I guess he saw me."

"I guess he did." Jimmy looked at the phone on the table next to the couch. Then, grinning, he reached for the cellular phone he had taken from the glove compartment of the stolen car. He also took out a gun and pointed it at Cally. "The cops may have your phone tapped." He pointed at the table next to the couch. "Go over there. I'm going to dial your number and tell you I'm turning myself in and I want you to call that public defender who is representing me. All you have to do is act nice and nervous, just like you are now. Make a mistake and you and this kid are dead."

He looked down at Brian. "One peep out of you and . . ." He left the threat unspoken.

Brian nodded to show he understood. He was too scared to even promise that he'd be quiet.

"Cally, you got all that straight?"

Cally nodded. How stupid I've been, she thought. I was fool enough to believe I'd gotten away from him. No chance. He even knows this phone number.

He finished dialing and the phone beside her rang. "Hello." Her voice was low and muffled.

"Cally, it's Jimmy. Listen, I'm in trouble. You probably know by now. I'm sorry I tried to get away. I hope that guard will be all right. I'm broke and I'm scared." Jimmy's voice was a whine. "Call Gil Weinstein. He's the public defender assigned to me. Tell him I'll meet him at St. Patrick's Cathedral when midnight Mass is over. Tell him I want to turn myself in and I want him to be with me. His home number is 555-0267. Cally, I'm sorry I messed up everything so badly."

Jimmy pressed the disconnect on the cellular phone and

watched as Cally hung up as well. "They can't trace a cellular phone call, you know that, don't you? Okay, now phone Weinstein and give him the same story. If the cops are listening, they must be jumping up and down right now."

"Jimmy, they'll think I . . ."

In two steps Jimmy was beside her, the gun to her head. "Make the call."

"Your lawyer may not be home. He may refuse to meet you."

"Naw. I know him. He's a jerk. He'll want the publicity. Get him."

Cally did not need to be told to make it quick. The moment Gil Weinstein was on the line, she rushed to say, "You don't know me. I'm Cally Hunter. My brother, Jimmy Siddons, just called. He wants me to tell you . . ." In a quavering voice she delivered the message.

"I'll meet him," the lawyer said. "I'm glad he's doing this, but if that prison guard dies, Jimmy is facing a death-penalty trial. He could get life without parole for the first killing, but now . . ." His voice trailed off.

"I think he knows that." Cally saw Jimmy's gesture. "I have to go now. Good-bye, Mr. Weinstein."

"You make a great accomplice, big sister," Jimmy told her. He looked down at Brian. "What's your name, kid?"

"Brian," he whispered.

"Come on, Brian. We're getting out of here."

"Jimmy, leave him alone. Please. Leave him here with me."

"No way. There's always the chance you'd go running to the cops even though the minute they talk to that kid, you're in big trouble yourself. After all, you *did* steal his mama's wallet. No, the kid comes with me. No one is looking for a guy with his little boy, are they? I'll let him go tomorrow morning when I get to where I'm headed. After that you can tell them anything you like about me. The kid'll even back you up, won't you, sonny?"

Brian shrank against Cally. He was so afraid of the man that he was trembling. Was the man going to make him go away with him?

"Jimmy, leave him here. Please." Cally thrust Brian behind her.

Jimmy Siddons's mouth twisted in anger. He grabbed Cally's arm and yanked her toward him, roughly twisting her arm behind her.

She screamed as she lost her grip on Brian and slipped to the floor.

With eyes that denied any history of affection between them, Jimmy stood over his sister, again holding the gun to her head. "If you don't do what I tell you, you'll get more of that . . . and worse. They won't take me alive. Not you, not nobody else is gonna send me to the death chamber. Besides, I got a girlfriend waiting for me. So just keep your mouth shut. I'll even make a deal. You don't say nothing, and I'll let the kid live. But if the cops try to close in on me, he gets a bullet in the head. It's as simple as that. Got it straight?"

He stuck the gun back inside his jacket, then reached down and roughly pulled Brian to his feet. "You and I are gonna get to be real pals, sonny," he said. "Real pals." He grinned. "Merry Christmas, Cally."

6

 The unmarked van parked across the street from Cally's apartment building was the lookout post for the detectives watching Cally's building for any sign of Jimmy Siddons. They had observed Cally come home at just a little after her usual time.

Jack Shore, the detective who had visited Cally in the morning, pulled off his earphones, swore silently, and turned to his partner. "What do you think, Mort? No, wait a minute. I'll tell you what I think. It's a trick. He's trying to buy time to get as far away from New York as possible while we take up the collection at St. Pat's looking for him."

Mort Levy, twenty years younger than Shore and less cynical, rubbed his chin, always a sign that he was deep in thought. "If it is a trick, I don't think the sister is a willing accomplice. You don't need a meter to hear the stress level in her voice."

"Listen, Mort, you were at Bill Grasso's funeral. Thirty years old, with four little kids, and shot between the eyes by that bum Siddons. If Cally Hunter had come clean with us and told us that she'd given that rat brother of hers money and the keys to her car, Grasso would have known what he was up against when he stopped him for running a light."

"I still believe that Cally had bought Jimmy's story about trying to get away because he'd been in a gang fight and the other gang was after him. I don't think she knew that he'd wounded a clerk in a liquor store. Up till then he hadn't been in really serious trouble."

"You mean he'd gotten away with it till then," Shore snapped. "Too bad that judge couldn't put Cally away as an accessory to murder instead of just for aiding a fugitive. She got off after serving fifteen months. Bill Grasso's widow is trimming the tree without him tonight."

His face reddened with anger. "I'll call in. Just in case that louse meant what he said, we've got to cover the cathedral. You know how many people go to midnight Mass there tonight? Take a guess."

Cally sat on the worn velour sofa, her hands clasped around her knees, her head bent, her eyes closed. Her entire body was trembling. She was beyond tears, beyond fatigue. Dear God, dear God, *why* did all this happen?

What should she do?

If anything happened to Brian, she would be responsible. She had picked up his mother's wallet, and that's why he'd followed her. If the child was right, his dad was very ill. She thought of the attractive young woman in the rose-colored coat and how she had been sure everything in her life was perfect.

Would Jimmy let the boy go when he got to wherever was his destination? How could he? she reasoned. Wherever that was, they'd start searching for Jimmy in that area. *And if he does let him go, Brian will tell how he followed me because I took the wallet,* she reminded herself.

But Jimmy had said he would shoot the child if the cops closed in on him. And he meant it, she was certain of that. So if I tell the cops, Brian doesn't have a chance, she thought.

If I don't say anything now and Jimmy does let him go, then I can honestly say that I didn't tell because he threatened to kill the kid if the cops got near him, and I knew he meant it. And I know he does mean it, Cally thought. That's the worst part.

Brian's face loomed in Cally's mind. The reddish brown hair that fell forward on his forehead, the large, intelligent blue eyes, the spatter of freckles on his cheeks and nose. When Jimmy dragged him in, her first impression was that he wasn't more than five; from the way he spoke, though, she was sure he was older. He was so scared when Jimmy made him go with him out the window and onto the fire escape. He had looked back at her, his eyes pleading.

The phone rang. It was Aika, the wonderful black woman who minded Gigi along with her own grandchildren each afternoon after the day-care center closed.

"Just checking to see if you're home, Cally," Aika said, her voice rich and comforting. "Did you find the doll man?"

"I'm afraid not."

"Too bad. You need more time to shop?"

"No, I'll come right over now and get Gigi."

"No, that's okay. She already ate dinner with my gang. I need milk for breakfast, so I've got to go out anyway. I'll drop her off in half an hour or so."

"Thanks, Aika." Cally put down the receiver, aware that she still had her coat on and that the apartment was dark except for the entryway light. She took off the coat, went into the bedroom, and opened the closet door. She gasped when she saw that when he took Frank's suede jacket and brown slacks, Jimmy had left other clothes crumpled on the floor, a jacket and pants, and a filthy overcoat.

She bent down and picked up the jacket. Detective Shore had told her that Jimmy had shot a guard and stripped him of his uniform. Obviously, this was the uniform—and there were bullet holes in the jacket.

Frantically, Cally wrapped the jacket and pants inside the overcoat. Suppose the cops came in with a search warrant! They'd never believe her, that Jimmy broke into her place. They'd be sure she gave him clothes. She'd go back to prison. And she'd lose Gigi for good! What should she do?

She looked around the closet, wildly searching for a solution. The storage box on the overhead shelf. In it she kept whatever summer clothes she and Gigi had. She yanked the box down, opened it, pulled out the contents, and threw them on the shelf. She folded the uniform and coat into the box, closed it, ran to the bed, and fished under it for the Christmas wrappings she had stored there.

With frantic fingers she wrapped candy-cane paper around the box and tied it with a ribbon. Then she carried it into the living room and put it under the tree. She had just completed the task when she heard the downstairs buzzer. Smoothing back her hair, and forcing a welcoming smile for Gigi, she went to answer it.

It was Detective Shore and the other detective who had been with him this morning who came up the stairs. "Playing games again, Cally?" Shore asked. "I hope not."

7

Brian huddled in the passenger seat as Jimmy Siddons drove up the East River Drive. He had never felt so afraid before. He'd been scared when the man made him climb up that fire escape to the roof. Then he'd practically been dragged from one roof to another as they went the length of the block, finally going down through an empty building and onto the street where this car was parked.

The man had pushed Brian into the car and snapped on the seat belt. "Just remember to call me Daddy if anyone stops us," he had warned him.

Brian knew the man's name was Jimmy. That was what the woman had called him. She had looked so worried about Brian. When Jimmy pulled him through the window, she had been crying, and Brian could tell how scared she was for him.

She knew his parents' names. Maybe she would call the cops. If she did, would they come looking for him? But Jimmy said he'd kill him if the cops came. Would he?

Brian huddled deeper in the seat. He was scared and hungry. And he had to go to the bathroom, but he was afraid to ask. His only comfort was the medal that now lay against his chest on the outside of his jacket. It had brought Grandpa home from the war. It was going to make Daddy well. And it was going to get him home safe, too. He was sure of it.

Jimmy Siddons glanced briefly at his small hostage. For the first time since he had broken out of the prison, he was beginning to relax. It was still snowing, but if it didn't get any worse than this, it was nothing to worry about. Cally wouldn't call the cops. He was positive of that. She knew him well enough to believe him when he said he would kill the kid if he was stopped.

I'm not going to rot in prison for the rest of my life, he thought, and I'm not giving them the chance to pump me full of poison. Either I make it, or I don't.

But I *will*. He smiled grimly. He knew there had to be an APB out on him and they'd be watching all the bridges and tunnels out of New York. But they had no idea where he was heading, and they certainly weren't looking for a father and son traveling in a car that wasn't reported stolen yet.

He'd pulled out all the presents he had seen the couple stash in the trunk. Now they were piled on the backseat, bundles of Christmas cheer. Those presents, coupled with the kid in the front, meant even if toll takers had been alerted to be on the lookout, they'd never glance twice at him now.

And in eight or nine hours he would be across the border and into Canada, where Paige would be waiting. And then he would find a nice deep lake that would be the final destination of this car and all the nice presents in the backseat.

And this kid with his St. Christopher medal.

The awesome power of the New York City Police Department ground methodically into gear as plans were laid to assure that Jimmy Siddons did not slip between their fingers, just in case, at the last minute, he panicked and decided not to surrender after midnight Mass.

As soon as their wiretap recorded Cally's phone calls from Jimmy, and to his lawyer, Jack Shore had called in the information. He had let the higher-ups know exactly what he thought of Siddons's "decision" to surrender. "It's an out-and-out crock," he had barked. "We tie up a couple of hundred cops till one-thirty or two in the morning, and he's halfway to Canada or Mexico before we find out that he's made us look like a bunch of fools."

Finally the deputy police commissioner in charge of the manhunt had snapped, "All right, Jack. We *know* what you think. Now let's get on with it. There's been no sign of him around his sister's place?"

"No, sir," Jack Shore had said and hung up, and then he and his partner, Mort, had gone to visit Cally. When they got back to the van, Shore again reported in to headquarters. "We just were back to Hunter's apartment, sir. She's fully aware of the consequences if she helps her brother in any way. The baby-sitter dropped off her kid as we were leaving, and my guess is Cally's in for the night."

Mort Levy frowned as he listened to his partner's conversation with the deputy police commissioner. There was something about that apartment that was *different* from the way it had looked this morning, but he couldn't figure out what it was. Mentally he reviewed the layout: the small entryway, the bathroom directly off it, the narrow combination living room–kitchen, the cell-like bedroom, barely large enough to hold a single bed, a cot for the little girl, and a three-drawer dresser.

Jack had asked Cally if she would mind if they looked around again, and she had nodded assent. Certainly no one was hiding in that place. They had opened the door to the bathroom, looked under the beds, poked in the closet. Levy had felt unwilling pity for Cally Hunter's attempts to brighten the dismal flat. All the walls were painted a bright yellow. Floral pillows were randomly piled on the old couch. The Christmas tree was bravely decorated with tons of tinsel and strings of red and green lights. A few brightly wrapped presents were placed under it.

Presents? Mort did not know why this word triggered something in his subconscious. He thought for a moment, then shook his head. Forget it, he told himself.

He wished Jack hadn't bullied Cally Hunter. It was easy to see that she was terrified of him. Mort hadn't been in on her case, which had been tried over two years ago, but from what he'd heard, he believed that Cally honestly thought that her troublesome kid brother had been in a gang fight and that the members of the other gang were hunting him.

What am I trying to remember about her apartment? Mort asked himself. *What was different?*

They were normally scheduled to go off duty at eight o'clock, but tonight both he and Jack were going back to headquarters instead. Like dozens of others, they would be working overtime at least until after midnight Mass at the cathedral. Maybe, just maybe, Siddons would show up as he had promised. Levy knew that Shore was aching to make the arrest personally. "I could spot that guy if he was wearing a nun's habit," he kept saying, over and over again.

There was a tap at the back door of the van, signifying that their replacements had arrived. As Mort stood up, stretched, and stepped down onto the street, he was glad that just before he left Cally Hunter's apartment, he had slipped her his card and whispered, "If you want to talk to anyone, Mrs. Hunter, here's a number where you can reach me."

8

 The crowds on Fifth Avenue had thinned out, although there were still some onlookers around the tree in Rockefeller Center. Others were still lined up waiting to see Saks's window display, and there was a steady stream of visitors slipping in and out of St. Patrick's Cathedral.

But as the car she was in pulled up behind the squad car where Officer Ortiz and Michael were waiting, Catherine could see that most of the last-minute shoppers were gone.

They're on their way home, she thought, to do the final gift wrapping and to tell each other that next year, for sure, they won't be rushing around to stores on Christmas Eve.

Everything at the last minute. That had been her own pattern until twelve years ago, when a third-year resident, Dr. Thomas Dornan, came into the administration office of St.

Vincent's Hospital, walked over to her desk, and said, "You're new here, aren't you?"

Tom, so easygoing, but so organized. If she were the one who was sick, Tom wouldn't have stuffed all her money and identification into his own bulging wallet. He wouldn't have dropped it into his pocket so carelessly that someone either reached in and grabbed it or picked it up off the ground.

That was the thought that was torturing Catherine as she opened the car door and, through the swirling snow, ran the few steps to the squad car. Brian would never have wandered away on his own, she was sure of that. He was so anxious to get to Tom, he hadn't even wanted to take the time to look at the Rockefeller Center tree. He must have set off on some mission. That was it. If somebody hadn't actually kidnapped him—and that seemed unlikely—he must have seen whoever took or picked up the wallet and followed that person.

Michael was sitting in the front seat with Officer Ortiz, sipping a soda. A brown paper bag with remnants of a packet of ketchup was standing on the floor in front of him. Catherine squeezed in beside him on the front seat and smoothed his hair.

"How's Dad?" he asked anxiously. "You didn't tell him about Brian, did you?"

"No, of course not. I'm sure we'll find Brian soon, and there was no need to worry him. And he's doing just great. I saw Dr. Crowley. He's a happy camper about Dad." She looked over Michael's head at Officer Ortiz. "It's been almost two hours," she said quietly.

He nodded. "Brian's description will keep going out every hour to every cop and car in the area. Mrs. Dornan, Michael and I have been talking. He's sure Brian wouldn't deliberately wander away."

"No, he's right. He wouldn't."

"You talked to the people around you when you realized he was missing?"

"Yes."

"And no one noticed a kid being pulled or carried away?"

"No. People remember seeing him, then they didn't see him."

"I'll level with you. I don't know any molester who would even attempt to kidnap a child from his mother's side and work his way through a crowd of people. But Michael thinks that maybe Brian would have taken off after someone he saw take your wallet."

Catherine nodded. "I've been thinking the same thing. It's the only answer that makes sense."

"Michael tells me that last year Brian stood up to a fourth-grade kid who shoved one of his classmates."

"He's a gutsy kid," Catherine said. Then the import of what the policeman had said hit her. *He thinks that if Brian followed whoever took my wallet, he may have confronted that person.* Oh God, no!

"Mrs. Dornan, if it's all right with you, I think it would be a good idea if we tried to get cooperation from the media. We might be able to get some of the local TV stations to show Brian's picture if you have one."

"The one I carried is in my wallet," Catherine said, her voice a monotone. Images of Brian standing up to a thief flashed in her mind. My little boy, she thought, would someone hurt my little boy?

What was Michael saying? He was talking to the cop Ortiz.

"My grandmother has a bunch of pictures of us," Michael was telling him. Then he looked up at his mother. "Anyhow, Mom, you gotta call Gran. She's going to start worrying if we're not home soon."

Like father, like son, Catherine thought. Brian looks like Tom. Michael thinks like him. She closed her eyes against the waves of near panic that washed through her. Tom. Brian. Why?

She felt Michael fishing in her shoulder bag. He pulled out the cellular phone. "I'll dial Gran," he told her.

9

 In her apartment on Eighty-seventh Street, Barbara Cavanaugh clutched the phone, not wanting to believe what her daughter was telling her. But there was no disputing the dreadful news that Catherine's quiet, almost emotionless voice had conveyed. Brian was missing, and had been missing for over two hours now.

Barbara managed to keep her voice calm. "Where are you, dear?"

"Michael and I are in a police car at Forty-ninth and Fifth. That's where we were standing when Brian . . . just suddenly wasn't next to me."

"I'll be right there."

"Mom, be sure to bring the most recent pictures you have of Brian. The police want to give them out to all the news media. And the news radio station is going to have me on in a few minutes to make an appeal. And Mom, call the nurses' station on the fifth floor of the hospital. Tell them to make absolutely sure that Tom isn't allowed to turn on the TV in his room. He doesn't have a radio. If he ever found out that Brian was missing . . ." Her voice trailed off.

"I'll call right away but, Catherine, I don't have any recent pictures here," Barbara cried. "All the ones we took last summer are in the Nantucket house." Then she wanted to bite her lip. She'd been asking for new pictures of the boys and hadn't received any. Only yesterday Catherine had told her that her Christmas present, framed portraits of them, had been forgotten in the rush to get Tom to New York for the operation.

"I'll bring what I can find," she said hurriedly. "I'm on my way."

For an instant after she finished delivering the message to the hospital, Barbara Cavanaugh sank into a chair and rested her forehead in her palm. Too much, she thought, too much.

Had there always been a feeling haunting her that everything was too good to be true? Catherine's father had died when she was ten, and there had always been a lingering touch of sadness in her eyes, until at twenty-two she met Tom. They were so happy together, so perfect together. The way Gene and I were from day one, Barbara thought.

For an instant her mind rushed back to that moment in 1943, when at age nineteen and a sophomore in college, she'd been introduced to a handsome young Army officer, Lieutenant Eugene Cavanaugh. In that first moment they'd both known that they were perfect for each other. They were married two months later, but it was eighteen years before their only child was born.

With Tom, my daughter has found the same kind of relationship with which I was blessed, Barbara thought, but now . . . She jumped up. She *had* to get to Catherine. Brian *must* have just wandered away. They just got separated, she told herself. Catherine was strong, but she must be close to the breaking point by now. Oh, dear God, let someone find him, she prayed.

She rushed through the apartment, yanking framed photographs from mantels and tabletops. She'd moved here from Beekman Place ten years ago. It was still more space than she needed, with a formal dining room, library, and guest suite. But now it meant that when Tom and Catherine and the boys came to visit from their home in Omaha, there was plenty of room for them.

Barbara tossed the pictures into the handsome leather carryall Tom and Catherine had given her for her birthday, grabbed a coat from the foyer closet, and, without bothering to double lock the door, rushed outside in time to press the button for the elevator as it began to descend from the penthouse.

Sam, the elevator operator, was a longtime employee. When he opened the door for her, his smile was replaced by a look of concern. "Good evening, Mrs. Cavanaugh. Merry Christmas. Any further word on Dr. Dornan?"

Afraid to speak, Barbara shook her head.

"Those grandkids of yours are real cute. The little one, Brian, told me you gave his mom something that would make his dad get well. I sure hope that's true."

Barbara tried to say, "So do I," but found that her lips could not form the words.

. . .

"Mommy, why are you sad?" Gigi asked as she settled onto Cally's lap.

"I'm not sad, Gigi," Cally said. "I'm always happy when I'm with you."

Gigi shook her head. She was wearing a red-and-white Christmas nightgown with figures of angels carrying candles. Her wide brown eyes and wavy golden-brown hair were legacies from Frank. The older she gets, the more she looks like him, Cally thought, instinctively holding the child tighter.

They were curled up together on the couch across from the Christmas tree. "I'm glad you're home with me, Mommy," Gigi said, and her voice became fearful. "You won't leave me again, will you?"

"No. I didn't want to leave you last time, sweetheart."

"I didn't like visiting you at that place."

That place. The Bedford correctional facility for women.

"I didn't like being there." Cally tried to sound matter-of-fact.

"Kids should stay with their mothers."

"Yes. I think so too."

"Mommy, is that big present for me?" Gigi pointed to the box that held the uniform and coat Jimmy had discarded.

Cally's lips went dry. "No, sweetheart, that's a present for Santa Claus. He likes to get something for Christmas, too. Now come on, it's past your bedtime."

Gigi automatically began to say, "I don't want to . . . ," then she stopped. "Will Christmas come faster if I go to bed now?"

"Uh-huh. Come on, I'll carry you in."

When she had tucked the blankets around Gigi and given her her "bee," the tattered blanket that was her daughter's indispensable sleeping companion, Cally went back to the living room and once again sank down onto the couch.

Kids should stay with their mothers . . . Gigi's words haunted her. Dear God, where had Jimmy taken that little boy? What would he do to him? What should she do?

Cally stared at the box with the candy-cane paper. *That's for Santa Claus.* A vivid memory of its contents flashed through her mind. The uniform of the guard Jimmy had shot, the side and sleeve still sticky with blood. The filthy overcoat—God knew where he'd found or stolen *that*.

Jimmy was *evil*. He had no conscience, no pity. Face it, Cally told herself fiercely—he won't hesitate to kill that little boy if it helps his chances to escape.

She turned on the radio to the local news. It was seven-thirty. The breaking news was that the condition of the prison guard who had been shot at Riker's Island was still critical, but was now stable. The doctors were cautiously optimistic that he would live.

If he lives, Jimmy isn't facing the death penalty, Cally told herself. They can't execute him now for the cop's death three years ago. He's smart. He won't take a chance on murdering the little boy once he knows that the guard isn't going to die. He'll let him go.

The announcer was saying, "In other news, early this evening, seven-year-old Brian Dornan became separated from his mother on Fifth Avenue. The family is in New York because Brian's father . . ."

Frozen in front of the radio, Cally listened as the announcer gave a description of the boy, then said, "Here is a plea from his mother, asking for your help."

As Cally listened to the low, urgent voice of Brian's mother, she visualized the young woman who had dropped the wallet. Early thirties at the most. Shiny, dark hair that just reached the collar of her coat. She'd only caught a glimpse of her face, but Cally was sure that she was very pretty. Pretty and well dressed and secure.

Now, listening to her begging for help, Cally put her hands over her ears, then ran to the radio and snapped it off. She tiptoed into the bedroom. Gigi was already asleep, her breathing soft and even, her cheek pillowed in her hand, the other hand holding the ragged baby blanket up to her face.

Cally knelt beside her. I can reach out and touch her, she thought. That woman can't reach out to her child. What should I do? But if I call the police and Jimmy does harm that little boy, they'll say it's my fault, just the way they said that the cop's death was my fault.

Maybe Jimmy will just leave him somewhere. He *promised* he would . . . Even Jimmy wouldn't hurt a little boy, surely? I'll just wait and pray, she told herself.

But the prayer she tried to whisper—"Please God, keep little Brian safe"—sounded like a mockery and she did not complete it.

Jimmy had decided that his best bet was to go over the George Washington Bridge to Route 4, then take Route 17 to the New York Thruway. It might be a little farther that way than going up through the Bronx to the Tappan Zee, but every instinct warned him to get out of New York City fast. It was good that the GW had no toll gate at the outgoing side where they might stop him.

Brian looked out the window as they crossed the bridge. He knew they were going over the Hudson River. His mother had cousins who lived in New Jersey, near the bridge. Last summer, when he and Michael spent an extra week with Gran after they came back from Nantucket, they had visited them there.

They were nice. They had kids just about his age, too. Just thinking about them made Brian want to cry. He wished he could open the window and shout, *"I'm here. Come get me, please!"*

He was so hungry, and he really had to go to the bathroom. He looked up timidly. "I . . . could I please . . . I mean, I have to go to the bathroom." Now that he'd said it, he was so afraid the man would refuse that his lip began to quiver. Quickly he bit down on it. He could just hear Michael calling him a crybaby. But even that thought made him feel sad. He wouldn't even mind seeing Michael right now.

"You gotta pee?"

The man didn't seem too mad at him. Maybe he wouldn't hurt him after all. "Uh-huh."

"Okay. You hungry?"

"Yes, sir."

Jimmy was starting to feel somewhat secure. They were on Route 4. The traffic was heavy but moving. Nobody was looking for this car. By now, the guy who parked it was probably in his pj's watching *It's a Wonderful Life* for the fortieth time. By tomorrow morning, when he and his wife started to holler about their stolen Toyota, Jimmy would be in Canada with Paige. God he was crazy about her. In his life, she was the closest he had ever come to a sure thing.

Jimmy didn't want to stop to eat yet. On the other hand, to be on the safe side, he probably should fill up the tank now. There was no telling what hours places would keep on Christmas Eve.

"All right," he said, "in a couple minutes we'll get some gas, go to the john, and I'll buy sodas and potato chips. Later on, we'll stop at a McDonald's and get a hamburger. But just remember when we stop for gas, you try to attract attention and . . ." He pulled the pistol from his jacket, pointed it at Brian, and made a clicking noise. *"Bang,"* he said.

Brian looked away. They were in the middle lane of the three-lane highway. A sign pointed to the exit marked Forest Avenue. A police car pulled abreast of them, then turned off into the parking lot of a diner. "I won't talk to anyone. I promise," he managed to say.

"I promise, *Daddy,*" Jimmy snapped.

Daddy. Involuntarily, Brian's hand curled around the St. Christopher medal. He was going to bring this medal to Daddy and then Daddy was going to get better. Then his dad would find this guy, Jimmy, and beat him up for being so mean to his kid. Brian was sure of it. As his fingers traced the raised image of the towering figure carrying the Christ child, he said in a clear voice, "I promise, *Daddy.*"

10

At lower Manhattan's One Police Plaza, the command post for the Jimmy Siddons manhunt, the escalating tension was visibly evident. Everyone was keenly aware that to make good his escape, Siddons would not hesitate to kill again. They also knew he had the weapon smuggled in to him.

"Armed and Dangerous" was the caption under his picture on the flyers that were being distributed all over the city.

"Last time, we got two thousand useless tips, followed up every useless one of them, and the only reason we ever got him behind bars last summer was because he was dumb enough to hold up a gas station in Michigan while a cop was on the premises," Jack Shore growled to Mort Levy, as in disgust he watched a team of officers answer the flood of calls on the hot line.

Levy nodded absently. "Anything more about Siddons's girlfriend?" he asked Shore.

An hour ago one of the prisoners in Siddons's cellblock had told a guard that last month Siddons had bragged about a girlfriend named Paige, who he said was a world-class stripper.

They were trying to trace her in New York, but on the hunch that she might have been involved with Siddons in Michigan, Shore had contacted the authorities there.

"No, nothing so far. Probably another dead end."

"Call for you from Detroit, Jack," a voice bellowed above the din in the room. Both men turned quickly. In two strides Shore was at his desk and had grabbed the phone.

His caller did not waste time. "Stan Logan, Jack. We met when you came out to pick up Siddons last year. I may have something interesting for you."

"Let's have it."

"We never could find out where Siddons was hiding before he tried to pull the holdup here. The tip about Paige may be the answer. We've got a rap sheet on a Paige Laronde who calls herself an exotic dancer. She left town two days ago. Told a friend she didn't know if she'd be back, that she expected to join her boyfriend."

"Did she say where she was going?" Shore snapped.

"She said California, then Mexico."

"California and Mexico! Hell, if he makes it to Mexico we may never find him."

"Our guys are checking the train and bus stations as well as the airports, to see if we can pick up her trail. We'll keep you posted," Logan promised, then added, "We're about to fax her rap sheet and publicity pictures. Don't show them to your kids."

Shore slammed down the phone. "If Siddons managed to get out of New York this morning, he could be in California right now, maybe even Mexico."

"It would be pretty tough to get a plane reservation at the last minute on Christmas Eve," Levy reminded him cautiously.

"Listen, somebody got a gun in to him. That same somebody may have had clothes and cash and an airline ticket waiting for him. Probably managed to get him to an airport in Philadelphia or Boston, where no one's looking for him. My guess is that he's met up with his girlfriend by now and the two of them are heading south of the border, if they're not already eating enchiladas. And I still say one way or the other the go-between had to be Siddons's sister."

Frowning, Mort Levy watched Jack Shore go to the communications room to await the faxes from Detroit. The next step would be to forward pictures of both Siddons and his girlfriend to the border patrol in Tijuana, with the warning to be on the lookout for them.

But we still have to cover the cathedral tonight on the one-in-a-million chance that Jimmy's offer to surrender was on the level, Mort thought. Somehow neither possibility rang true to him—not Mexico, not the surrender. Would this Paige be smart enough to lie to her friend on the chance that the cops might come looking for her?

The coffee and sandwiches they had ordered were just being delivered. Mort went over to get his ham on rye. Two of the women officers were talking together.

He heard one of them, Lori Martini, say, "Still no sign of that missing kid. For sure some nut must have picked him up."

"What missing kid?" Levy asked.

Soberly he listened to the details. It was the one kind of case no one in the department could work on without becoming emotionally involved. Mort had a seven-year-old son. He knew what must be going through that mother's mind. And the father so sick he hadn't even been told his son was missing. And all this at Christmastime. God, some people really get it in spades, he thought.

"Call for you, Mort," a voice shouted from across the room.

Carrying the coffee and sandwich, Mort returned to his desk. "Who is it?" he asked as he took the receiver.

"A woman. She didn't give her name."

As Mort pressed the phone to his ear, he said, "Detective Levy."

He heard the sound of frightened breathing. And then a faint click as the line went dead.

WCBS reporter Alan Graham approached the squad car where he'd interviewed Catherine Dornan an hour earlier when he had done an update on the story.

It was eight-thirty, and the intermittent gusts of snow had become a steady flow of large white flakes again.

Through his earphone, Graham heard the anchorman give the latest information about the escaped prisoner. "The condition of Mario Bonardi, the injured prison guard, is still extremely critical. Mayor Giuliani and Police Commissioner Bratton have paid a second visit to the hospital where he is in intensive care after delicate surgery. According to the latest report, the police are following up on a tip that his assailant, alleged murderer Jimmy Siddons, may be meeting a girlfriend in

California with the final destination, Mexico. The border patrol at Tijuana has been alerted."

One of the newsmen had been tipped off that Jimmy's lawyer claimed Siddons was turning himself in after midnight Mass at St. Patrick's. Alan Graham was glad that the decision had been made not to air that story. None of the police brass really believed it, and they didn't want the worshipers distracted by the rumor.

There were few pedestrians now on Fifth Avenue. It occurred to Graham that there was something almost obscene about the breaking stories they were covering this Christmas Eve: an escaped cop killer; a prison guard clinging to life; a seven-year-old missing boy, who was now the suspected victim of foul play.

He tapped on the window of the squad car. Catherine glanced up, then opened it halfway. Looking at her, he wondered how long she would be able to maintain her remarkable composure. She was sitting in the passenger seat of the car next to Officer Ortiz. Her son Michael was in the back with a handsome older woman whose arm was around him.

Catherine answered his unasked question. "I'm still waiting," she said quietly. "Officer Ortiz has been good enough to stay with me. I don't know why, but I feel as though somehow I'll find Brian right here." She turned slightly. "Mom, this is Alan Graham from WCBS. He interviewed me right after I spoke with you."

Barbara Cavanaugh saw the compassion on the face of the young reporter. Knowing that if there were anything to tell, they would have heard it by now, she still could not stop herself from asking, "Any word?"

"No, ma'am. We've had plenty of calls to the station, but they were all to express concern."

"He's vanished," Catherine said, her voice lifeless. "While Tom and I have raised the boys to basically trust people, they also know how to deal with emergencies. Brian knew enough to go to a policeman if he was lost. He knew to dial 911. Somebody has taken him. Who would take and hold a seven-year-old child unless . . . ?"

"Catherine, dear, don't torture yourself," her mother urged. "Everyone who heard you on the radio is praying for Brian. You must have faith."

Catherine felt frustration and anger rising inside her. Yes, she supposed she should have "faith." Certainly Brian had faith—he believed in that St. Christopher medal, probably enough to have followed whoever picked up my wallet. He knew it was inside, she reasoned, and felt he had to get it back. She looked back at her mother, and at Michael beside her. She felt her anger ebb. It wasn't her mother's fault that any of this had happened. No, faith—even in something as unlikely as a St. Christopher medal—was a good thing.

"You're right, Mom," she said.

From the receiver in his ear, Graham heard the anchorman say, "Over to you, Alan."

Stepping back from the car, he began, "Brian Dornan's mother is still keeping watch at the spot where her son disappeared shortly after 5:00 P.M. Authorities believe Catherine Dornan's theory that Brian may have seen someone steal her wallet and followed that person. The wallet contained a St. Christopher medal, which Brian was desperately anxious to bring to his father's hospital bed."

Graham handed the microphone to Catherine. "Brian believes the St. Christopher medal will help his father get well. If I had had Brian's faith, I would have guarded my wallet more carefully because the St. Christopher medal was in it. I want my husband to get better. I want my child," she said, her voice steady despite her emotion. "In the name of God, if anyone knows what happened to Brian, who has him, or where he is, please, *please* call us."

Graham stepped back from the squad car. "If anyone who knows anything about Brian's whereabouts is listening to that young mother's pain, we beg you to call this number, 212-555-0748."

11

Her eyes filled with tears, her lip quivering, Cally turned off the radio. *If anyone knows what happened to Brian . . .*

I *tried,* she told herself fiercely. I tried. She had dialed Detective Levy's number, but when she heard his voice, the enormity of what she was about to do overwhelmed her. They would arrest her. They would take Gigi away from her again and would put her with a new foster family. *If anyone knows anything about Brian's whereabouts . . .*

She reached for the phone.

From inside the bedroom she heard a wail and spun around. Gigi was having another nightmare. She rushed inside, sat down on the bed, gathered her child in her arms, and began rocking her. "Sshh, it's okay, everything's fine."

Gigi clung to her. "Mommy, Mommy. I dreamed that you

were gone again. Please don't go, Mommy. Please don't leave me. I don't want to live with other people ever, ever."

"That won't happen, sweetheart, I promise."

She could feel Gigi relax. Gently she laid her back on the pillow and smoothed her hair. "Now go back to sleep, angel."

Gigi closed her eyes, then opened them again. "Can I watch Santa Claus open his present?" she murmured.

Jimmy Siddons lowered the volume on the radio. "Your mom sure is flipping out about you, kid."

Brian had to keep himself from reaching out to the dashboard and touching the radio. Mom sounded so worried. He had to get back to her. Now she believed in the St. Christopher medal too. He was sure of it.

There were a lot of cars on the highway, and even though it was really snowing now, they were all going pretty fast. But Jimmy was in the far right lane, so no cars were coming up on that side. Brian began to plan.

If he could open the door real fast and roll out onto the road, he could keep rolling to the side. That way nobody would run over him. He pressed the medal for an instant, and then his hand crept to the handle on the door. When he put faint pressure on it, it moved slightly. He was right. Jimmy hadn't put the lock on after they stopped for gas.

Brian was about to throw open the door when he remembered his seat belt. He'd have to unfasten that just as the door swung open. Careful not to attract Jimmy's attention, he laid the index finger of his left hand on the seat belt's release button.

Just as Brian was about to pull on the handle and push the release, Jimmy swore. A car, weaving erratically, was coming up behind them on the left. An instant later it was so close it was almost touching the Toyota. Then it cut in front of them. Jimmy slammed on the brakes. The car skidded and fishtailed, as around them came the sound of metal impacting metal. Brian held his breath. Crash, he begged, *crash!* Then someone would help him.

But Jimmy righted the car and drove around the others. Just ahead, Brian could hear the wail of sirens and see the brilliance of flashing lights gathered around another accident, which they quickly drove past as well.

Jimmy grinned in savage satisfaction. "We're pretty lucky, aren't we, kiddo?" he asked Brian, as he glanced down at him.

Brian was still clutching the handle.

"Now you weren't thinking of jumping out if we'd gotten stuck back there, were you?" Jimmy asked. He clicked the control that locked the doors. "Keep your hand away from there. I see you touch that handle again and I'll break your fingers," he said quietly.

Brian didn't have the slightest doubt he would do just that.

12

 It was five after ten. Mort Levy sat at his desk, deep in thought. He had only one explanation for the disconnected call: Cally Hunter. The tap from the police surveillance van outside Cally's building confirmed that she had dialed him. The men on duty there offered to go up and talk to her if Mort wanted them to. "No. Leave her alone," he ordered. He knew it would be pointless. She'd only repeat exactly what she'd told them before. But she knows something and she is afraid to tell, he thought. He had tried to phone her twice, but she had not answered. He knew she was there, though. The lookouts in the van would have notified them if she'd left the apartment. So why wasn't she answering? Should he go over to see her himself? Would it do any good?

"What's with you?" Jack Shore asked impatiently. "You forgot how to hear?"

Mort looked up. The rotund senior detective stood glowering down at him. No wonder Cally's afraid of you, Mort thought, remembering the fear in her eyes at Jack's anger and open hostility.

"I'm thinking," Mort said curtly, resisting the impulse to suggest that Shore try it sometime.

"Well, think with the rest of us. We've gotta go over the plans to cover the cathedral." Then Shore's scowl softened. "Mort, why don't you take a break?"

He isn't as bad as he tries to seem, Mort thought. "I don't see you taking a break, Jack," he replied.

"It's just that I hate Siddons worse than you do."

Mort got up slowly. His mind was still focused on the elusive memory of some important clue that had been overlooked, something he knew was there, right in front of him, but that he just couldn't make himself see. They'd seen Cally Hunter at seven-fifteen this morning. She'd already been dressed for work. They had seen her again nearly twelve hours later. She looked exhausted and desperately worried. She was probably in bed asleep now. But every nerve in his body was telling him that he should talk to her. Despite her denial, he believed she held the key.

As he turned away from his desk, the phone rang. When he picked it up, he again heard the terrified breathing. This time he took the initiative. "Cally," Mort said urgently. "Cally, *talk* to me. Don't be afraid. Whatever it is, I'll try to help you."

Cally could not even think of going to bed. She had listened to the all-news station, hoping but at the same time fearing that the cops had found Jimmy, praying that little Brian was safe.

At ten o'clock she had turned on the television to watch the

Fox local news, then her heart sank. Brian's mother was seated next to the anchorman, Tony Potts. Her hair seemed looser now, as though she'd been standing outside in the wind and snow. Her face was very pale, and her eyes were filled with pain. There was a boy sitting next to her who seemed to be about ten or eleven years old.

The anchorman was saying, "You may have heard Catherine Dornan's appeals for help in finding her son Brian. We've asked her and Brian's brother, Michael, to be with us now. There were crowds of people on Fifth Avenue and Forty-ninth Street shortly after five o'clock this evening. Maybe you were one of them. Maybe you noticed Catherine with her two sons, Michael and Brian. They were in a group listening to a violinist playing Christmas carols, and singing along. Seven-year-old Brian disappeared from his mother's side. His mother and brother need your help in finding him."

The anchorman turned to Catherine. "You're holding a picture of Brian."

Cally watched as the picture was held up, listened as Brian's mother said, "It's not very clear, so let me tell you a little more about him. He's seven but looks younger because he's small. He has dark reddish brown hair and blue eyes and freckles on his nose . . ." Her voice faltered.

Cally shut her eyes. She couldn't bear to look at the stark agony on Catherine Dornan's face.

Michael put his hand over his mother's. "My brother's wearing a dark blue ski jacket just like mine, 'cept mine is green, and a red cap. And one of his front teeth is missing." Then he burst out, "We gotta get him back. We can't tell my Dad that Brian is missing. Dad's too sick to be worried." Michael's voice became even more urgent. "I know my dad.

He'd try to do something. He'd get out of bed and start looking for Brian, and we can't let him do that. He's sick, real
sick."

Cally snapped off the set. She tiptoed into the bedroom
where Gigi was at last sleeping peacefully and went over to
the window that led to the fire escape. She could still see
Brian's eyes as he glanced over his shoulder, begging her to
help him, his one hand in Jimmy's grasp, his other holding the
St. Christopher medal as though it would somehow save him.
She shook her head. That medal, she thought. He hadn't cared
about the money. He followed her because he believed that
medal would make his father get well.

Cally ran the few steps back into the living room and
grabbed Mort Levy's card.

When he answered, her resolve almost crumbled again, but
then his voice was so kind when he said, "Cally, *talk* to me.
Don't be afraid."

"Mr. Levy," she blurted out, "can you come here, quick?
I've *got* to talk to you about Jimmy—and that little boy who's
missing."

13

 All that was left of the snack Jimmy had purchased when they stopped for gas were the empty Coca-Cola cans and the crumpled bags that had held potato chips. Jimmy had thrown his on the floor in front of Brian, while Brian had placed his in the plastic wastebasket attached under the dashboard. He couldn't even remember what the chips had tasted like. He was so hungry that, scared as he felt, being hungry was all he could think about.

He knew that Jimmy was really mad at him. And ever since the time they'd nearly crashed and Jimmy realized that he had been planning to try to jump out of the car, he'd seemed real nervous. He kept opening and closing his fingers on the steering wheel, making a scary snapping sound. The first time he did it, Brian had flinched and jumped, and Jimmy had grabbed him by the shoulder, snarling at him to stay away from the door.

The snow was coming down faster now. Ahead of them someone braked. The car swung around in a circle, then kept going. Brian realized that it hadn't slammed into another car only because all the drivers on the road were trying to keep from getting too close to other cars.

Even so, Jimmy began to swear, a low steady stream of words, most of which Brian had never heard, even from Skeet, the kid in his class who knew all the good swear words.

The spinning car confirmed Jimmy's growing sense that near as he was to escaping the country something could still go wrong any minute. It didn't sound as though that prison guard he shot was going to make it. If the guard died . . . Jimmy had meant it when he told Cally that they wouldn't take him alive.

Then Jimmy tried to reassure himself. He had a car that probably nobody even realized was missing yet. He had decent clothes and money. If they'd been stuck back there when that crazy fool caused the accident, the kid might have managed to jump out of the car. If that jerk who just spun around had hit the Toyota, I might have been hurt, Jimmy thought. On my own, maybe I could've bluffed it, but not with the kid along. On the other hand, nobody knew he had the kid, and in a million years no cop was on the lookout for a guy in a nice car with a bunch of toys in the backseat and a little boy beside him.

They were near Syracuse now. In three or four hours he'd be across the border with Paige.

There was a McDonald's sign on the right. Jimmy was hungry, and this would be a good place to get something to eat. It would have to last him until he reached Canada. He'd pull up to the drive-in window, order for the two of them, then get back on the road fast.

"What's your favorite food, kid?" he asked, his tone almost genial.

Brian had spotted the McDonald's sign and held his breath, hoping that this meant they were going to get something to eat. "A hamburger and french fries, and a Coke," he said timidly.

"If I stop at McDonald's, can you look like you're sleeping?"

"Yes, I promise."

"Do it then. Lean against me with your eyes closed."

"Okay." Obediently Brian slumped against Jimmy and squeezed his eyes shut. He tried not to show how scared he was.

"Let's see what kind of actor you are," Jimmy said. "And you'd better be good."

The St. Christopher medal had slipped to the side. Brian straightened it so that he could feel it, heavy and comforting against his chest.

It was scary to be so close to this guy, not like being sleepy when he was driving with Dad and curling up against him and feeling Dad's hand patting his shoulder.

Jimmy pulled off the highway. They had to wait on line at the drive-in window. Jimmy froze when he saw a state trooper pull in behind them, but had no choice except to stay put and not draw attention to himself. When it was their turn and he placed the order and paid, the attendant didn't even glance into the car. But at the pickup spot, the woman looked over the counter to where the light from behind her shone on Brian.

"I guess he just can't wait to see what Santa Claus is going to bring him, can he?"

Jimmy nodded and tried to smile in agreement as he reached for the bag.

She leaned way forward and peered into the car. "My goodness, is he wearing a St. Christopher medal? My dad was named after him and used to try to make a big deal of it, but my mom always jokes about St. Christopher being dropped from the calendar of saints. My dad says it's too bad Mom wasn't named Philomena. She's another saint the Vatican said didn't exist." With a hearty laugh the young woman handed over the bag.

As they drove back onto the highway, Brian opened his eyes. He could smell the hamburgers and the french fries. He sat up slowly.

Jimmy looked at him, his eyes steely, his face rigid. Through lips that barely parted, he quietly ordered, "Get that goddamn medal off your neck."

Cally had to talk to him about her brother and the missing child. After promising to be right over, Mort Levy hung up the phone, stunned. What possible connection could there be between Jimmy Siddons and the little boy who disappeared on Fifth Avenue?

He dialed the lookout van. "You recorded that call?"

"Is she crazy, Mort? She can't be talking about the Dornan kid, can she? Want us to pick her up for questioning?"

"That's just what I *don't* want you to do!" Levy exploded. "She's scared to death as it is. Sit tight until I get there."

He had to inform his superiors, starting with Jack Shore, about Cally Hunter's call. Mort spotted Shore leaving the chief of detectives' private office, was out of his chair and across the room in seconds. He grabbed Shore's arm. "Come back inside."

"I told you to take a break." Shore tried to shake off his hand. "We just heard from Logan in Detroit again. Two days ago a woman whose description matches Siddons's girlfriend got a ride from a private car service over the border to Windsor. Logan's guys think that Laronde told her girlfriend about California and Mexico to throw them off her trail. The girlfriend was questioned again. This time it occurred to her to mention that she offered to buy Laronde's fur coat because it wouldn't be needed in Mexico. Laronde refused."

I never bought that Mexico story, Mort Levy thought. He didn't relinquish his grip on Shore's arm as he shoved open the chief's door.

Five minutes later, a squad car was racing up the East Side Drive to Avenue B and Tenth Street. A bitterly frustrated Jack Shore had been ordered to wait in the lookout van while Mort and the chief, Bud Folney, went upstairs to talk to Cally.

Mort knew that Shore would not forgive him for insisting that he stay out of it. "Jack, when we were there earlier, I knew there was something she was holding back. You've scared her to death. She thinks you'd do anything to see her back behind bars. For God's sake, can't you look at her as a human being? She's got a four-year-old child, her husband is dead, and she got the book thrown at her when she made the mistake of helping the brother she'd practically raised."

Now Mort turned to Folney. "I don't know how Jimmy Siddons ties into that missing child, but I do know that Cally has been too frightened to talk. If she tells us now whatever she knows, it will be because she feels that the department . . . you . . . aren't out to get her."

Folney nodded. He was a soft-spoken, lean man in his late forties, with a scholarly face. He had in fact spent three years as a high school teacher before realizing his passion was law enforcement. It was widely believed among the ranks that one day he'd be police commissioner. Already he was one of the most powerful men in the department.

Mort Levy knew that if there was anyone who could help Cally, assuming she had in some way been forced to cover for Jimmy again, it was Folney. But the missing child—how could Siddons be involved in this?

It was a question they were all frantic to ask.

When the squad car pulled up behind the surveillance van, Shore made one last appeal. "If I keep my mouth shut . . ."

Folney answered, "I suggest you start right now, Jack. Get in the van."

14

 Pete Cruise had been about to call it a day. He'd discovered where Cally Hunter lived when he tried to interview her after she was released from prison, and now he was hoping her brother would show up. But there'd been nothing to watch for hours except the on-again-off-again falling snow. Now at least it seemed to have stopped for good. The van that he knew was a police van was still parked across the street from Cally's apartment, but probably all they were doing was monitoring her calls. The likelihood of Jimmy Siddons suddenly showing up at his sister's house now was about the same as two strangers having matching DNA.

All the hours of hanging around Hunter's building were a waste, Pete decided. From the time he'd seen Cally come home shortly before six, and the two detectives stop in around seven, it had been a big nothing.

He'd kept his powerful portable radio on the whole time he waited, switching between the police band, his station, WYME, and the WCBS news station. No word of Siddons at all. Shame about that missing kid.

When the ten o'clock news came on WYME, Pete thought for the hundredth time that the anchor in that slot sounded like a wimp. But she did have some real emotion when she talked about the missing seven-year-old. Maybe we need a missing kid every day, Pete thought sarcastically, then was immediately ashamed of himself.

There was a lot of activity in Hunter's building, people coming and going. Many of the churches had moved up the midnight services to ten o'clock. No matter what time they schedule them, some people will always be late, Pete thought as he saw an elderly couple hurry from the building and turn up Avenue B. Probably heading for St. Emeric's.

The woman who had brought Hunter's kid home earlier was coming up the block. Was she headed for Hunter's apartment? Cally planning to go out? he wondered.

Pete shrugged. Maybe Hunter had a late date or was going to church herself. Obviously, today wasn't the day to get the story that was going to make his name as a reporter.

It'll happen, Pete promised himself. I won't always be working on this lousy ten-watt station. His buddy who worked at WNBC loved to ride Pete about his job. A favorite put-down was that the only audience for WYME were two cockroaches and three stray cats. "This is station Why-Me," he'd joke.

Pete started his car. He was just about to pull out when a squad car raced down the block and stopped in front of Cally's building.

Through narrowed eyes, Pete observed three men emerge. One he recognized as Jack Shore crossed the street and got into the van. Then in the light from the building entrance he could make out Mort Levy. He didn't get a good look at the other one.

Something was breaking. Pete turned off the engine, suddenly interested again.

While she waited for Mort Levy, Cally took Gigi's Christmas presents from their hiding place behind the couch and set them in front of the tree. The secondhand doll's carriage didn't look that bad, she decided, with the pretty blue satin coverlet and pillowcase. She'd put the baby doll she'd picked up for a couple of dollars last month in it, but it wasn't nearly as cute as the one that she'd wanted to buy from the peddler on Fifth Avenue. That one had Gigi's golden-brown hair and was wearing a blue party dress. *If she hadn't been looking for that peddler, she wouldn't have seen the wallet, and the boy wouldn't have followed her, and . . .*

She put that thought aside. She was past feeling now. Carefully, she stacked the presents she'd wrapped with candy-cane paper: an outfit from The Gap—leggings and a polo shirt; crayons and a coloring book; some furniture for Gigi's dollhouse. Everything, even the two pieces of the Gap outfit, was in separate boxes so at least it looked as though Gigi had a stack of gifts to open.

She tried to avoid looking at the largest package under the tree, the package that Gigi thought was their gift for Santa Claus.

Finally she phoned Aika. Aika's grandchildren always went home to sleep, so she was sure she could come over and stay

with Gigi in case the cops arrested Cally after she told them
about Jimmy and the little boy.

Aika answered on the first ring. "Hello." Her voice was
filled with her normal warmth. If only they'd let Gigi stay with
Aika if they put me in prison again, Cally thought. She swallowed over the lump in her throat, then said, "Aika, I'm in
trouble. Can you come over in about half an hour and maybe
stay overnight?"

"You bet I can." Aika did not ask questions, simply
clicked off.

As Cally replaced the receiver, the buzzer from the downstairs door resounded through the apartment.

"The switchboard's on fire, Mrs. Dornan," Leigh Ann
Winick, the producer of Fox 5 Ten o'Clock News told Catherine as, carefully avoiding the floor cables, she and Michael left
the broadcast area. "It looks as though everyone in our view-
ing area wants you to know that they're rooting and praying
for Brian and your husband."

"Thank you." Catherine tried to smile. She looked down at
Michael. He had been trying so hard to keep up his spirits for
her sake. It was only when she had listened to his on-camera
plea that she had fully realized what this was doing to him.

Michael's hands were in his pockets, his shoulders hunched
under his ears. It was exactly the same posture Tom unconsciously fell into when he was worried about a patient.
Catherine squared her own shoulders and put her arm around
her older son as the door from the studio closed behind them.

The producer said, "Our operators are thanking everyone
in your name, but is there anything else you'd like us to tell
our audience?"

Catherine drew a deep breath, and her arm tightened around Michael. "I wish you'd tell them that we think I dropped my wallet, and that Brian apparently followed whoever picked it up. The reason he was so anxious to get it back is that my mother had just given me a St. Christopher medal that my father wore through World War II. My father believed the medal kept him safe. It even has a dent where a bullet glanced off it, a bullet that might have killed him. Brian has the same wonderful faith that St. Christopher or what he represents is going to take care of us again . . . and so do I. St. Christopher will carry Brian back to us on his shoulders, and he will help my husband get well."

She smiled down at Michael. "Right, pal?"

Michael's eyes were shining. "Mom, do you really believe that?"

Catherine drew a deep breath. *I believe, Lord, help my unbelief.* "Yes, I do," she said firmly.

And maybe because it was Christmas Eve, for the first time, she really did.

15

State Trooper Chris McNally tuned out as Deidre Lenihan droned on about just seeing a St. Christopher medal, and how her father was named after St. Christopher. She was a well-meaning young woman, but every time he stopped for coffee at this McDonald's, she seemed to be on duty and always wanted to talk.

Tonight Chris was too preoccupied with thoughts of getting home. He wanted to get at least some sleep before his kids got up to open all their Christmas presents. He also had been thinking about the Toyota he had just seen pull out in front of him. He'd been thinking of buying one himself, although he knew his wife wouldn't want a brown one. A new car meant monthly payments to worry about. He noticed the remnant of a bumper sticker on the Toyota, a single word, *inheritance*. He knew the sticker had originally said, "We're spending our grandchildren's inheritance." We could use an inheritance, he thought.

"And my father said . . ."

Chris forced himself to refocus. Deidre's nice, he thought, but she talks too much. He reached for the bag she was dangling in her hand, but it was clear she was not going to relinquish it yet, not until she had told how her dad said it was too bad that her mother hadn't been named Philomena.

Still she wasn't finished. "Years ago my aunt worked in Southampton and belonged to St. Philomena's parish. When they had to rename it, the pastor had a contest to decide which saint they should choose and why. My aunt suggested St. Dymphna because she said she was the saint of the insane and most of the people in the parish were nuts."

"Well, I was named after St. Christopher myself," Chris said, managing to snare the bag. "Merry Christmas, Deidre."

And it will be Christmas before I get a bite out of this Big Mac, he thought as he drove back onto the Thruway. With one hand, he deftly opened the bag, freed the burger, and gratefully took a large bite. The coffee would have to wait until he got back to his post.

He'd be off duty at midnight, and then, he thought, smiling to himself, it would be time to grab a little shut-eye. Eileen would try to keep the kids in bed till six, but lots of luck. It hadn't happened last year and it wouldn't happen this year if he knew his sons.

He was approaching exit 40 and drove the car to the official turnaround, from which he could observe errant drivers. Christmas Eve was nothing like New Year's Eve for nabbing drinkers, but Chris was determined that no one who was speeding or weaving on the road was going to get past him.

He'd witnessed a couple of accidents where some drunk turned the holiday into a nightmare for innocent people. Not tonight if he could help it. And the snow had made driving that much more treacherous.

As Chris opened the lid on his coffee, he frowned. A Corvette doing at least eighty was racing up the service lane. He snapped on his dome lights and siren, shifted into gear, and the squad car leaped in pursuit.

Chief of Detectives Bud Folney listened with no expression other than quiet attentiveness as a trembling Cally Hunter told Mort Levy about finding the wallet on Fifth Avenue. She had waived her Miranda warning, saying impatiently, "This can't wait any longer."

Folney knew the basics of her case: older sister of Jimmy Siddons, had served time because a judge had not believed her story that she thought she was helping her brother get away from a rival gang bent on killing him. Levy had told him that Hunter seemed to be one of the hard-luck people of this world—raised by an elderly grandmother, who died, leaving her to try to straighten out her louse of a younger brother when she was only a kid herself; then her husband killed by a hit-and-run driver when she was pregnant.

About thirty, Folney thought, and could be pretty with a little meat on her. She still had the pale, haunted expression he had seen on other women who had been imprisoned and carried with them the horror that someday they might be sent back.

He looked around. The neat apartment, the sunny, yellow paint on the cracked walls, the bravely decorated but skimpy Christmas tree, the new coverlet on the battered doll carriage, they all told him something about Cally Hunter.

Folney knew that, like himself, Mort Levy was desperate to know what connection Hunter could give them between Siddons and the missing Dornan child. He approved of Mort's gentle approach. Cally Hunter had to tell it her way. It's a good thing we didn't bring in the raging bull, Folney thought. Jack Shore was a good detective, but his aggressiveness often got on Folney's nerves.

Hunter was talking about seeing the wallet on the sidewalk. "I picked it up without thinking. I guessed it belonged to that woman, but I wasn't sure. I honestly wasn't sure," she burst out, "and I thought if I tried to give it back to her, she might say something was missing from it. That happened to my grandmother. And then you'd send me back to prison and . . ."

"Cally, take it easy," Mort said. "What happened then?"

"When I got home . . ."

She told them about finding Jimmy in the apartment, wearing her deceased husband's clothes. She pointed to the big package under the tree. "The guard's uniform and coat are in there," she said. "It was the only place I could think to hide them in case you came back."

That's it, Mort thought. When we looked around the apartment the second time, there was something different about the closet. The box on the shelf and the man's jacket were missing.

Cally's voice became ragged and uneven as she told them about Jimmy taking Brian Dornan and threatening to kill him if he spotted a cop chasing him.

Levy asked, "Cally, do you think Jimmy can be trusted to let Brian go?"

"I wanted to think so," she said tonelessly. "That was what I told myself when I didn't call you immediately. But I know he's desperate. Jimmy will do anything to keep from going to prison again."

Folney finally asked a question. "Cally, why did you call us now?"

"I saw Brian's mother on television, and I knew that if Jimmy had taken Gigi, I'd want you to help me get her back." Cally clasped her hands together. Her body swayed slightly forward then back in the ancient posture of grief. "The look on that little boy's face, the way he put that medal around his neck and was holding on to it like it was a life preserver . . . if anything happens to him, it's my fault."

The buzzer sounded. *If that's Shore . . .* Folney thought as he jumped up to answer it.

It was Aika Banks. When she entered the apartment, she looked at the policemen searchingly, then rushed to Cally and hugged her. "Baby, what is it? What's wrong? Why do you need me to stay with Gigi? What do these people want?"

Cally winced in pain.

Aika peeled up her friend's sleeve. The bruises caused by Jimmy's fingers were now an ugly purple. Any doubts that Bud Folney had about Hunter's possible cooperation with her brother disappeared. He squatted in front of her. "Cally, you're not going to get into trouble. I promise you. I believe you found that wallet. I believe you didn't know what was best for you to do. But now you've got to help us. *Have you any idea where Jimmy might have gone?*"

Ten minutes later, when they left Cally's apartment, Mort Levy was carrying the bulky gift-wrapped package that held the guard's uniform.

Shore joined them in the squad car and impatiently fired

questions at Mort. As they were driven downtown, they agreed that the search for Jimmy Siddons would be based on the assumption that he might be trying to reach Canada.

"He's got to be in a car," Folney said flatly. "There's no way he'll travel on public transportation with that child."

Cally had told them that from the time he was twelve years old, Jimmy could hot-wire and steal any car; she was sure he must have had one waiting near the apartment.

"My guess is that Siddons would want to get out of New York State as soon as possible," Folney said. "Which means he'd drive through New England to the border. But it's only a guess. He could be on the Thruway, headed for I87. That's the fastest route."

And Siddons's girlfriend was probably in Canada. It all fit together.

They also accepted Cally's absolute certainty that Jimmy Siddons would not be taken alive and that his final act of vengeance would be to kill his hostage.

So they were faced with an escaped murderer with a child, possibly driving a car they could not describe, probably headed north in a snowstorm. It would be like looking for a needle in a haystack. Siddons would be too smart to attract attention by speeding. The border was always mobbed with holiday traffic on Christmas Eve. He dictated a message to be sent to state police throughout New England as well as New York. "Has threatened to kill the hostage," he emphasized.

They calculated that if Siddons had left Cally Hunter's apartment shortly after six, depending on driving conditions, he'd be between two and three hundred miles away. The alert that went out to the state police contained Cally's final certainty: *On a chain around his neck, the child may be wearing a bronze St. Christopher medal the size of a silver dollar.*

Pete Cruise watched as the detectives emerged from Cally Hunter's building some twenty minutes after arriving there. He noted that Levy was carrying a bulky package. Shore immediately jumped out of the van and joined them.

This time Pete got a good look at the third man, then whistled silently. It was Bud Folney, chief of detectives and in line to be the next police commissioner. Something was breaking. Something big.

The squad car took off with its dome light flashing. A block away its siren was turned on. Pete sat for a moment, debating what to do. The cops in the van might stop him if he tried to go in to see Cally, but obviously something major was going down here, and he was determined to scoop everyone on this.

As he was wondering about looking for a back entrance to the building, he saw the woman he knew to be Cally's babysitter leave. In a flash he was out of the car and following her. He caught up with her when she turned the corner and they were out of sight of the cops in the van. "I'm Detective Cruise," he said. "I've been instructed to see you safely home. How is Cally doing?"

"Oh, that poor girl," Aika began. "Officer, you people have to believe her. She thought she was doing the right thing when she didn't phone you about her brother kidnapping that little boy . . ."

Even though Brian was hungry, the hamburger was hard to swallow. His throat felt like there was something stuck in it. He knew that Jimmy was the reason for that. He took a giant swallow of Coke and tried to think about how Daddy would beat Jimmy up for being so mean to him.

But now when he thought about Daddy it was hard to remember anything except all the plans they had made for Christmas Eve. Daddy had planned to come home early, and they were all going to trim the tree together. Then they were going to have dinner and go around their neighborhood singing Christmas carols with a bunch of their friends.

That was all he could think about now, because that was all he wanted, to be home and have Daddy and Mommy smiling a lot the way they always did when they were together. When they came to New York because Dad was sick, Mom had told him and Michael that their big presents, the ones they really wanted, would be waiting for them when they got back home. She said that Santa Claus would keep the presents on his sleigh until he knew they were in their own house again.

Michael had said, "Yeah, really," under his breath to Brian. But Brian believed in Santa Claus. Last year Dad had pointed out marks on the roof of the garage where Santa's sleigh had landed and where the reindeer had stood. Michael told him he heard Mom tell Dad it was a good thing Dad hadn't broken his neck sliding around on the icy roof and making tracks all over it, but Brian didn't mind what Michael said, because he didn't believe it. Just like he didn't mind that Michael sometimes called him the Dork; he knew he wasn't a dork.

He knew things were bad when you wished your jerk brother, who could be such a pain in the neck, was there with you, and that was just how he felt now.

As Brian swallowed over that feeling of something in his throat, the plastic container almost jumped out of his hand. He realized Jimmy had switched lanes fast.

Jimmy Siddons swore silently. He had just passed a state trooper's car stopped in back of a sports car. The sight of a trooper made him sweat all over, but he shouldn't have switched lanes like that. He was getting jumpy.

Sensing the animosity that bristled from Jimmy, Brian put the uneaten hamburger and the soda back in the bag and, moving slowly so Jimmy could see what he was doing, leaned down and put the bag on the floor. Then he straightened up, huddled against the back of the seat and hugged his arms against his sides. The fingers of his right hand groped until they closed around the St. Christopher medal, which he had laid on the seat next to him when he opened the package of food.

With a sense of relief he closed his hand over it and mentally pictured the strong saint who carried the little kid across the dangerous river, who had taken care of his grandfather, who would make Dad get better and who . . . Brian closed his eyes . . . He didn't finish the wish, but in his mind he could see himself on the shoulders of the saint.

16

 Barbara Cavanaugh was waiting for Catherine and Michael in the green room at Channel 5. "You both did a great job," she said quietly. Then, seeing the exhaustion on her daughter's face, she said, "Catherine, please come back to the apartment. The police will get in touch with you there as soon as they have any word about Brian. You look ready to drop."

"I can't, Mother," Catherine said. "I know it's foolish to wait on Fifth Avenue. Brian isn't going to get back there on his own, but while I'm out and about I at least feel as though I'm doing something to find him. I don't really know what I'm saying except that when I left your apartment, I had my two little boys with me, and when I go back they're going to be with me, too."

Leigh Ann Winick made a decision. "Mrs. Dornan, why

not stay right here at least for the present? This room is comfortable. We'll send out for some hot soup or a sandwich or whatever you want. But you've said yourself, there's no point in just waiting on Fifth Avenue indefinitely."

Catherine considered. "And the police will be able to reach me here?"

Winick pointed to the phone. "Absolutely. Now tell me what I can order for you."

Twenty minutes later, as Catherine, her mother, and Michael were sipping steaming hot minestrone, they watched the green room's television monitor. The news bite was about Mario Bonardi, the wounded prison guard. Although still critical, his condition had stabilized.

The reporter was with Bonardi's wife and teenage children in the waiting room of the intensive care unit. When asked for a comment, a weary Rose Bonardi said, "My husband is going to make it. I want to thank everyone who has been praying for him today. Our family has known many happy Christmases, but this will be the best ever because we know what we so nearly lost."

"That's what we'll be saying, Michael," Catherine said determinedly. "Dad is going to make it and Brian is going to be found."

The reporter with the Bonardi family said, "Back to you at the news desk, Tony."

"Thanks, Ted. Glad to hear that it's going so well. That's the kind of Christmas story we want to be able to tell." The anchor's smile vanished. "There is still no trace of Mario Bonardi's assailant, Jimmy Siddons, who was awaiting trial for the murder of a police officer. Police sources are quoted as saying that he may be planning to meet his girlfriend,

Paige Laronde, in Mexico. Airports, train stations, and bus terminals are under heavy surveillance. It was nearly three years ago, while making his escape after an armed robbery, that Siddons shot and fatally wounded Officer William Grasso, who had stopped him for a traffic violation. Siddons is known to be armed and should be considered extremely dangerous."

As the anchorman spoke, Jimmy Siddons's mug shots were flashed on the screen.

"He looks mean," Michael observed as he studied the cold eyes and sneering lips of the escaped prisoner.

"He certainly does," Barbara Cavanaugh agreed. Then she looked at her grandson's face. "Mike, why don't you close your eyes and rest for a little while?" she suggested.

He shook his head. "I don't want to go to sleep."

It was one minute of eleven. The newscaster was saying, "In an update, we have no further information about the whereabouts of seven-year-old Brian Dornan, who has been missing since shortly after five o'clock today.

"On this very special evening, we ask you to continue to pray that Brian is safely returned to his family, and wish you and all of your loved ones a very Merry Christmas."

In an hour it will be Christmas, Catherine thought. *Brian, you have to come back, you have to be found. You have to be with me in the morning when we go see Dad. Brian, come back. Please come back.*

The door of the green room opened. Winick ushered in a tall man in his late forties, followed by Officer Manuel Ortiz. "Detective Rhodes wants to talk to you, Mrs. Dornan," Winick said. "I'm outside if you need me."

Catherine saw the grave look on the faces of both Rhodes

and Ortiz, and fear paralyzed her. She was unable to move or speak.

They realized what she was thinking. "No, Mrs. Dornan, it isn't that," Ortiz said quickly.

Rhodes took over. "I'm from headquarters, Mrs. Dornan. We have information about Brian, but let me begin by saying that as far as we know he's alive and unharmed."

"Then where is he?" Michael burst out. 'Where's my brother?"

Catherine listened as Detective Rhodes explained about her wallet being picked up by a young woman who was the sister of escaped prisoner Jimmy Siddons. Her mind did not want to accept that Brian had been abducted by the murderer whose face she had just seen on the television screen. No, she thought, no, that can't be.

She pointed to the monitor. "They just reported that that man is probably on his way to Mexico. Brian disappeared six hours ago. He could be in Mexico right now."

"At headquarters we don't buy that story," Rhodes told her. "We think he's heading for Canada, probably in a stolen car. We're concentrating the search in that direction."

Suddenly Catherine could feel no emotion. It was like when she was in the delivery room and was given the shot of Demerol and all the pain miraculously stopped. *And she'd looked up to see Tom wink at her. Tom, always there for her. "Feels better doesn't it, Babe?" he had asked. And her mind, no longer clouded with pain, had become so clear.* It was that way now, as well. "What kind of car are they in?"

Rhodes looked uncomfortable. "We don't know," he said. "We're only guessing that he's in a car, but we feel sure it's the right guess. We have every trooper throughout New York and New England on the alert for a man traveling with a young boy who is wearing a St. Christopher medal."

"Brian is wearing the medal?" Michael exclaimed. "Then he'll be all right. Gran, tell Mom that the medal will take care of Brian like it took care of Grandpa."

"Armed and dangerous," Catherine repeated.

"Mrs. Dornan," Rhodes said urgently. "If Siddons is in a car, he's probably listening to the radio. He's smart. Now that Officer Bonardi is out of danger, Siddons knows he isn't facing a death sentence. Capital punishment had not been reinstated when he killed the police officer three years ago. And he did tell his sister that he'd let Brian go tomorrow morning."

Her mind was so clear. "But you don't believe that, do you?"

She did not need to see the expression on his face to know that Detective Rhodes did not believe that Jimmy Siddons would voluntarily release Brian.

"Mrs. Dornan, if we're right and Siddons is heading for the Canadian border, he's not going to get there for at least another three or four hours. Although the snow has stopped in some areas, the roads are still going to be something of a mess all night. He can't be traveling fast, and he doesn't know that we know he has Brian. That's being kept from the media. In Siddons's mind, Brian will be an asset—at least until he reaches the border. We will find him before then."

The television monitor was still on with the volume low. Catherine's back was to it. She saw Detective Rhodes's face change, heard a voice say, "We interrupt this program for a news bulletin. According to a report that has just been broadcast by station WYME, seven-year-old Brian Dornan, the boy who has been missing since this afternoon, has fallen into the hands of alleged murderer Jimmy Siddons, who told his sister that if the police close in on him, he will put a bullet through the child's head. More later, as news comes in."

17

After Aika left, Cally made a cup of tea, wrapped herself in a blanket, turned the television on, and pressed the MUTE button. This way I'll know if there's any news, she thought. Then she turned on the radio and tuned in a station playing Christmas music, but she kept the volume low.

"*Hark, the herald angels sing . . .*" Remember how Frank and I sang that together when we were trimming the tree? she thought. Five years ago. Their one Christmas together. They'd just learned that she was pregnant. She remembered all the plans they'd made. "Next year we'll have help trimming the tree," Frank had said.

"Sure we will. A three-month-old baby will be a big help," she'd said, laughing.

She remembered Frank lifting her up so that she could place the star on the top of the tree.

Why?

Why had everything gone so wrong? There wasn't a next year. Just one week later Frank was killed by a hit-and-run driver. He'd been on his way home from a trip to the deli for a carton of milk.

We had so little time, Cally thought, shaking her head. Sometimes she wondered if those months were just a dream. It seemed so long ago now.

"O come, all ye faithful, joyful and triumphant..." "Adeste Fideles." Was it just yesterday that I was feeling so good about life? Cally wondered. At work the hospital administrator had said, "Cally, I've been hearing wonderful reports on you. They tell me you've got the makings of a born nurse. Have you ever thought of going to nursing school?" Then she'd talked about scholarships and how she was going to look into it.

That little boy, Cally thought. Oh God, don't let Jimmy hurt him. I should have called Detective Levy immediately. I know I should have. Why didn't I? she wondered, then immediately answered her own question: Because I wasn't just afraid for Brian. I was afraid for myself, too, and that may cost Brian his life.

She got up and went in to look at Gigi. As usual, the little girl had managed to work one foot out from under the covers. She did it every night, even when the room was cold.

Cally tucked the covers around her daughter's shoulders, then touched the small foot and tucked that in, too. Gigi stirred. "Mommy," she said drowsily.

"I'm right here."

Cally went back to the living room and glanced over at the television for a moment, then rushed to turn up the volume. No! No! she thought as she heard the reporter explain that police now had information that the missing boy had been kidnapped by escaped cop killer Jimmy Siddons. The police will blame the leak on me, she thought frantically. They'll think I told someone. I know they will.

The phone rang. When she picked it up and heard Mort Levy's voice, the pent-up emotions that had seemed so frozen erupted suddenly. "I didn't do it," she sobbed. "I didn't tell anyone. I swear, I swear I didn't tell."

The steady rise and fall of Brian's chest told Jimmy Siddons that his hostage was asleep. Good, he thought, better for me. The problem was that the kid was smart. Smart enough to know that if he had managed to throw himself out of the car next to the breakdown lane, he wouldn't risk getting run over. If that jerk hadn't spun out and caused the fender-bender, it would be all over for me now, Jimmy thought. The kid would have gotten out and the troopers would have been on my tail right then.

It was past eleven o'clock. The kid should be tired. With luck he'd sleep for a couple of hours anyhow. Even with the snow on the roads, they should be at the border in, at most, three or four hours. It'll still be dark for a long time after that, Jimmy thought with satisfaction. He knew he could count on Paige to be waiting on the Canadian side. They'd worked out a rendezvous point in the woods about three miles from the customs check.

Jimmy debated about where he should leave the Toyota. There was nothing to tie him to it as long as he made sure he wiped it clean of fingerprints. Maybe he'd ditch it in one of the wooded areas.

On the other hand . . . He thought of the Niagara River, where he would make the border crossing. It had a strong current, so chances were it wouldn't be frozen. With luck, the car might never surface.

What about the kid? Even as he asked himself the question, Jimmy knew there was no way he'd take a chance on the kid being found near the border and able to talk about him.

Paige had told all her friends she was going to Mexico.

Sorry, kid, Jimmy thought. That's where I want the cops looking for me.

He reflected for a moment, then decided the river would take care of the car *and* the kid.

That decision made, Jimmy felt some of the tension ease from his body. With every mile, he felt more sure that he was going to make it, that Canada and Paige and freedom were within reach. And with each mile he felt more anxious—and more determined—that nothing happen to screw it up.

Like last time. He'd been all set. He'd had Cally's car, a hundred bucks, and was heading for California. Then he ran a lousy caution light on Ninth Avenue and got pulled over. The cop, a guy about thirty, thought he was a big shot. He had come to the driver's window and said real sarcastically, "Driver's license and registration, *sir.*"

That's all he would have needed to see, Jimmy thought, remembering the moment as though it were yesterday, a license issued to James Siddons. He had had no choice. He would have been arrested on the spot. He'd reached into his breast pocket, pulled out his gun, and fired. Before the cop's body hit

the ground, Jimmy was out of the car and on the street, blending into the crowd around the bus terminal. He had looked at
the departure schedule board and rushed to buy a ticket on a
bus leaving in three minutes, destination: Detroit.

That was a lucky decision, Jimmy thought. He'd met Paige
the first night, moved in with her, then got some phony ID and
a job with a low-life security firm. For a while he and Paige
had even had a kind of normal life. Their only real arguments
were when he got sore at the way she encouraged the guys
who made passes at her in the strip joint. But she said it was
her job to make them *want* to make passes at her. For the first
time, everything was actually working out. Until he was dumb
enough to hit the service station without taking enough time
to case it.

He focused his attention back on the snow-covered road
ahead of him. He could tell from the feel of the tires that it was
getting icy. Good thing this car had snow tires, Jimmy
thought. He flashed back to the couple who owned the car—
what had the guy said to his wife? Something about can't wait
to see Bobby's face? Yeah, that was it, Jimmy thought, grinning as he imagined their faces when they found an empty
space where their car had been parked, or more likely another
car taking up the space.

He had the radio turned on, but the volume was low. It was
tuned to a local station to get an update on the weather, but
now the sound was fading and static was breaking up the signal. Impatiently Jimmy twiddled the dial until he found an all-
news station, then froze as an announcer's urgent voice
reported: "Police have reluctantly confirmed the story broken
by station WYME that seven-year-old Brian Dornan, missing

since five o'clock this evening, has fallen into the hands of alleged murderer Jimmy Siddons, who is believed to be heading for Canada."

Swearing steadily, Jimmy snapped off the radio. Cally. She must have called the cops. The Thruway's probably already lousy with them, all looking for me—and the kid, he reasoned frantically. He glanced to the left, at the car just passing him. Probably dozens of unmarked cars around here, he thought.

Calm. Keep it calm, he told himself. They didn't know what kind of car he was driving. He wasn't going to be dumb enough to speed or, worse yet, crawl so far below the speed limit that they'd get suspicious.

But the kid was a problem. He had to get rid of him right away. He thought the situation through quickly. He'd get off at the nearest exit, take care of him, dump him fast, and then get back on the road. He looked at the boy sleeping beside him. Too bad, kid, but that's the way it's got to be, he said to himself.

On the right he saw an exit sign. That's it, Jimmy thought, that's the one I'll take.

Brian stirred as though starting to wake up, then fell back asleep. Drowsily, he decided that he must have been dreaming, but he thought he had heard his name.

18

 Al Rhodes saw the haunted look on the face of Catherine Dornan when she realized the implications of Brian being with Jimmy Siddons. He watched as she closed her eyes, ready to catch her if she fainted.

But then she opened her eyes quickly and reached out to put her arms around her older son. "We mustn't forget that Brian has the St. Christopher medal," she said softly.

The mask of adult bravado that Michael had managed to maintain throughout the evening's ordeal began to crumble. "I don't want anything to happen to Brian," he sobbed.

Catherine stroked his head. "Nothing is going to happen to him," she said calmly. "Believe that, and hold on to it."

Rhodes could see the effort it took for her to talk. Who the hell leaked to the media that Brian Dornan was with Jimmy

Siddons? he wondered angrily. Rhodes could feel his fist itching to connect with the louse who had so thoughtlessly jeopardized the kid's life. His anger was further fed by the realization that if Siddons was listening to the radio, the first thing he'd do was get rid of the boy.

Catherine was saying, "Mother, remember how Dad used to tell us about the Christmas Eve when he was only twenty-two years old and in the thick of the Battle of the Bulge, and he took a couple of soldiers in his company into one of the towns on the fringe of the battle line? Why don't you tell Michael about it?"

Her mother took up the story. "There'd been a report of enemy activity there but it turned out not to be true. On the way back to their battalion, they passed the village church. Midnight Mass had just started. They could see that the church was packed. In the midst of all that fear and danger, everyone had left their homes for the service. Their voices singing 'Silent Night' drifted out into the square. Dad said it was the most beautiful sound he'd ever heard."

Barbara Cavanaugh smiled at her grandson. "Grandpa and the other soldiers went into the church. Grandpa used to tell me how scared all of them had been until they saw the faith and courage of those villagers. Here these people were, surrounded by fierce fighting. They had almost no food. Yet those villagers believed that somehow they'd make it through that terrible time."

Her lower lip quivered, but her voice was steady as she continued. "Grandpa said that was when he *knew* he was going to come home to me. And it was an hour later that the St. Christopher medal kept the bullet from going through his heart."

Catherine looked over Michael's head to Officer Ortiz.

"Would you take us to the cathedral now? I want to go to midnight Mass. We'd need to be in a seat where you could find me quickly if you have any news."

"I know the head usher. Ray Hickey," Ortiz said. "I'll take care of it."

She looked at Detective Rhodes. "I will be notified immediately if you have any word at all . . . ?"

"Absolutely." He could not resist adding, "You're very brave, Mrs. Dornan. And I can tell you this for sure: every law enforcement officer in the northeast is dedicated to getting Brian back safely."

"I believe that, and the only way I can help is to pray."

"The leak didn't come from our guys," Mort Levy reported tersely to Chief of Detectives Folney. Apparently some hotshot kid from WYME was watching Cally's apartment and saw us go in, knew something was up, and followed Aika Banks home. He told her he was a cop and pumped her. His name is Pete Cruise."

"Damn good thing it wasn't one of ours. When all this is over, we'll hang Cruise out to dry for impersonating an officer," Folney said. "In the meantime we've got plenty to do here."

He was standing in front of an enlarged map of the northeast that had been attached to the wall of his office. It was crisscrossed with routes outlined in different colors. Folney picked up a pointer. "Here's where we're at, Mort. We've got to assume that Siddons had a car waiting when he left his sister's place. According to her, he left shortly after six. If we're right, and he got in a car immediately, he's been on the road about five and a half hours."

The pointer moved. "The light snow band extends from the city to about Herkimer, exit 30 on the Thruway. It's heavier throughout New England. But even so, Siddons probably isn't more than four to six hours from the border."

Folney gave a decisive thump to the map. "Amounts to looking for a needle in a haystack."

Mort waited. He knew the boss didn't want comments.

"We've got a special alert along the border," Folney continued. "But with the heavy traffic, he could still be missed, and we all know that someone like Siddons probably knows how to get into Canada without going through a checkpoint." Now he waited for comments.

"How about staging an accident on the major roads to force a one-laner about twenty miles before the border?" Mort suggested.

"I wouldn't rule that out. But on the same principle as erecting a barrier, traffic would build up in two minutes, and Siddons might just try to get off at the nearest exit. If we go ahead with that plan we'll have to put barriers at all the exits, as well."

"And if Siddons feels trapped . . . ?" Mort Levy hesitated. "Siddons has a screw loose, sir. Cally Hunter believes her brother is capable of killing both Brian and himself rather than get captured. I think she knows what she's talking about."

"And if she had had the guts to call us the minute Jimmy left her house with that boy, he wouldn't have gotten out of Manhattan."

Both men turned. Jack Shore was in the doorway. He looked past Mort Levy to Bud Folney. "A new development, sir. A state trooper, Chris McNally, got a hamburger about twenty minutes ago at the travel plaza between Syracuse, exit 39, and Weedsport, exit 40, on the Thruway. He didn't pay much attention at the time, but the woman at the pickup station, a Miss Deidre Lenihan, was talking about a St. Christopher medal that some kid was wearing."

Bud Folney snapped, "Where is the Lenihan woman now?"

"Her shift ended at eleven. Her mother said her boyfriend was picking her up. They're trying to track them down now. But if Cally Hunter had called us earlier none of this would have happened, we could have been at every travel plaza between here and . . ."

Bud Folney almost never raised his voice. But his increasing frustration over the agonizing twists in the manhunt for Jimmy Siddons made him suddenly shout, "Shut up, Jack! 'If only's' don't help now. Do something useful. Get the radio stations in that area to broadcast a plea to Deidre Lenihan to call her mother. Say she's needed at home or something. And for God's sake, don't let anyone connect her to Siddons or that child. Got it?"

19

From his perch just off the road, Chris McNally kept a watchful eye on the cars passing before him. The snow had finally ended, but the roadway remained icy. At least the drivers were being careful, he thought, although they were all probably frustrated at having to crawl along at thirty-five miles an hour. Since he'd picked up his hamburger, he had only ticketed one driver, a hotshot in a sports car.

Although he was focused on the flow of traffic on the highway, he still could not get his mind off the report of the missing child. The minute the alert had come in about the little boy who was being held hostage by an escaped cop killer, a little boy wearing a St. Christopher medal, Chris had phoned the McDonald's he had just visited and had asked to speak to Deidre Lenihan, the woman who had waited on him. Even though he hadn't really been paying any attention, he remembered that she had been going on about just such a medal and a little boy. Now he was sorry he hadn't been more in the mood to gab with her, especially since they told him she had just left for the evening with her boyfriend.

Despite the tenuous nature of the tip, he nonetheless had reported the possible lead to his supervisor, who had passed it along to One Police Plaza. They had decided it was worth acting on and had asked the local radio station to broadcast an appeal that Deidre call in to police headquarters. From Deidre's mother they had even gotten a description of the boyfriend's car, then they had gotten his license number and put out an all-points call to try and find them.

Deidre's mother had also told them, however, that she thought tonight was going to be special for her daughter, that the boyfriend had let her know his Christmas present was going to be an engagement ring. Chances were they wouldn't be out on the road now, but someplace a little more romantic.

But even if Deidre did hear the radio appeal and did call in, what could she tell them? That she had seen a kid wearing a St. Christopher medal? They knew that already. Did she know the make and model of the car? Had she seen the license plate? From what Chris knew of Deidre, good-hearted as she was, she was not too alert and was observant only when something struck her fancy. No, it was unlikely that she could provide any more significant information.

All of which made Chris even more frustrated. I might have been around that kid myself, he thought. I might have been in line behind them at McDonald's—why didn't I notice anything more?

The thought of having possibly been close to the kidnapped

child practically drove him wild. My kids are home in bed right now, he thought. That little boy should be with his family, too. The problem was, he realized, thinking back over his conversation with Deidre, the car with the little boy could have come through there anywhere between a few minutes and an hour before she told him about it. Still, it was the only lead they had, so they had to treat it seriously.

His radio went on. It was headquarters. "Chris," the dispatcher said, "the boss wants to talk to you."

"Sure."

When the captain got on, his voice was urgent. "Chris, the New York City police think your tip is the closest thing they have to a chance of saving that kid's life. We're going to keep on beating the bushes looking for the Lenihan woman, but in the meantime, rack your brain. Try to remember if there was anything else she might have said, anything that might be of some help . . ."

"I'm trying, sir. I'm on the Thruway now. If it's all right with you, I'd like to start driving west. If the guy was on the McDonald's line about the same time as I was, he's got about a ten to fifteen minute lead on me at this point. If I can pick up a little time on him, I'd sure like to be in the vicinity when word does come through from Deidre. I'd like to be there when we get him."

"Okay, go ahead. And, Chris, for God's sake, *think.* Are you sure that she didn't say anything more specific about either the kid with the St. Christopher medal or maybe about the car he was in?"

Just.

The word jumped into Chris's mind. Was it his imagination, or had Deidre said, *"I just saw a kid wearing a St. Christopher medal"?*

He shook his head. He couldn't remember for sure. He did know that the car ahead of him in the line at McDonald's had been a brown Toyota with New York plates.

But there hadn't been a kid in the car, or at least not that he could see. That much he *was* sure of.

Even so . . . if Deidre had said *"just,"* maybe she did mean the Toyota. What had been the license number on that car? He couldn't remember. But he had noticed something about it. What was it?

"Chris?" The supervisor's voice was sharp, effectively breaking his reverie.

"I'm sorry, sir, I was trying to remember. I think Deidre said *'just'* seen the kid wearing the medal. If she meant that literally, then it could have been the car directly in front of me on line. That was a brown Toyota with New York plates."

"Do you remember any part of the number?"

"No, I'm just getting a blank. My mind was probably a million miles away."

"And the car, was there definitely a little boy in it?"

"I didn't see one."

"That's not much help. Every third car on the road is probably a Toyota, and tonight they're all so dirty you can't tell one color from another. They probably all look brown."

"No, this one was definitely brown. That much *is* for sure. I just wish I could remember Deidre's exact words."

"Well, don't drive yourself crazy. Let's hope we hear from the Lenihan woman, and in the meantime I'll send one of the other cars to cover your station. Head west. We'll check in later."

At least it feels as if I'm doing something, Chris thought as he signed off, turned the key and pressed his foot on the gas.

The squad car leaped forward. One thing I do know is how to drive, he thought grimly as he steered the vehicle onto the breakdown lane and began passing the cautious motorists along the way.

And as he drove, he continued to try to remember what exactly he had seen in front of him. It was there, imprinted in his mind, he was sure of that. If only he could call it up. As he strained, he felt as though his subconscious were trying to shout out the information. If only he could hear it.

In the meantime, every inch of his six-foot-four-inch being was warning him that time was running out for the missing boy.

Jimmy was seething. What with all the cars going like old ladies were driving them, it had taken him half an hour to get to the nearest exit. Jimmy knew he had to get off the Thruway *now* so he could get rid of the kid. A sign told him he was within a half mile of exit 41 and a town named Waterloo. Waterloo for the kid, he thought with grim satisfaction.

The snow had stopped, but he wasn't sure that was good for him. The slush was turning to ice, and that slowed him up more. Plus, without the snow, it was easier for any cops who might be driving by to get a look at him.

He switched to the right lane. In a minute he'd be able to get off the Thruway. Suddenly the brake lights flashed on the car ahead of him, and Jimmy watched with increasing anger and frustration as the rear of that car fishtailed. "Jerk!" Jimmy screamed. "Jerk! Jerk! Jerk!"

Brian sat up straight, eyes wide open, fully alert. Jimmy began to curse, a steady stream of invective flowing as he realized what had happened. A snowplow four or five cars in front had just switched into the exit lane. Instinctively, he steered the Toyota into the middle lane and barely managed to avoid the fishtailing car. As he pulled abreast of the snowplow, they were just passing the exit.

He slammed the wheel with his fist. Now he'd have to wait till exit 42 to get off the Thruway. How far was that? he wondered.

But as he glanced back at the exit he'd just missed, he realized he actually had been lucky. There was a pileup on the ramp. It must have just happened. That was why the plow had switched lanes. If he had tried to get off there, he could have been stuck for hours.

Finally he saw a sign that informed him the next exit was in six miles. Even at this pace, it shouldn't take more than fifteen minutes. The wheels were gripping the road better. This stretch must have been sanded. Jimmy felt for the gun under his jacket. Should he take it out and hide it under the seat?

No, he decided. If a cop tried to stop him, he needed it just where it was. He glanced at the odometer on the dashboard. He'd set it when he and the kid started driving. It showed that they had gone just over three hundred miles.

There was still a long way to go, but just knowing that he was this close to the Canadian border and Paige was so exciting a sensation he could almost taste it. This time he'd make it work, and whatever he did, this time he wouldn't be dumb enough to be caught by the cops.

Jimmy felt the kid stirring beside him, trying to settle back into sleep. What a mistake! he thought. I should have dumped him five minutes after I took him. I had the car and the money. Why did I think I needed him?

He ached for the moment when he could be rid of the kid and be safe.

20

 Officer Ortiz escorted Catherine, her mother, and Michael to the Fiftieth Street entrance to St. Patrick's Cathedral. A security guard stationed outside was waiting for them. "We have seats for you in the reserved section, ma'am," he told Catherine as he pushed the heavy door open.

The magnificent sound of the orchestra led by the organ and accompanied by the choir filled the great cathedral, which was already packed with worshipers.

"Joyful, joyful," the choir was singing.

Joyful, joyful, Catherine thought. Please God, yes, let this night end like that.

They passed the crèche where the life-sized figures of the Virgin, Joseph, and the shepherds were gathered around the empty pile of hay that was the crib. She knew that the statue of the infant Christ child would be placed there during the Mass.

The security guard showed them to their seats in the second row on the middle aisle. Catherine indicated that her mother should go in first. Then she whispered, "You go between us, Michael." She wanted to be on the outside, at the end of the row, so she could be aware the minute the door opened.

Officer Ortiz leaned over. "Mrs. Dornan, if we hear anything, I'll come in for you. Otherwise when Mass is over, the guard will lead you out first, and I'll be waiting outside in the car."

"Thank you," Catherine said, then immediately sank to her knees. The music changed to a swirling paean of triumph as the procession began—the choir, the acolytes, deacon, priests, and bishops, preceding the cardinal, who was carrying the crook of the shepherd in his hand. *Lamb of God,* Catherine prayed, *please, please save my lamb.*

Chief of Detectives Folney, his gaze still riveted to the map of the Thruway on the wall of his office, knew that with each passing minute, the chances of finding Brian Dornan alive grew slimmer. Mort Levy and Jack Shore were across the desk from him.

"Canada," he said emphatically. "He's on his way to Canada, and he's getting close to the border."

They had just received further word from Michigan. Paige Laronde had closed all her bank accounts the day she left Detroit. And in a burst of confidence, she had told another dancer that she had been in touch with a guy who was a genius at creating fake IDs.

It was reported that she had said, "Let me tell you, with the kind of papers I got for my boyfriend and me, we can both just *disappear.*"

"If Siddons makes it over the border . . ." Bud Folney muttered more to himself than to the others.

"Nothing from the Thruway guys?" he asked for the third time in fifteen minutes.

"Nothing, sir," Mort said quietly.

"Call them again. I want to talk to them myself."

When he got through to Chris McNally's supervisor and heard for himself that absolutely nothing was new, he decided he wanted to speak to Trooper McNally himself.

"A lot of good that'll do," Jack Shore muttered to Mort Levy.

But before Folney could be connected with McNally, another call came in. "Hot lead," an assistant said, rushing into Folney's office. "Siddons and the kid were seen by a trooper about an hour ago at a rest area on Route 91 in Vermont near White River Junction. He said the man matches Siddons's description to a T, and the boy was wearing some kind of medal."

"Forget McNally," Folney said crisply. "I want to talk to the trooper who saw them. And right now, call the Vermont police and have them put up barriers at all the exits north of the sighting. For all we know, the girlfriend may be holed up waiting for him in a farmhouse on this side of the border."

While Folney waited, he looked over at Mort. "Call Cally Hunter and tell her what we've just learned. Ask her if she knows if Jimmy has ever been to Vermont and if so, where did he go? There might be some place in particular he could be headed."

21

Brian could tell that the car was going faster. He opened his eyes, then shut them as fast as he could. It was easier to stay lying down, curled up on the seat, pretending to be asleep, instead of having to try not to act scared when Jimmy looked at him.

He also had been listening to the radio. Even though the volume was turned way down, he could hear what they were saying, that cop killer Jimmy Siddons, who had shot a prison guard, had kidnapped Brian Dornan.

His mother had been reading a book named *Kidnapped* to him and Michael. Brian liked the story a lot, but when they went to bed, Michael told him he thought it was dumb. He had said that if anyone tried to kidnap him, he'd kick the guy and punch him and run away.

Well, I can't run away, Brian thought. And he was sure that

trying to hurt Jimmy by punching him wouldn't work. He wished that he'd been able to open the car door earlier and roll out like he had planned to. He'd have curled up in a ball just like they taught the kids to do in gym class. He would have been okay.

But now the car door near him was locked, and he knew that before he could even pull up the lock and open the door, Jimmy would grab him.

Brian was almost crying. He could feel his nose filling up and his eyes getting watery. He tried to think about how Michael might call him a crybaby. Sometimes that helped him when he was trying not to cry.

It didn't help now, though. Even Michael would probably cry if he was scared and he had to go to the bathroom again. And it said right on the radio that Jimmy was dangerous.

But even though he was crying, Brian made sure he didn't make a sound. He felt the tears on his cheeks, but he didn't move to brush them away. If he moved his hand, Jimmy would notice and know he was awake, and for now he had to keep pretending.

Instead, he clasped the St. Christopher medal even tighter and made himself think about how when Dad was able to go back home, they were going to put up their own Christmas tree and open the presents. Just before they had left for New York, Mrs. Emerson who lived next door had come in to say good-bye, and he had heard her say to his mom, "Catherine, no matter when it is, the night you put up your tree, we're all going to come and sing Christmas carols under your window."

Then she'd hugged Brian and said, "I *know* your favorite carol."

"Silent Night." He'd sung it all by himself in the first-grade Christmas pageant at school last year.

Brian tried to sing it to himself now, in his mind . . . but he couldn't get past "Silent night." He knew if he kept thinking about it, he wouldn't be able to keep Jimmy from knowing that he was crying.

Then he almost jumped. Someone on the radio was talking about Jimmy and him again. The man was saying that a state trooper in Vermont was sure he had seen Jimmy Siddons and a young boy in an old Dodge or Chevrolet at a rest stop on Route 91 in Vermont, and the search was being concentrated there.

Jimmy's grim smile vanished as quickly as it had come. The first surge of relief at hearing the news bulletin was followed by instant caution. *Had* some fool claimed he'd spotted them in Vermont? he wondered. It was possible, he decided. When he had been hiding out in Michigan, some two-bit drifter swore he'd seen Jimmy in Delaware. After he got caught at the gas-station job and was taken back to New York, he had found out that the marshals had kept the heat on in Delaware for months.

Even so, being on the Thruway was really beginning to spook him. The road was good and he could make time, but the nearer you got to the border, the more troopers there might be on the road. He decided that when he got off at the next exit, and got rid of the kid, he'd swing over to Route 20. Now that it wasn't snowing, he should be able to make okay time there.

Follow your hunch, Jimmy reminded himself. The only time he hadn't was when he had tried to hold up that gas station. He still remembered that at the time something had warned him there was a problem.

Well, after this, there'll be no more problems, he thought, looking down at Brian. Then when he looked up, he grinned. The sign looming before him read EXIT 42, GENEVA, ONE MILE AHEAD.

Chris McNally had passed the fender-bender on the exit 41 ramp. Two police cars were on the scene already, so he decided there was no need for him to stop. He had traveled fast, and he hoped that by now he had caught up to any cars that had been ahead of him on line at McDonald's.

Provided, of course, they hadn't taken one of the earlier exits.

A brown Toyota. That's what he kept looking for. Finding it was the one chance. He knew it. What was it about the license plate? He clenched his teeth, again trying hard to remember. There had been something about it . . . Think, damn it, he told himself, *think.*

He didn't for one minute believe the report that Siddons and the kid had been spotted in Vermont. Every gut instinct kept telling Chris that they were nearby.

Exit 42 to Geneva was coming up. That meant the border was only another hundred miles or so away. Most of the cars were doing fifty to sixty miles an hour now. If Jimmy Siddons was in this vicinity, he could look forward to being out of the country in less than two hours.

What was there about the license plate of the Toyota? he asked himself once more.

Chris's eyes narrowed. He could see a dark Toyota in the

passing lane that was moving fast. He switched lanes and drove up beside it, then glanced in. He prayed that it held a single man or a man with a young boy. Just a chance to find that child. Give me a chance, he prayed.

Without turning on his siren or dome light, Chris continued past the Toyota. He had been able to see a young couple inside. The guy was driving with his arm around the girl, not a good idea on an icy road. Another time he'd have pulled him over.

Chris stepped on the gas. The road was clearer, the traffic was better spaced. But everything was moving faster and faster, and closer and closer to Canada.

His radio was on low when a call came in for him. "Officer McNally?"

"Yes."

"New York City Chief of Detectives Bud Folney calling you from One Police Plaza. I just spoke to your supervisor again. The Vermont sighting is a washout. The Lenihan woman can't be found. Tell me what you reported earlier about a brown Toyota."

Knowing his boss had dismissed that, Chris realized that this Folney must be really pressing him.

He explained that if Deidre had been talking about the car directly ahead of him in the McDonald's line, she was talking about a brown Toyota with New York plates.

"And you can't remember the license."

"No, sir." Chris wanted to strangle the words in his throat. "But there was something unusual about it."

He was almost at exit 42. As he watched, a vehicle two cars ahead switched into the exit lane. His casual glance became a stare. "My God," he said.

"Officer? What is it?" In New York, Bud Folney instinctively knew that something was happening.

"*That's it.*" Chris said. "It wasn't the license plate I noticed. It was the bumper sticker. There's just a piece of it left and it says *inheritance.* Sir, I'm following that Toyota down the exit ramp right now. Can you check out the license?"

"Don't lose that car," Bud snapped. "And hang on."

Three minutes later the phone rang in apartment 8C, in 10 Stuyvesant Oval, in lower Manhattan. A sleepy and anxious Edward Hillson picked it up. "Hello," he said. He felt his wife's nervous grasp on his arm.

"What? My car? I parked it around the corner at five or so. No, I didn't lend it to anyone. Yes. It's a brown Toyota. What are you telling me?"

Bud Folney got back to Chris. "I think you have him, but for God's sake remember, he's threatened to kill the child before he lets himself get captured. So be careful."

22

 Michael was so sleepy. All he wanted to do was lean against Gran and close his eyes. But he couldn't do that yet, not until he was sure that Brian was okay. Michael struggled to suppress his growing fear. *Why didn't he grab me if he saw that lady pick up Mom's wallet? I could have run after her and helped him when he got caught by that guy.*

The cardinal was at the altar now. But when the music stopped, instead of starting to offer Mass, he began to speak. "On this night of joy and hope . . ."

Off to the right, Michael could see the television cameras. He had always thought it would be cool to be on television, but whenever he had thought about it, the circumstances he envisioned had to do with winning something or with witnessing some great event. That would be fun. Tonight, when he and Mom were on together, it wasn't fun.

It was awful to hear Mom begging people to help them find Brian.

". . . in a year that has brought so much violence to the innocent . . ."

Michael straightened up. The cardinal was talking about them, about Dad being sick and Brian being missing and believed to be with that escaped killer. He was saying, "Brian Dornan's mother, grandmother, and ten-year-old brother are with us at this Mass. Let our special prayer be that Dr. Thomas Dornan will recover fully and that Brian will be found unharmed."

Michael could see that Mom and Gran were both crying. Their lips were moving, and he knew they were praying. His prayer was the advice he would have given Brian if he could hear him: *Run, Brian, run.*

Now that he was off the Thruway, Jimmy felt somewhat relieved, despite a gnawing sense that things were closing in on him.

He was running low on gas but was afraid to risk stopping at a station with the kid in the car. He was on Route 14 south. That connected with Route 20 in about six miles. Route 20 led to the border.

There was a lot less traffic here than on the Thruway. Most people were home by now anyway, asleep or getting ready for Christmas morning. It was unlikely that anyone would be looking for him here. Still, he reasoned, the best thing to do was to get on some of the local streets in Geneva, find someplace like a school where there'd be a parking lot, or find a wooded area, somewhere he could stop without being noticed and do what he had to do.

As he took the next right-hand turn, he glanced in the rearview mirror. His antennae went up. He thought he had seen headlights reflected there as he made the turn, but now he didn't see them anymore.

I'm getting too jumpy, he thought.

A block later it suddenly was like they'd sailed off the edge of the earth. As far as he could see, there were no cars ahead. They were in a residential area, quiet and dark. The houses were mostly unlit, except some of them still had Christmas-tree lights glowing from bushes and evergreens on the snow-covered lawns.

He couldn't be sure if the kid was really asleep or faking it. Not that it mattered. This was the sort of place he needed. He drove six blocks and then saw what he was looking for: a school, with a long driveway that had to lead to a parking area.

His eyes missed nothing as he carefully searched the area for any sign of an approaching car or someone out walking. Then he stopped the car and opened the window halfway, listening intently for any hint of trouble. The cold instantly turned his breath to steam. He could hear nothing but the hum of the Toyota's engine. It was quiet out there. Silent.

Still, he decided to drive around the block one more time, just to be sure he wasn't being followed.

As he put his foot on the accelerator, and as the car slowly moved forward, he kept his gaze glued to the rearview mirror. Damn. He'd been right. There *was* a car behind him, running without lights. Now it was moving, too. The lights from a brilliantly lit tree reflected on its rooftop dome.

A squad car. Cops! Damn them, Jimmy swore under his breath. Damn them! Damn them! He tromped on the gas pedal. It might be his last ride, but he'd make it a good one.

He looked down at Brian. "Quit pretending. I know you're awake," he shouted. "Sit up, damn you. I shoulda ditched you as soon as I was out of the city. Lousy kid."

Jimmy floored the accelerator. A quick look in the rearview mirror confirmed that the pursuing car had also speeded up and was now openly following him. But so far there seemed to be only one of them.

Clearly Cally had told the cops he had the kid, he reasoned. She'd probably also told them that he said he'd kill the kid first if they tried to close in on him. If that cop behind him knew that, it explained why he wasn't trying to pull him over right now.

He glanced at the speedometer: fifty . . . sixty . . . seventy. Damn this car! Jimmy thought, suddenly wishing he had something more powerful than a Toyota. He hunched over the wheel. He couldn't outrun them, but he still might have a chance to get away.

The guy chasing him didn't have backup yet. What would he do if he saw the kid had been shot and pushed out of the car? He'd stop to try to help him, Jimmy reasoned. I'd better do it right away, he thought, before he has time to call in help.

He reached inside his jacket for his gun. Just then the car hit a patch of ice and began to skid. Jimmy dropped the gun in his lap, turned the wheels in the direction of the skid, then managed to straighten the car just inches away from crashing into a tree at the edge of the sidewalk.

Nobody can drive like I can, he thought grimly. Then he picked up the gun again and released the safety catch. If the cop stops for the kid, I'll make it to Canada, he promised himself. He released the lock on the passenger door and reached across the terrified boy to open it.

23

Cally knew she had to call police headquarters to see if there was any word about little Brian. She had told Detective Levy she didn't think Jimmy would try to reach Canada through Vermont. "He got in trouble up there when he was about fifteen," she'd said. "He never did time there, but I think some sheriff really scared Jimmy. He told him he had a long memory and warned him never to show up in Vermont again. Even though that was at least ten years ago, Jimmy is superstitious. I think he'd stick to the Thruway. I know he went to Canada a couple of times when he was a teenager, and both times he went that way."

Levy had listened to her. She knew he wanted to trust her, and she prayed that this time he had. She also prayed that she was right and they got the boy back safely, so she could know that in some small way she had helped.

Someone other than Levy answered his phone, and she was told to wait. Then Levy came on. "What is it, Cally?"

"I just had to know if there's been any word . . . I've been praying that what I told you about Jimmy taking the Thruway helped."

Levy's voice softened even though he still spoke quickly. "Cally, it did help, and we're very grateful. I can't talk now, but whatever prayers you know, keep saying them."

That means they must have located Jimmy, she thought. But what was happening to Brian?

Cally sank to her knees. *It doesn't matter what happens to me,* she prayed. *Stop Jimmy before he hurts that child.*

Chris McNally had known it the minute Jimmy spotted him. The radio was open between him and headquarters and was tied in to One Police Plaza in Manhattan. "He knows he's being followed," Chris reported tersely. "He's taking off like a bat out of hell."

"Don't lose him," Bud Folney said quietly.

"We've got a dozen cars on the way, Chris," the dispatcher snapped. "They're running silent and on dim lights. They'll surround you. We're bringing in a chopper, too."

"Keep them out of sight!" Chris pressed his foot on the accelerator. "He's going seventy. There's not many cars out, but these streets aren't completely cleared. This is getting dangerous."

As Siddons raced across an intersection, Chris watched in horror as he barely missed slamming into another car. Siddons was driving like a maniac. There was going to be an accident, he knew it. "Passing Lakewood Avenue," he reported. Two blocks later he saw the Toyota skid and almost hit a tree. A minute after that, he yelled, "The boy!"

"What is it?" Folney demanded.

"The passenger door of the Toyota just opened. The inside light's on, so I can see the kid struggling. Oh God . . . Siddons has his gun out. It looks like he's going to shoot him."

24

"Kyrie Eleison," the choir sang.

Lord have mercy, Barbara Cavanaugh prayed.

Save my lamb, Catherine begged.

Run, Dork, run, get away from him, Michael shouted in his mind.

Jimmy Siddons was crazy. Brian had never been in a car before that was going so fast. He wasn't sure what was going on, but there must be someone following them.

Brian looked away from the road for a moment and glanced at Jimmy. He had his gun out. He felt Jimmy tugging at his seat belt, releasing it. Then he reached across Brian and opened the door beside him. He could feel the cold air rushing in.

For a moment he was paralyzed with fear. Then he sat up

very straight. He realized what was about to happen. That Jimmy was going to shoot him and push him out of the car.

He had to get away. He was still clutching the medal in his right hand. He felt Jimmy poke him in the side with the gun, pushing him toward the open door and the roadway rushing beneath them. Holding onto the seat-belt buckle with his left hand, he swung out blindly with his right. The medal arced and slammed into Jimmy's face, catching him in his left eye.

Jimmy yelled and took his hand off the wheel, instinctively slamming his foot on the brake. As he grabbed his eye, the gun went off. The bullet whistled past Brian's ear as the out-of-control car began to spin around. It jumped the curb, went up into a corner lawn, and caught on a bush. Still spinning, it slowed as it dragged the bush back across the lawn and out onto the edge of the road.

Jimmy was swearing now, one hand again on the wheel, the other aiming the gun. Blood dripped into his eye from a gash across his forehead and cheek.

Get out. Get out. Brian heard the command in his head as though someone were shouting it at him. Brian dove for the door and rolled out onto the snow-covered lawn just as a second bullet passed over his shoulder.

"Jesus Christ, the kid's out of the car," Chris yelled. He jammed on the brakes and skidded to a stop behind the Toyota. "He's getting up. Oh my God."

Bud Folney shouted, "Is he hurt?" but Chris didn't hear him. He was already out of his car and running toward the boy. Siddons was in control of the Toyota again and had turned it, clearly planning to run over Brian. In what seemed like an eternity but was actually only seconds, Chris had crossed the space between him and Brian and gathered the boy in his arms.

The car was racing toward them, its passenger door still open and its interior still illuminated so that the maniacal anger in Jimmy Siddons's face was clearly visible. Clutching Brian tightly against him, Chris dove to the side and rolled down a snowy incline just as the wheels of the Toyota passed inches from their heads. An instant later, with a sickening sound of metal crashing and glass breaking, the vehicle careened off the porch of the house and flipped over.

For a moment there was silence, and then the quiet was shattered as sirens screamed and wailed. Lights from a dozen squad cars brightened the night as swarms of troopers raced to surround the overturned vehicle. Chris lay in the snow for a few seconds, hugging Brian to him, listening to the convergence of sounds. Then he heard a small relieved voice ask, "Are you St. Christopher?"

"No, but right now I feel like him, Brian," Chris said heartily. "Merry Christmas, son."

25

Officer Manuel Ortiz slipped noiselessly through the side door of the cathedral and instantly caught Catherine's eye. He smiled and nodded his head. She jumped up and ran to meet him.

"Is he . . ."

"He's fine. They're sending him back in a police helicopter. He'll be here by the time Mass is over."

Noticing that one of the television cameras was trained on them, Ortiz raised his hand and made a circle of his thumb and forefinger, a symbol that for this moment, on this most special of days, everything was A-OK.

Those seated nearby witnessed the exchange and began to clap softly. As others turned, they stood, and applause began to slowly rumble through the giant cathedral. It was a full five minutes before the deacon could begin to read the Christmas Gospel, " 'And it came to pass . . .' "

"I'm going to let Cally know what's happened," Mort Levy told Bud Folney. "Sir, I know she should have called us earlier, but I hope . . ."

"Don't worry. I'm not going to play Scrooge tonight. She worked with us. She deserves a break," Folney said crisply. "Besides, the Dornan woman has already said she's not going to press charges against her." He paused for a moment, thinking. "Listen, there's got to be some toys left in the station houses. Tell the guys to get busy and round some up for that little girl of Cally's. Have them meet us at Cally's building in forty-five minutes. Mort, you and I are going to give them to her. Shore, you go home."

It was Brian's first helicopter ride, and even though he was incredibly tired, he was too excited to even think about closing his eyes. He was sorry Officer McNally—Chris, as he had said he should call him—hadn't been able to come with him. But he had been with Brian when they took Jimmy Siddons away, and he had told him not to worry, that this was one guy who would never get out of prison again. And then he'd gotten the St. Christopher medal out of the car for Brian.

As the helicopter came down it looked like it was almost landing on the river. He recognized the Fifty-ninth Street Bridge and the Roosevelt Island tramway. His dad had taken him for a ride on that. He wondered suddenly if his father knew what had happened to him.

He turned to one of the officers. "My dad's in a hospital near here. I have to go see him. He might be worried."

The officer, who was by now familiar with the story of the whole Dornan family, said, "You'll see him soon, son. But now, your mother's waiting for you. She's at midnight Mass at St. Patrick's Cathedral."

When the buzzer sounded at Cally's Avenue B apartment, she answered it with the resigned belief that she was going to be arrested. Detective Levy had called to say only that he and another officer were coming by. But it was two beaming, self-appointed Santa Clauses who arrived at her door, laden with dolls and games and a sparkling white wicker doll's carriage.

As she watched, unbelieving, they placed the gifts under and around the Christmas tree.

"Your information about your brother was a tremendous help," Bud Folney said. "The Dornan boy is okay and on his way back to the city. Jimmy is on his way back to prison; he's our responsibility once again, and I promise we won't let him get away this time. From now on I hope it gets a lot better for you."

Cally felt as though a giant weight had been lifted from her. She could only whisper, "Thank you . . . thank you . . ."

Folney and Levy chorused, "Merry Christmas, Cally," and were gone.

When they left, Cally at last knew she could go to bed and sleep. Gigi's even breathing was an answered prayer. From now on, she'd be able to hear it every night, and listen without fear that her little girl would be taken away from her again. Everything *will* get better, she thought. I know it now.

As she fell asleep, her last thought was that when Gigi saw that the big package with Santa's present was missing from under the Christmas tree, she could honestly tell her that Santa Claus had come and taken it away.

The recessional was about to start when once again the side door of the cathedral opened and Officer Ortiz entered. This time he was not alone. He bent down to the small boy beside him and pointed. Before Catherine could get to her feet, Brian was in her arms, the St. Christopher medal he was wearing pressed against her heart.

As she held him close, she said nothing, but felt the silent tears of relief and joy course down her cheeks, knowing that he once again was safe, and firm in her belief now that Tom was going to make it, too.

Barbara also did not speak, but leaned over and laid her hand on her grandson's head.

It was Michael who broke the silence with whispered words of welcome. "Hi, Dork," he said with a grin.

Christmas Day

Christmas morning dawned cold and clear. At ten o'clock, Catherine, Brian, and Michael arrived at the hospital.

Dr. Crowley was waiting for them when they got off the elevator on the fifth floor. "My God, Catherine," he said, "are you okay? I hadn't heard about what happened until I got here this morning. You must be exhausted."

"Thanks, Spence, but I'm fine." She looked at her sons. "We're all fine. But how is Tom? When I called this morning, all they would say was that he had a good night."

"And he did. It's an excellent sign. He had a very good night. A lot better than yours, that's for sure. I hope you don't mind, but I decided it was best if I told Tom about Brian. The press have been calling here all morning, and I didn't want to risk his hearing about it from an outsider. When I told him, I started with the happy ending, of course."

Catherine felt relief rush through her. "I'm glad he knows, Spence. I didn't know how to tell him. I couldn't be sure how he'd take it."

"He took it very well, Catherine. He's a lot stronger than you might think." Crowley looked at the medal around Brian's neck. "I understand you went through a lot to make sure you'd be able to give that medal to your dad. I promise all of you that between St. Christopher and me, we'll make sure he gets well."

The boys tugged at Catherine's hands.

"He's waiting for you," Spence said, smiling.

The door of Tom's room was partly open. Catherine pushed it the rest of the way and stood looking at her husband.

The head of the bed was elevated. When Tom saw them, his face brightened with that familiar smile.

The boys ran to him, then carefully stopped just inches from the bed. They both reached out and grasped his hand. Catherine watched his eyes fill with tears when he looked at Brian.

He's so pale, she thought. I can tell that he hurts. But he *is* going to get better. She did not need to force the radiant smile that her lips formed as Michael lifted the chain with the St. Christopher medal from Brian's neck and together they put it on Tom. "Merry Christmas, Dad," they chorused.

As her husband looked over their sons' heads and his lips formed the words *I love you,* other words sang through Catherine's being.

All is calm . . . all is bright.

Acknowledgments

When Michael Korda, my editor, called to suggest I write a Christmas story, my reply was, "Michael, I am hanging up this phone."

"Alvirah and Willy," he said quickly, and I paused. Alvirah and Willy are my continuing characters. It's been a year since I wrote about them, and I've missed them.

All Through the Night is the result of that phone call. I hope you enjoy it. Love and thanks as always to Michael Korda for starting me on the path to telling it. Blessings to Michael and Senior Editor Chuck Adams for being my mentors, rooters, and coaches literally all through the night.

Grazie to Associate Director of Copy Editing Gypsy da Silva and to Carol Bowie; to agent Sam Pinkus, who researched the world of probate courts and family services for me; to my publicist Lisl Cade and daughter Carol Higgins Clark for their always prescient comments and suggestions; and last but surely not least to my husband, John Conheeney.

For John, with love,
and
For Bishop Paul G. Bootkoski, in loving friendship.

1

Prologue

 There were twenty-two days to go before Christmas, but Lenny was doing his Christmas shopping early this year. Secure in the knowledge that no one knew he was there, and standing so still and quiet that he hardly could hear himself breathe, he watched from the confessional as Monsignor Ferris went about the rounds of securing the church for the night. With a contemptuous smile, Lenny waited impatiently as the side doors were checked and the lights in the sanctuary extinguished. He shrank back when he saw the monsignor turn to walk down the side aisle, which meant that he would pass directly by the confessional. He cursed silently when a floorboard in the enclosure squeaked. Through a slit in the curtain he could see the clergyman stop and tilt his head, as if listening for another sound.

But then, as if satisfied, Monsignor Ferris resumed his jour-

ney to the back of the church. A moment later, the light in the
vestibule was extinguished, and a door opened and closed.
Lenny allowed himself an audible sigh—he was alone in St.
Clement's church on West 103rd Street in Manhattan.

Sondra stood in the doorway of a townhouse across the street
from the church. The building was under repair, and the tem-
porary scaffolding around the street level shielded her from
the view of passersby. She wanted to be sure that Monsignor
had left the church and was in the rectory before she left the
baby. She had been attending services at St. Clement's for the
last couple of days and had become familiar with his routine.
She also knew that during Advent he would now be conduct-
ing a seven o'clock recitation of the rosary service.

Weak from the strain and fatigue of the birth only hours
earlier, her breasts swelling with the fluid that preceded her
milk, she leaned against the door frame for support. A faint
whimper from beneath her partially buttoned coat made her
arms move in the rocking motion instinctive to mothers.

On a plain sheet of paper that she would leave with the
baby she had written everything she could safely reveal:
"Please give my little girl to a good and loving family to raise.
Her father is of Italian descent; my grandparents were born
in Ireland. Neither family has any hereditary diseases that I
am aware of, so she should be healthy. I love her, but I cannot
take care of her. If she asks about me someday, show her this
note, please. Tell her that the happiest hours of my life will always be the ones when I held her in my arms after she was
born. For those moments it was just the two of us, alone in the
world."

Sondra felt her throat close as she spotted the tall, slightly stooped figure of the monsignor emerge from the church and walk directly to the adjacent rectory. It was time.

She had bought baby clothes and supplies, including a couple of shirts, a long nightgown, booties and a hooded jacket, bottles of formula and disposable diapers. She had wrapped the baby papoose-style, in two receiving blankets and a heavy woolen robe, but because the night was so cold, at the last minute she had brought along a brown paper shopping bag. She had read somewhere that paper was a good insulator against the cold. Not that the baby would be out in the frigid air for long, of course—just until Sondra could get to a phone and call the rectory.

She unbuttoned her coat slowly, shifting the baby only as needed, remembering to be especially careful of her head. The faint glow from the streetlight made it possible for her to see her infant's face clearly. "I love you," Sondra whispered fiercely. "And I will always love you." The baby stared up at her, her eyes fully open for the first time. Brown eyes stared into blue eyes, long dark-blond hair brushed against sprigs of the blond hair curling on the little forehead; tiny lips puckered and turned, seeking Mother's breast.

Sondra pressed the baby's head against her neck; her lips lingered on the soft cheek; her hand caressed the infant's back and legs. Then, in a decisive move, she slipped the tiny figure into the shopping bag, reached for the secondhand blue stroller folded next to her and tucked the handle under one arm.

She waited until several people had walked past her hiding place, then hurried to the curb and looked up and down the street. A block away traffic was stopped at the red light, but she saw no pedestrians coming in either direction.

A solid wall of parked cars on both sides of the street helped to protect Sondra from any curious eyes as she darted across the street to the rectory. There she ran up the three steps to the narrow stoop and opened the stroller. After engaging the brake, she laid the baby snugly under the stroller's hood and laid the bundle of clothes and bottles at her feet. She knelt for a moment and took one last look at her child. "Goodbye," she whispered. Then she stood and quickly ran down the steps and headed toward Columbus Avenue.

She would make the call to the rectory from a street phone two blocks away.

Lenny prided himself on being in and out of a church in less than three minutes. You never know about silent alarms, he thought, as he opened his backpack and pulled out a flashlight. Keeping the narrow beam pointed toward the floor, he quickly began to make his usual rounds. He went to the poor box first. Donations had been down lately, he'd noticed, but this one yielded a better than usual take, somewhere between thirty and forty dollars.

The offering boxes below the votive candles turned out to be the most satisfactory of any of the last ten churches he had hit. There were seven of them, placed at intervals in front of the statues of the saints. Quickly he smashed the locks and grabbed the cash.

In the last month he'd come to Mass here a couple of times to study the layout; he had observed that the priest consecrated the bread and wine in plain goblets, so he didn't bother to break into the tabernacle, since there'd be nothing special there. He was just as glad to avoid doing that anyway. The couple of years he'd spent in parochial school had had an effect on him, he acknowledged, making him queasy about doing certain things. It definitely got in his way when it came to robbing churches.

On the other hand, he had no qualms about leaving with the prize that had brought him here in the first place, the silver chalice with the star-shaped diamond at the base. It had belonged to Joseph Santori, the priest who founded St. Clement's parish one hundred years ago, and it was the one treasure this historic church contained.

A painting of Santori hung above a mahogany cabinet in a recess to the right of the sanctuary. The cabinet was ornate, its grillwork designed to both protect and display the chalice. After one of the masses he had attended, Lenny had drifted over to read the plaque beneath the cabinet.

At his ordination in Rome, Father, later Bishop, Santori was given this cup by Countess Maria Tomicelli. It had been in her family since the days of early Christianity. At age 45, Joseph Santori was consecrated as a bishop and assigned to the See of Rochester. Upon his retirement at age 75, he returned to St. Clement's, where he spent his remaining years working among the poor and the elderly. Bishop Joseph Santori's reputation for holiness was so widespread that after his death, a petition was signed to ask the Holy See to consider him for beatification, a cause that remains active today.

The diamond definitely would bring a few bucks, Lenny thought as he swung his hatchet. With two hard blows he smashed the hinges of the cabinet. He yanked open the doors and grabbed the chalice. Afraid that he might have triggered a silent alarm, he quickly ran to the side door of the church, unlocked it and pushed it open, anxious now to get out.

As he turned west toward Columbus Avenue, the cold air quickly dried the perspiration that had covered his face and back. Once on the avenue, he knew he could disappear into the crowds of shoppers. But as he passed the rectory, the wail of an approaching police siren shattered the calm.

He could see two couples down the block, headed in the same direction he was going, but he didn't dare to start running to catch up with them. That would be a sure giveaway. Then he spotted the stroller on the rectory steps. In an instant he was carrying it down to the sidewalk. There appeared to be nothing in it but a couple of shopping bags. Shoving his backpack in the foot of the stroller, he walked quickly to catch up with the couples ahead of him. Once he was near them, he strolled sedately just behind.

The police car roared past the group and screeched to a halt in front of the church. At Columbus Avenue, Lenny quickened his steps, no longer worried about detection. On such a chilly night, all pedestrians were hurrying, anxious to reach their destinations. He would just blend in. There was no reason for anyone to pay attention to the average-sized, sharp-faced man in his early thirties, who was wearing a cap and a plain, dark jacket and pushing a cheap, well-worn stroller.

The street phone Sondra had planned to call from was in use. Wildly anxious with impatience and already heartsick about the baby she had abandoned, she tried to decide whether to interrupt the caller, a man wearing the uniform of a security guard. She could explain that it was an emergency.

I can't do that, she thought despairingly. Tomorrow, if there's a story in the newspapers about the baby, he might remember me and talk to the police. Dismayed, she shoved her hands in her pockets, groping for the coins she needed and the paper on which she'd written the phone number of the rectory, unnecessary because she knew it by heart.

It was December 3rd, and already Christmas lights and decorations glittered from the windows of the shops and restaurants along Columbus Avenue. A couple walking hand in hand passed Sondra, their faces radiant as they smiled at each other. The girl appeared to be about eighteen, her own age, Sondra thought, although she felt infinitely older—and infinitely removed from the air of careless joy this couple displayed.

It was getting colder. Was the baby wrapped warmly enough? she worried. For an instant she shut her eyes. O, God, please make this man get off the phone, she prayed, I need to make this call now.

An instant later she heard the click of the receiver being replaced. Sondra waited until the caller was a few paces away before she grabbed the receiver, dropped in the coins and dialed.

"St. Clement's rectory." The voice was that of an elderly man. It had to be the old priest she had seen at Mass.

"Please, may I speak to Monsignor Ferris, right away."

"I'm Father Dailey. Perhaps I can help you. Monsignor is outside with the police. We have an emergency."

Quietly, Sondra broke the connection. They had found the baby already. She was safe now, and Monsignor Ferris would see that she was placed in a good home.

An hour later Sondra was on the bus to Birmingham, Alabama, where she was a student in the music department of the university, a violin student whose astonishing talent had already marked her for future stardom on the concert stage.

It was not until he was in the apartment of his elderly aunt that Lenny heard the faint mewling of the infant.

Startled, he looked into the stroller. He saw the shopping bag begin to move and quickly tore it open; he stared in shock at the tiny occupant. Unbelieving, he unpinned the note from the blanket, read it and mouthed an expletive.

From the bedroom at the end of the narrow hallway, his aunt called: "Is that you, Lenny?" There was no hint of a welcome in the greeting, spoken with a strong accent that betrayed her Italian roots.

"Yes, Aunt Lilly." There was no way he could simply hide the baby. He had to figure out what to do. What should he tell her?

Lilly Maldonado walked down the hall to the living room. At seventy-four, she both looked and moved like someone ten years younger than her age. Her hair, pulled back in a tight bun, was still generously sprinkled with black strands; her brown eyes were large and lively, and her short, ample body moved in quick, sure steps.

Along with Lenny's mother, her younger sister, she had emigrated to the United States from Italy shortly after World War II. A skilled seamstress, she had married a tailor from her native village in Tuscany and worked side by side with him in their tiny Upper West Side shop until his death five years ago. Now she worked out of her apartment, or went to the homes of her devoted clients, whom she charged far too little for dressmaking and alterations.

But as her customers joked among themselves, in exchange for Lilly's low prices, they were forced to lend considerable sympathetic attention to her endless stories about her trouble-some nephew Lenny.

On her knees, a heap of pins beside her, her alert eyes care-fully measuring as she chalked hem lengths, Lilly would sigh, then launch into her litany of complaints. "My nephew. He's always driving me crazy. Trouble from the day he was born. When he was in school: Don't ask. Arrested. Went away to a prison for kids twice. Did that straighten him out? No. Never can hold a job. Why not? My sister, his mama, God rest her, always was too easy on him. I love him, of course—after all, he's my flesh and blood—but he drives me crazy. How much can I put up with, him coming in at all hours? What's he *living* on, I ask you?"

But now, after earnest prayer to her beloved St. Francis of Assisi, Lilly Maldonado had made a decision. She had tried everything, and none of it had made a difference. Clearly nothing was going to change Lenny, and so she was going to wash her hands of him once and for all.

The light in the foyer was dim, and she was so intent on de-livering her speech that she did not immediately notice the stroller behind him.

Her arms folded, her voice firm, Lilly said, "Lenny, you asked if you could stay a few nights. Well, that was three weeks ago, and I don't want you here anymore. Pack your bags and get out."

Lilly's loud, strident tone startled the already stirring in-fant, and the faint mewling broke into a wail.

"What?" Lilly exclaimed. Then she saw the stroller. In a quick move, she shoved her nephew aside and looked down into it. Shocked, she snapped, "What have you done now? Where did you get that baby?"

Lenny thought fast. He didn't want to leave this apartment. It was a perfect place to live, and staying with his aunt gave him the aura of respectability. He had read the note from the baby's mother, so he quickly came up with a plan.

"She's mine, Aunt Lilly. A girl I was crazy about is the mother. But she's moving to California and wants to put the baby up for adoption. I don't want to. I want to keep her."

The wail was now a demanding screech. Tiny fists flailed the air.

Lilly opened the bundle at the infant's feet. "The baby's hungry," she announced. "At least your girlfriend sent some formula." She plucked out one of the bottles and thrust it at Lenny. "Here, warm this up."

Her expression changed as she unwrapped the blankets from around the tiny infant, picked her up and cradled her in warm and comforting arms. "Beautiful, *bella*. How could your mama not want you?" She looked at Lenny. "What do you call her?"

Lenny thought of the star-shaped diamond in the chalice. "Her name is Star, Aunt Lilly."

"Star," Lilly Maldonado murmured as she soothed the sobbing baby. "In Italy we would call her Stellina. That means 'little star.' "

Through narrowed eyes, Lenny watched the bonding between the infant and the aging woman. No one would be looking for the baby, he thought. It wasn't like he had kidnapped it, and anyhow, if anything ever did come up about the kid, he'd have the note to prove she had been abandoned. He knew the word for grandmother in Italian was *nonna.* As he turned and hurried into the kitchen to warm the bottle, Lenny told himself with satisfaction, "Star, my little girl, I've found me a home—and you've got yourself a *nonna.*"

2

Seven Years Later

 Frowning, Willy Meehan sat at the piano his wife, Alvirah, had bought him for his sixty-second birthday. With intense concentration, he attempted to read the notes in the *John Thompson's Book for Mature Beginners*. Maybe it will be easier if I sing along, he thought. "Sleep, my child, and peace attend thee," he began.

Willy has such a good voice, Alvirah thought, as she came into the room. "All Through the Night" is one of my favorite carols, she reflected, as she looked affectionately at her husband of more than forty years. In profile, his resemblance to the late Tip O'Neill, the legendary Speaker of the House of Representatives, was even more startling than when viewed full on, she decided. With his shock of white hair, his craggy features, his keen blue eyes and warm smile, Willy was often the recipient of startled glances of recognition, even though it was several years since O'Neill's passing.

Now, to her loving eyes, he looked simply splendid in the dark blue suit he'd worn out of respect for Bessie Durkin Maher, whose wake they were about to attend. Alvirah had reluctantly switched from the size twelve navy suit she'd been planning to wear to a black dress that was a size larger. She and Willy had just returned the previous evening from their post-Thanksgiving cruise in the Caribbean, and the sumptuous food had dealt a mortal blow to her diet.

"Guardian angels God will send thee," Willy sang as he played.

The dear Lord God sure did send his angels to us, Alvirah thought as—not wanting to disturb Willy—she tiptoed to the window to enjoy the breathtaking view of Central Park.

Only a little over two years ago Alvirah, then a cleaning woman, and Willy, a plumber, had been living in Jackson Heights in Queens, in the apartment they had rented long ago as newlyweds. She had been bone weary after a particularly hard day at Mrs. O'Keefe's, who always felt that she didn't get her money's worth unless Alvirah moved every stick of furniture in the house when she vacuumed. Still, as they did every Wednesday and Saturday evening, they had paused to watch television when the lottery numbers were announced as the balls popped into place. They'd almost had a collective heart attack when one after another, their numbers, the ones they always played, came up.

And then we realized we'd won forty million dollars, Alvirah thought, still incredulous at their good luck.

We weren't just *lucky,* though, we were blessed, she corrected herself, as she drank in the view. It was quarter of seven, and Central Park was softly beautiful with fresh snow that had left a shimmering white coverlet on the trees and fields. In the distance, festive Christmas lights illuminated the area surrounding the Tavern on the Green. The headlights of cars and taxis were a moving river of brightness as they wound their way along the curving roads. Anywhere else they would just look like traffic, she mused. The horse-drawn carriages, not visible to her now, but no doubt present in the park, always reminded her of the stories her mother told about growing up near Central Park in the early part of the century. Likewise the skaters waltzing on the Wollman Rink ice reminded her of evenings years ago when she had rollerskated to organ music at St. Raymond's in the Bronx.

After winning the lottery, with its yearly income of two million dollars, minus taxes, she and Willy had moved to this luxurious apartment. Living on Central Park always had been one of her fantasies, and besides, the apartment was a good investment. However, they still kept their old rental apartment in Jackson Heights, just in case New York State went broke and quit paying them.

Truthfully, though, Alvirah had made good use of her newfound wealth, giving quite a lot to charity while managing to enjoy herself immensely. Plus she'd had some memorable experiences. She had gone to Cypress Point Spa in Pebble Beach and almost got murdered there because of her nose for news. The experience paid off when she became a contributing columnist for the *New York Globe,* and, as one thing always leads to another, with the aid of the recording device in her sunburst lapel pin, she had solved a number of crimes, gradually earning herself a reputation as a real sleuth, though still an amateur, to be sure.

Willy's skills as a plumber were now utilized exclusively by his oldest sibling, Sister Cordelia, who tended to the poor and elderly on the Upper West Side of Manhattan. She kept Willy busy repairing sinks and toilets and heating units in the tenements of her charges.

Before they left on the cruise, he had worked double time fixing up the second floor of the abandoned furniture store where Cordelia ran a clothing thrift shop. Called Home Base, it was also an unofficial after-school center for young children, from the first to the fifth grade, whose parents were working.

Yes, Alvirah had decided, having money was a fine thing, so long as one never forgot how to live without it, something she and Willy intended never to do. It's nice that we can help out other people, she thought, but if we were to lose every dime of the money, we'd be happy as long as we're together.

"*All through the night,*" Willy concluded with a decisive crescendo. "Ready to go, hon?" he asked as he pushed back the piano bench.

"All set," Alvirah said as she turned to face him. "You sounded just great. You play with so much feeling. So many people just rush through these sweet songs."

Willy smiled benevolently. While he heartily regretted the moment he had casually mentioned to Alvirah that he wished he had taken piano lessons as a child, he realized that he was beginning to derive intense satisfaction whenever he managed to play through a song without a single mistake.

"The reason I played so slowly was because I couldn't read the notes any faster," he joked. "Anyhow, we'd better get going."

. . .

The funeral home was on Ninety-sixth Street, just off River-side Drive. As their cab made its laborious way uptown, Alvi-rah reflected on her friends Bessie and Kate Durkin. She had known Bessie and Kate for many years. Kate had worked as a salesperson in Macy's, and Bessie had been the live-in house-keeper for a retired judge and his ailing wife.

When the judge's wife died, Bessie had handed in her resig-nation, saying she could not possibly stay under the same roof with the judge without the presence of another woman.

A week later, Judge Aloysius Maher had requested her hand in marriage, and so, after sixty years of maidenhood, Bessie promptly accepted the offer. Once married, she had settled in to make his large and handsome townhouse on the Upper West Side her own.

After over forty years of marriage, and a blessedly happy one at that, Willy and Alvirah had reached the point where they typically thought about the same subject even before they discussed it. "Bessie knew just what she was doing when she quit her job," Willy commented, his words melding seam-lessly with Alvirah's own unspoken thought. "She knew if she didn't grab the judge before other women got their hooks into him, she didn't stand a chance. She always treated that house as if she owned it, and it would have killed her to be booted out of it."

"True, she loved it all right," Alvirah agreed. "And to be fair, she kept her part of the bargain. She was a marvelous housekeeper and could cook like an angel. The judge couldn't get to the table fast enough. You have to admit she waited on him hand and foot."

Willy had never been a fan of Bessie Durkin's. "She knew what she was doing. The judge only lasted eight years. Then

Bessie got the house *and* a pension, invited Kate to move in, and Kate's waited on *her* hand and foot ever since."

"Kate's a saint," Alvirah said in agreement, "but of course the house will be hers now that Bessie's gone, and she'll have an income. She should be able to manage just fine."

Cheered by her own optimistic statement, she glanced out the window. "Oh, Willy, don't you love the Christmas decorations in all the windows?" she asked. "It's such a shame Bessie died so near the holidays; she always loved them so."

"It's only the fourth of December," Willy pointed out. "She made it through Thanksgiving."

"That's true," Alvirah conceded. "I'm glad we were with them. Remember how much she enjoyed her turkey? She ate every bite of it."

"And everything else in sight," Willy said dryly. "Here we are."

As their taxi pulled up to the curb, an attendant at the Reading Funeral Home opened the door for them and, in a subdued tone, told them that Bessie Durkin Maher was reposing in the east parlor. The heavy, sweet smell of flowers drifted through the hushed atmosphere as they walked sedately down the corridor.

"These places give me the creeps," Willy commented. "They always smell of dead carnations."

In the east parlor they joined a group of some thirty mourners, including Vic and Linda Baker, the couple who had rented the top floor apartment of Bessie's townhouse. They were standing at the head of the casket next to Bessie's sister Kate, and, like family, were accepting condolences with her.

"What's *that* all about?" Willy whispered to Alvirah as they waited their turn to speak to Kate.

Thirteen years younger than her formidable sister, Kate was a wiry seventy-five-year-old with a cap of short gray hair and warm blue eyes that were now welling with tears.

She's been bullied all her life by Bessie, Alvirah thought, as she enveloped Kate in her arms. "It's for the best, Kate," she said firmly. "If Bessie had survived that stroke she'd have been a total invalid, and that wasn't for her."

"No," Kate agreed, brushing away a tear. "She wouldn't have wanted that. I guess I've always thought of Bessie as both my sister *and* my mother. She might have been set in her ways, but she had a good heart."

"We'll miss her terribly," Alvirah said, as behind her Willy breathed a deep sigh.

As Willy gave Kate a brotherly hug, Alvirah turned to Vic Baker. So formal was his mourning attire that Alvirah immediately was reminded of one of the Addams Family characters. Baker, a stocky man in his mid-thirties, with a boyish face, dark brown hair and shrewd china-blue eyes, was wearing a black suit with a black tie. Beside him, his wife, Linda, also dressed in black, was holding a handkerchief to her face.

Trying to squeeze out a tear no doubt, Alvirah thought dryly. She had met Vic and Linda for the first time on Thanksgiving. Aware of her sister's failing health, Kate had invited Alvirah and Willy, Sister Cordelia, Sister Maeve Marie and Monsignor Thomas Ferris, the pastor of St. Clement's who resided in the rectory a few doors from Bessie's townhouse on West 103rd Street, to share the holiday dinner with them.

Vic and Linda had stopped in as they were having coffee, and it seemed to Alvirah that Kate had pointedly not invited them to stay for dessert. So what were they doing acting like the chief mourners? Alvirah asked herself as she dismissed Linda's apparent sadness, assuming it to be phony.

A lot of people would think she's good-looking, Alvirah conceded as she took in Linda's even features, but I'd hate to get on the wrong side of her. There's a coldness to her eyes that I don't trust, and that spiky hairdo with all those brassy gold highlights is the pits.

". . . as though she were my own mother," Linda was saying, a quiver in her voice.

Willy, of course, had heard the remark and couldn't help adding his own. "You rented that apartment less than a year ago, didn't you?" he asked.

Without waiting for an answer, he took Alvirah's arm and propelled her toward the kneeling bench.

In death as in life, Bessie Durkin looked to be in charge of the situation. Attired in her best print dress, wearing the narrow strand of faux pearls the judge had given her on their wedding day, her hair styled and combed, Bessie had the satisfied expression of someone who had successfully made a lifelong habit of getting other people to do things her way.

Later, when Alvirah and Willy were leaving, they said good-bye to Kate, promising to be at the funeral Mass at St. Clement's and ride in the car with her to the cemetery. "Sister Cordelia is coming too," Kate told them. "Willy, I've been worried about her this week that you've been away. She's been under so much strain. The city inspectors are giving her a terrible time about Home Base."

"We expected as much," Willy said. "I called today, but she was out and didn't get back to me. I had expected to see her here tonight."

Glancing across the room, Kate saw Linda Baker bearing down on them. She dropped her voice. "I asked Sister back to the house after the funeral," she whispered. "I want you to come too, and Monsignor will be there."

They said their good-nights, and because Willy said he had to get some fresh air just to get the overwhelming smell of flowers off him, they agreed to walk a ways before hailing a taxi.

"Did you notice how Linda Baker came running when she saw us talking to Kate?" Alvirah asked Willy as they strolled arm in arm toward Columbus Avenue.

"I sure did. I have to say there was something about that woman that bothered me. And now I'm worried about Cordelia too. She's no spring chicken, and I think she's bitten off more than she can chew by trying to mind those kids after school."

"Willy, they're just being kept warm and safe until their mothers can pick them up from work. How can anyone find fault with that?"

"The city can. Like it or not, there are rules and regulations about minding kids. Hold on, I've had enough of this cold air. Here comes a cab."

3

"Like it or not, there are rules and regulations," Sister Cordelia said with a sigh, as she unconsciously repeated Willy's exact words the next day. "They've given me a deadline—January 1st—and Inspector Pablo Torres told me he was already breaking every rule in the book to stretch it that far."

It was one o'clock, and after a Mass of Resurrection, Bessie Durkin had been lowered into her final resting place, alongside three generations of Durkins in Calvary Cemetery.

Willy and Alvirah, Sister Cordelia and her assistant, Sister Maeve Marie, who was a twenty-nine-year-old former NYPD policewoman, and Monsignor Thomas Ferris were at the table in Bessie's townhouse, enjoying the Virginia ham, homemade potato salad and sourdough biscuits prepared by Kate.

"Is there anything else I can get anyone?" Kate asked meekly before she took her place at the table.

"Kate, sit down," Alvirah ordered. She turned to Cordelia. "What are the specific problems that are so terrible, Cordelia?" she asked.

For a moment the troubled frown on the face of the seventy-year-old nun disappeared. Cordelia's eyes softened as she looked at her sister-in-law and smiled. "It's nothing even you can fix, Alvirah. We have thirty-six kids, ages six to eleven, who come to us after school. I asked Pablo if he'd rather have them on the streets. I asked him what we're doing wrong. We give them a snack. We've rounded up some trustworthy high school kids who help them with their homework and play games with them. There are always adult volunteers in the thrift shop, so there's plenty of supervision at all times. The kids' mothers or fathers pick them up by six-thirty. We don't charge anything, of course. The nurses at the schools have checked any kids we take in. They've never complained about anything."

Cordelia sighed and shook her head.

"We know the property is in the process of being sold," Sister Maeve explained, "but it's at least a year before we have to get out. We've freshly spackled and painted the whole second floor where the kids stay when they're there, so there isn't a peeling chip anywhere. Apparently it's still a problem though, because they say that lead paint was used years ago. Sister Superior asked Pablo if he'd taken a look at some of the places where these kids live and compared the conditions there to those at Home Base. He said he doesn't make the rules. He said there have to be two exits, and they can't include the fire escape."

"The staircase is wide enough for five kids to come down together, but they don't count that. Maeve, we could go on and on," Sister Cordelia interrupted. "The bottom line is that in under four weeks we have to close the doors on the Home Base program, and if any of those kids show up, we have no choice but to send them home to an empty apartment with no security and no supervision."

Monsignor Ferris reached for his empty cup as Kate held up the teapot. "Thank you, yes, Kate. And I think it's time to share our good news with the others."

Kate looked shy. "Why don't you, please, Monsignor?"

"Gladly. Bessie, God rest her, realized the end was near, and the day after Thanksgiving she asked me to stop in."

Let this news be what I think it is, Alvirah prayed silently.

The quiet composure that was a habitual expression on Monsignor Ferris's kindly face was brightened by the obviously happy tidings he was about to impart. He smoothed his silver hair, which still was somewhat disheveled from the wind at the graveside service, then he smiled. "Bessie told me that, of course, in her will she left this house to her sister, as well as an income that would ensure Kate's comfort, but Kate had indicated to her that she would like to turn the house over to Sister Cordelia for the Home Base program."

"Saints preserve us!" Cordelia said fervently. "Oh, Kate."

"Kate would want to stay on, living in the fourth floor apartment the Bakers are now occupying. Bessie quite frankly wasn't enthusiastic about the idea but felt it was Kate's decision to make, and she asked me to make sure nothing went wrong with all the arrangements."

"You know Bessie always treated me as if I couldn't find my own way to the store," Kate said fondly.

"I told Bessie that with the rectory just three doors down, there'd be no problem keeping an eye on everything, although I also told her that Kate is very much able to handle her own affairs," the monsignor explained.

"I'll love having Home Base here," Kate said. "I've wanted to volunteer to help ever since you opened it, Cordelia, but Bessie needed me."

Monsignor Ferris stood, smiling as he watched the news register on Sister Cordelia's face. "I've always believed foresight should be considered a cardinal virtue," he announced. "I happen to have a bottle of champagne cooling in the ice bucket. I think a toast to the Durkin sisters, Bessie and Kate, is in order."

This is such wonderful news. So why am I so worried? Alvirah asked herself. Why am I sure that something is going to go wrong? Mentally she examined the possibilities in much the same way she might use her tongue to seek out the source of a toothache. It only took an instant to find the source of her concern: the Bakers.

"Are you sure you can get the Bakers out, Kate?" she asked. "It isn't so easy to get rid of tenants these days."

"Absolutely sure," Kate said firmly. "The lease is for one year, and it's up in January. There is a specific clause saying that the renewal is solely at the discretion of the owner. You remember how we had that young man in that apartment who was an exercise nut? At least once a week he'd drop a barbell, and always in the middle of the night. Bessie was sure the house would cave in. You know how she loved this place. After she finally got rid of him, she added the renewal clause to the lease for the new tenants."

"Looks as though you've thought of everything," Willy observed.

"I do feel sorry about telling them they have to move, but I'll be honest—I'll be glad when they're gone," Kate said. "Vic Baker is always underfoot, looking for things to fix around here. You'd think he *owned* the house."

When they left an hour later, Willy and Alvirah walked Monsignor Ferris to the door of the rectory. The already cloudy sky was now completely overcast. The wind had become sharp, and the raw, damp cold was bone penetrating.

"They're predicting a long winter," Alvirah said. "Can you imagine in a couple of weeks, having to tell those little kids that they can't go to Home Base, where they're safe and warm and comfortable?"

It was a rhetorical question, of course, and as she asked it, even Alvirah was only half listening. Instead, her attention was directed across the street, where a young woman in a sweat suit was standing, staring at the rectory.

"Monsignor Tom," she said. "See that woman. Don't you think there's something odd about the way she's just standing there?"

He nodded. "I saw her there yesterday, and then she was at early Mass this morning. I caught up to her before she left and asked if I could help her in any way. She just shook her head and almost rushed away. If she has a problem she wants to discuss, I think I'm going to have to let her come to me."

Willy put a restraining hand on Alvirah's arm. "Don't forget we're due at Home Base to help Cordelia with the rehearsal for the Christmas pageant," he reminded her.

"Meaning mind my own business. Well, I suppose you're right," Alvirah agreed cheerfully.

She glanced across the street again. The young woman was walking rapidly away, headed west. Alvirah squinted to get a good look at her classic profile even as she admired her regal carriage. "She looks familiar," she said flatly. "I'll have to put on my thinking cap."

4

They're talking about me, Sondra thought as she hurried away. The townhouse she had been standing in front of was no longer under repair, as it had been before. There was no scaffolding to shield her today as she tried to decide what to do.

But what *could* she do? Certainly she couldn't buy back that moment seven years ago when she had crossed the street, opened the stroller and left her baby on the rectory stoop. If only. If only, she thought. Then: Dear God, where can I turn? What happened to her? Who took my little girl? She fought back tears.

A cab with its light on was stopped in traffic. She raised her hand to signal the driver. "The Wyndham, on West Fifty-eighth between Fifth and Sixth," she said as she got into the backseat.

"First visit to New York?" the cabbie asked.

"No." But I haven't been here in seven years, she thought. Her first visit had been when she was twelve and her grandfather brought her here from Chicago to a Midori concert at Carnegie Hall. He had brought her twice again after that. "Someday you will play on that stage," he had promised her solemnly. "You have the gift. You can be as successful as she."

A violinist whose hands had been limited by arthritis, cutting short his career, her grandfather had made his living as a music teacher and critic. And supported me, Sondra thought sadly—when he was sixty years old he took me in.

She had been only ten when her young parents had been killed in an accident. Granddad devoted himself to me, taught me everything he knew about music, she reminded herself. And he used every spare penny he could find to take me to hear the great violinists.

Her talent had earned her a full scholarship to the University of Birmingham, and it was there, in the spring of her freshman year, that she met Anthony del Torre, a pianist visiting the campus for a concert. What followed should never have happened.

How could I have told Granddad that I got involved with a man I knew was married? she asked herself now. *I couldn't have kept the baby. There was no money to pay for help. I had years of schooling ahead of me. And if I had told him what had happened, it would have broken his heart.*

As the cab made its way through the slow traffic, Sondra thought back to that wrenching time. She thought about how she had saved money to come to New York, she remembered checking into a cheap hotel on November 30th, buying the baby clothes and diapers, the bottles and formula and stroller.

She had located the hospital closest to the hotel and had planned to go to the emergency room when she went into labor. She would, of course, have to give a false name and address. But the baby had come so quickly on December 3rd; there had been no time to get to the hospital.

Early in the pregnancy, she had decided that New York was where she would leave the baby. She loved the city. From her very first visit there with her granddad, she knew that someday she would live in Manhattan. She had instantly felt at home there. On that first visit, her grandfather had taken her to St. Clement's, the church he had attended throughout his boyhood. "Whenever I wanted a special favor, I would kneel in the pew nearest Bishop Santori's picture and his chalice," he told her. "From them I always received comfort. Sondra, I went there when I realized there was no hope for the stiffening fingers. That was the nearest I ever came to despair."

In the several days before the baby was born, Sondra had slipped in and out of St. Clement's; each time she had knelt in that pew. She had watched the clergymen there; she'd seen the kindness in the face of Monsignor Ferris and knew that she could trust him to find a good home for her baby.

Where is my baby now? Sondra wondered in despair. She'd been in agony since yesterday. As soon as she checked into the hotel, she had phoned the rectory and said she was a reporter following up on the story of the baby who had been left on the stoop of the rectory on December 3rd, seven years ago.

The astonishment in the secretary's voice had warned her of what was to come. "*A baby left at St. Clement's?!* I'm afraid you're wrong. I've been here twenty years, and nothing like that has ever happened."

The cab turned onto Central Park South. I used to daydream that maybe the people who adopted the baby were pushing her in her carriage here, along the park, Sondra thought, where the baby could see the horses and carriages. Late yesterday afternoon she had gone to the public library and called up the microfilm of the New York newspapers of December 4th, seven years ago. The only reference to St. Clement's that day was an article about a theft there, stating that the chalice of Bishop Santori, the founding pastor to whom many of the devout prayed, had been stolen.

That's probably why the police were there when I called that night; that's why the monsignor was outside, Sondra thought, her distress growing. And I believed it was because they'd found the baby.

Then who *had* taken the baby? She had left her in a paper shopping bag for added warmth. Maybe some kids had come by and pushed the stroller away and abandoned it, without ever realizing she was there. Suppose the baby had died of exposure.

I'd go to prison, Sondra thought. What would that do to Granddad? He keeps telling me that all the sacrifices he's made over the years have been worthwhile because of what I've become. He's so proud that I'll be playing a concert at Carnegie Hall on December 23rd. It's what he always dreamed of—first for himself, and then for me.

The celebrity-studded charity affair would introduce her to the New York critics. Yo-Yo Ma, Plácido Domingo, Kathleen Battle, Emanuel Ax and the brilliant young violinist Sondra Lewis were the main attractions. She still could hardly believe it.

"We're here, miss," the cabbie said, an edge in his voice. With a start, Sondra realized that his irritation was due to the fact that he'd already told her that once.

"Oh, sorry." The fare was $3.40. She fished in her wallet for a five-dollar bill. "That's fine," she said, opening the door and starting to get out.

"I don't think you really wanted to give me a forty-five dollar tip, miss."

Sondra looked at the fifty-dollar bill the cabbie was holding out to her. "Oh, thank you," she stammered.

"That's a big mistake, lady. Lucky for you I don't take advantage of pretty young women."

As Sondra exchanged the fifty for a five-dollar bill, she thought—too bad you weren't around when I traded my baby for my grandfather's good opinion of me and my own chance at success.

5

When they reached the building on Amsterdam Avenue—formerly the Goldsmith and Son Furniture Emporium—that now housed Sister Cordelia's clothing thrift shop, Alvirah and Willy went directly to the second floor.

It was four o'clock, and the children who regularly came to Home Base to take advantage of the after-school facilities were sitting cross-legged on the floor around Sister Maeve Marie. The large area had been transformed into a kind of bright and cheery auditorium. The faded linoleum was polished to the point that even the floorboards beneath the worn spaces glistened.

The walls were painted sunshine yellow and decorated with drawings and cutouts the children had made. Old-fashioned radiators whistled and thudded, but thanks to Willy and his near-magical ability to fix the unfixable, there was no mistaking the warmth they provided.

"Today is very special," Sister Maeve Marie was saying. "We're going to begin practice for our Christmas pageant."

Willy and Alvirah slipped into seats near the staircase and watched affectionately. A regular volunteer at Home Base, Alvirah was in charge of the party that was to follow the pageant, and Willy would be playing Santa Claus.

The children's expectant and lively eyes were riveted on Sister Maeve Marie as she explained, "Today we're going to start learning the songs about Christmas and Chanukah that we'll be performing at the pageant. Then we'll study our lines."

"Isn't it wonderful that Cordelia and Maeve are making sure that everybody has a speaking part?" Alvirah whispered.

"Everybody? Well, let's hope it's a *short* speaking part," Willy replied.

Alvirah smiled. "You don't mean that."

"Want to bet?"

"Sshh." She patted his hand as Sister Maeve Marie read off the names of the children who would be assigned to tell the story of Chanukah. "Rachel, Barry, Sheila . . ."

Cordelia appeared from downstairs and, with her practiced eye, glanced over the children. Seeing mischief about, she walked over to Jerry, the lively seven-year-old who was poking the six-year-old seated next to him.

She tapped him lightly. "Keep that up, and I'll find a new Saint Joseph," she warned, then turned and joined Alvirah and Willy. "When I got back, there was another message from Pablo Torres," she said. "He'd gone to bat for us, and I do believe he tried his best, but he says there was no way he could get an extension on keeping this place open. I think he was as happy as I was to hear about Bessie's townhouse. He knows the block and said he's sure there won't be any problem transferring our operation there. We can even take in more kids."

One of the volunteer salespeople at the thrift shop came rushing up the stairs. "Sister, Kate Durkin is on the phone, asking to talk to you. Hurry; she's crying her eyes out."

6

 No traces remained of the festive luncheon they had enjoyed only a few hours earlier. But once again, Willy, Alvirah, Monsignor Ferris and Sister Cordelia sat at the same table they had dined at earlier in the day. Kate was with them, quietly weeping.

"I spoke to the Bakers an hour ago," she said. "I told them that I was turning the house over to Home Base and that I couldn't renew their lease."

"And you say they produced a new will?" Willy asked incredulously.

"Yes. They said Bessie had changed her mind, that she hadn't been a bit happy at the prospect of having the house wrecked by a bunch of kids. They also told me that she said the repairs Vic has made and the painting he's done showed her that they'd keep the house in pristine condition, just the way she wanted it. You know how much she loved this house."

She married the judge to get it, Alvirah thought wryly. "When did she sign it?"

"Just a few days ago, on November 30th."

"She showed me the previous will when I stopped in to see her on November 27th," Monsignor Ferris said. "She seemed quite happy with it then. That was when she asked me to make sure that Kate could stay in the apartment after she transferred the house to the Home Base program."

"Bessie left me an income, and according to the new will, I'm allowed to live in the apartment in the *Bakers'* home rent free. As though I'd stay here with those people!" The tears now ran freely down Kate's face. "I can't believe Bessie would do this to me. To leave this house to perfect strangers like that. She knew I didn't like the Bakers. And to get an apartment somewhere else is impossible. You know what the prices are in Manhattan."

Kate's scared and she's angry and she's hurt, Alvirah thought. But even worse . . . She looked across the table and thought that for the first time since she'd known her, Cordelia looked her age.

Catching her sister-in-law's eye, she said, "Cordelia, we'll think of something to keep Home Base going, I promise."

Cordelia shook her head. "Not in under four weeks," she said. "Not unless the age of miracles isn't over."

Monsignor Ferris had been carefully studying the copy of the new will that Vic Baker had presented to Kate.

"From my experience, it looks absolutely legitimate," he commented. "It's on Bessie's stationery, we know that she was a good typist, and that certainly is her signature. Take a look, Alvirah."

Alvirah skimmed the page and a half and then reread it carefully. "It certainly *sounds* like Bessie," she admitted. "Listen, Willy. 'A home is like a child, and as one nears the end, it becomes important to surrender that home to the protection of those who would care for it in the most fitting manner. I cannot be comfortable knowing that the daily presence of many small children will totally change the appearance and character of the pristine house for which I have sacrificed so much.' "

"Does she mean being married to Judge Maher?" Willy asked. "He wasn't a bad little guy."

Alvirah shrugged and continued to read. " 'Therefore I leave my home to Victor and Linda Baker, who will care for it in a manner suited to its genteel quality.' "

"Genteel quality, indeed!" she snorted as she laid the will on the table. "What could be more genteel than giving a helping hand to children?" She turned to the monsignor. "Who witnessed this miserable piece of paper?"

"Two of the Bakers' friends," Monsignor Ferris said. "We'll get a lawyer, of course, just to see if there's anything to be done, but it certainly looks legitimate to me."

Willy had been observing Alvirah for the past several minutes. "Your brain cells are working, honey. I can tell," he said.

"They sure are," Alvirah conceded as she reached to turn on the microphone in her sunburst pin. "This will may sound like Bessie in most ways, but Kate, did you ever hear her use the word 'pristine'?"

"No, I don't think so," Kate said slowly.

"What kind of things *did* she say when she talked about the house?" Alvirah asked, persisting in her probe of the new will.

"Oh, you know Bessie. She'd brag that you could eat a seven-course meal off the floor—that sort of thing."

"Exactly," Alvirah said. "I know it looks bad, but every bone in my body says that this will is a phony. And Kate, Cordelia—I promise you that if there's any way to prove it, then I'll find that way. I'm on the job!"

7

 Sister Maeve Marie had remained at Home Base and continued the rehearsal for the Christmas pageant, although in her mind she conjured up the worst possible scenario to explain why Sister Cordelia, Willy and Alvirah had raced off to see Kate Durkin.

"Something's gone wrong, and Kate's all upset," was all that Cordelia had time to tell her before she left.

Was it possible that Kate had been robbed or mugged? Maeve Marie wondered. She knew that sometimes felons would look through the death notices in the paper and would burglarize the deceased's home when they thought the bereaved were at the funeral. A former New York City cop herself, with four policemen brothers, Maeve Marie thought instantly of potential criminal activity.

All the children at Home Base had been assigned their parts

for the pageant and told to practice their lines at home. The Chanukah story would be recited at the beginning of the pageant, immediately followed by the Chanukah song. Next would come the scene in which the decree from Caesar Augustus was read, proclaiming a census and telling everyone to go to the village of his ancestors to be registered.

The play had been written by Cordelia and Alvirah, and Maeve Marie had complimented them on including so many speaking parts in that first scene. The kids loved that. Plus the lines were both simple and familiar.

"But my father's village is so far away."

"It is such a long journey, and there is no one to care for the children."

"We must find someone, because nothing is more important than that our children are safe."

Cordelia had confessed that she was taking a few liberties with some of the dialogue, but she had invited the housing inspectors to the pageant and she wanted to be sure to get the message across to them: *Nothing is more important than that our children are safe.*

The only children who had not been assigned lines at random were the three wise men, the shepherds, the Virgin Mary and Saint Joseph. The ones selected for those parts were the best singers in the group and would lead the singing in the stable scene.

Jerry Nuñez, the biggest cutup among the younger children, was to be Saint Joseph, and Stellina Centino, a grave and oddly composed seven-year-old, was Mary.

Stellina and Jerry lived on the same block, and Jerry's mother picked up both children at the end of the day. "Stellina's mama took off for California when she was a baby,"

Mrs. Nuñez explained to the nuns. "And her dad is away a lot. Her great-aunt Lilly raised her, but now lately Lilly's been sick a lot, poor woman. And she worries so much. You wouldn't believe how she worries about Stellina. She says, 'Gracie, I'm eighty-two; I gotta live another ten years anyhow so I can raise her. That's my prayer.' "

Stellina is such a beautiful child, Maeve thought as she blocked out the final tableau for the pageant. Curly dark-blond hair that was clasped at the nape of her neck by a barrette fell down her back. Her porcelain complexion was enhanced by wide dark-brown eyes, fringed with long black lashes.

Jerry, never one to be still, began to make faces at one of the shepherds. Before Maeve Marie had a chance to admonish him, Stellina said, "Jerry, when you are Saint Joseph, you have to be very good."

"Okay," Jerry agreed instantly, assuming a frozen posture of almost exaggerated decorum.

"The chorus of angels will begin to sing, the shepherds will see the angels and listen, and you, Tommy, will point to them and . . . then what do you say?" Sister Maeve Marie asked.

"I say, 'Shark, the hellish angels sing,' " six-year-old Tommy suggested.

Sister Maeve Marie tried not to smile. Lead us not into Penn Station, she thought—that's what my brothers used to tell me to say. Tommy had a smart-aleck big brother at home; chances were, he had been coaching his younger brother. "Tommy, you have to get it right, and if you don't listen, you can't be the head shepherd," she said firmly.

The rehearsal ended at six. Not a bad first practice, Maeve

Marie decided as she complimented the children on their performances. The nice thing was that the kids were enjoying it.

She had enjoyed it as well, although the pleasure she took in seeing the children learn their parts was tempered by her concern and growing sense of unease: *Where was Cordelia, and what had gone wrong?*

As she helped to sort out jackets and mittens and scarves, Maeve noticed that, as usual, Stellina had carefully hung up her beautifully tailored blue winter jacket, which, the little girl had proudly explained, her nonna had made for her.

By six-thirty all the children except Jerry and Stellina were gone, most having waited for an adult or older sibling to walk them home. At quarter of seven, Sister Maeve Marie brought the two of them downstairs to the thrift shop, which was closed now. Five minutes later, Gracie Nuñez hurried in.

"My boss," she said, rolling her eyes. "We had to get out some skirts. Two of the girls didn't show. Woulda been worth my job to tell her I had kids to worry about. God bless you, Sister. You have no idea what it means to know that the kids are safely with you. Jerry, say good night and thank you to Sister."

Stellina did not need to be reminded. "Good night, Sister," she said quietly. "And thank you very much." Then with a rare smile she added, "Nonna is so happy that I'm to be the Blessed Mother. She listens to me recite my lines every night, and when she does, she calls me Madonna."

Maeve locked the door behind them and quickly began turning off the lights. Cordelia must either still be with Kate Durkin or she stopped in for a visit with some of the old girls, Maeve decided. She sighed with concern over what kind of news she would hear when she got home.

As she was putting on her coat she heard a tapping on the

front window. She turned to see the face of a man who appeared to be fortyish, his features illuminated by the streetlight. Maeve stared at him with an ex-cop's intuitive sense of unease.

"Sister, is my little girl still here? I mean Stellina Centino," he called.

Stellina's *father!* Maeve hurried to the door and opened it. With professional detachment she studied the thin-faced man, immediately distrusting both his vague good looks and his hangdog expression. "I'm sorry, Mr. Centino," she said coolly, "we didn't expect you. Stellina went home as usual with Mrs. Nuñez."

"Oh, yeah, okay," Lenny Centino said. "I forgot. My job keeps me out of town a lot. Okay, Sister, I'll see you next week. I plan to be picking her up some nights. Take her to dinner and maybe even a movie. I wanna give Star a treat. I'm proud of her. She's turning into some good-looking kid."

"You should be proud. She's a beautiful child in every way," Maeve Marie said shortly. She stood in the doorway and watched him leave. She sensed something disturbing and unsettling about that man.

Still troubled by concern for Sister Cordelia, she made a final check of the premises, turned on the security system and walked home through the dusting of snow that was promising to turn into another full-blown storm.

She found Sister Cordelia sitting with Sister Bernadette and Sister Catherine, two elderly retired nuns who shared their apartment-convent. "Maeve, I confess to being weary to the soul," Cordelia said, and then proceeded to tell her about the newfound will left by Bessie Durkin Maher.

Instantly suspicious, Maeve asked questions about the new document: "Aside from the use of the word 'pristine,' is there anything to suggest the will is a fake?"

Cordelia smiled wanly. "Only Alvirah's instinct," she said.

Sister Bernadette, who would be ninety on her next birthday, had been nodding in an easy chair. "Alvirah's instinct, and something the Lord told us, Cordelia," she said. "You all know what I mean."

Smiling at their puzzled expressions, she murmured, " 'Suffer the little children to come unto me.' I don't think Bessie would have forgotten that, however house proud she was."

8

Stellina kept the key to the apartment in a zippered pocket of her coat. Nonna had given it to her but had made her promise that she would never tell anyone it was there. Now she always used it when she got home so Nonna wouldn't have to get up if she was resting.

It used to be that when she came home from school she would find Nonna sewing in the small room where Daddy always slept when he was home. Then they'd have milk and cookies, and if Nonna had clothes to deliver, or someone to fit for a hem or a new dress, Stellina would accompany her great-aunt and help carry the bags and boxes to the ladies' homes.

But Nonna had been going to the clinic a lot lately, and that was why Mrs. Nuñez had suggested Stellina should be at Home Base each day after school.

Some nights, if Nonna was feeling well, Stellina would arrive home to find her in the kitchen, dinner cooking on the stove and the apartment filled with the good, warm smell of pasta sauce. But tonight she found Nonna lying in bed, with her eyes closed. Stellina could see though that she wasn't asleep, because her lips were moving. She's probably praying, Stellina thought. Nonna prayed a lot.

Stellina bent down to kiss her. "Nonna, I'm home."

Nonna opened her eyes and sighed. "I was so worried. Your papa came home. He said he was going to Home Base. He said he wanted to take you out. I don't want you to go out with him. If ever he shows up there, asking for you, say that Nonna wants you to go home with Mrs. Nuñez."

"Daddy's home?" Stellina asked, trying to hide her distress at the news. She wouldn't tell even Nonna that she was sorry he had reappeared, but she was. Whenever Daddy was home, he and Nonna argued a lot. And Stellina didn't like to go out with him, either, because sometimes they visited people and he would argue with them too. Sometimes the people gave him money and he'd argue about that, usually saying that something he gave them was worth a lot more than the money he'd received.

Nonna leaned on her elbow, sat up, then got out of bed very slowly. "You must be hungry, *cara*. Come. I'll fix dinner for you."

Stellina reached out her arm to help steady Nonna as she got up.

"Such a good girl," Nonna murmured as she headed into the kitchen.

Stellina was hungry, and Nonna's pasta was always so good, but tonight it was hard for her to eat because of her concern for her great-aunt. Nonna looked so worried, and her breathing was fast, as though she had been running.

The click of the lock in the front door told them that Daddy was home. Immediately Nonna began to frown, and Stellina's mouth went dry. She knew that there would be an argument soon.

Lenny came into the kitchen and ran over to Stellina and picked her up. He swung her around and kissed her. "Star, baby," he said. "I've missed you."

Stellina tried to pull away. He was hurting her.

"Put her down, you roughneck!" Nonna shouted. "Get out of here! Stay out of here! You're not welcome! Go away! Leave us alone!"

Lenny didn't display his usual anger. He just smiled. "Aunt Lilly, maybe I *will* go for good, but if I do, I'll take Star with me. Neither you nor anyone else can stop me. Don't forget, I'm her daddy."

Then he turned around and went out, slamming the door behind him. Stellina could see that Nonna was trembling, and there was perspiration on her forehead. "Nonna, Nonna, it's all right," she said. "He won't take me away."

Nonna began to cry. "Stellina," she said, "if I ever get sick and can't be here with you, you must never, ever go away with your daddy. I will ask Mrs. Nuñez to take care of you. But *promise* me, never go away with him. He is not a good man. He gets in trouble."

As Stellina tried to comfort her, she heard her great-aunt whisper, "He is the father. He is the guardian. Dear God, dear God, *what am I to do?*"

She wondered why her Nonna was crying.

9

As usual when she was trying to solve a possible crime, Alvirah did not sleep the sleep of the just. From the time she and Willy turned out the light following the eleven o'clock news, which they had watched in bed, Alvirah was restless. She spent the next six hours dozing, her light sleep filled with vague, unsettling dreams; then she woke with a start.

Finally at five-thirty, deciding to take pity on Willy, who had frequently mumbled in his sleep, "Are you all right, honey?" she got up, put on her favorite old chenille robe, fastened on her sunburst pin with its tiny concealed recording microphone, got her pen and the tabbed notebook in which she kept the record of her ongoing investigations, made herself a cup of tea, settled down at the small dining table overlooking Central Park, turned on the microphone in her pin and began to think out loud.

"It's not beyond Bessie, who was always a true stickler and pain in the neck about her house, to leave it to people who she thought would keep it up a certain way. I mean, it's not as though she was throwing her sister out. After all, she did make sure that Kate would have the upstairs apartment, which is where she had planned to live anyway when she donated the ownership of the house to Home Base."

Alvirah's jaw jutted out unconsciously as she went on. "Bessie was never one to fall all over children, as I recall. In fact, I remember when someone asked her if she was sorry she hadn't had a family, she said, 'People with children and people without them feel sorry for each other.' "

For a moment Alvirah paused, thinking how much she and Willy would have loved to have had a family. By now her grandchildren would probably be the age of the kids she'd seen yesterday at Home Base. She shook her head. Well, never mind. It wasn't to be, she reminded herself briskly.

"So let's assume," she went on, "that Bessie really did get upset at the prospect of kids running around her precious house and getting finger marks on the walls and scratches on the woodwork, and, of course, by knowing that the furniture she'd been polishing since she went to work for the judge and his wife fifty years ago would be replaced by kids' paraphernalia."

Remembering to check the microphone, Alvirah pushed the STOP, REWIND and PLAY buttons, and listened for a moment to the tape.

It's working, she told herself gratefully, and I sound as if I'm working up a head of steam. *Well, I am!* she decided.

Clearing her throat, she resumed her indignant recital. "So the only real clue we have so far to show that this new will might be false is that Bessie was never known to use the word 'pristine.' "

She picked up her pen and turned to the next unused section of her loose-leaf notebook, the one that followed "The case of the death of Trinky Callahan." At the top of the page, she wrote "The case of Bessie's will," then entered the first item in her investigation: "Use of the word 'pristine.' "

Now Alvirah began to write quickly. Witnesses to the will: Who were they? What were their backgrounds? Time: The will was signed November 30th. Did Kate meet the witnesses? What did she think was going on if she was there and they asked to see Bessie?

Now I'm using the old gray matter, Alvirah thought. She had recently been rereading Agatha Christie's Hercule Poirot books. While working on the crimes she had helped to solve, she had tried to follow his method of deductive reasoning.

As she made the last entry in her plan of action, Alvirah looked at the clock: seven-thirty—time to close the notebook and turn off the microphone, she decided. Willy would be awake soon, and she wanted to have breakfast ready for him.

Then, sometime today, I have to sit down alone with Kate and go over these questions with her, she thought.

Suddenly another idea came to her, and she snapped the microphone on again. Since she had written that first article for the *New York Globe* about visiting Cypress Point Spa after winning the lottery, she and the editor there, Charley Evans, had become fast friends. He could get the lowdown on Vic and Linda Baker for her right away. "The little gray cells are really waking up," she announced. "It's time to get the *Globe* researchers to dig up the dirt on the Bakers. Dollars to donuts, this isn't the first time that pair of phonies pulled a fast one."

. . .

The 7:00 A.M. Mass at St. Clement's usually had an attendance of about thirty people, mostly the older, retired parishioners. But now that it was the season of Advent, the number attending was at least double that. In his brief homily, Monsignor Ferris spoke about Advent as the season of waiting. "We are in the time when we anticipate the birth of the Savior," he said. "We anticipate the moment in Bethlehem when Mary gazed for the first time at her infant Son."

A faint sob from the congregation riveted his attention on the pew near the painting of Bishop Santori. The pretty young woman whom he had noticed earlier, standing across the street from the rectory, sat there. Her face was buried in her hands, and her shoulders were shaking. I have got to make her talk to me, he thought, but then he saw her reach into her purse, put on dark glasses and slip down the aisle and out the door.

At nine-thirty, Kate Durkin began going through everything left in her late sister's room. It would be a crying shame just to leave Bessie's clothes hanging in the closet when so many people need something to wear, she decided.

The four-poster bed which for eight years Bessie had shared with Judge Aloysius Maher, and from which she had gone to her Maker, seemed somehow to stand in silent reproach as Kate took dresses and jackets from the closet. Some of the items she recognized as being at least twenty years old. Bessie was always telling me that there was no point in giving them away, because maybe I could use them someday, Kate thought. What she didn't seem to realize is that I'd have had to grow five inches for any of them to fit. It's a wonder she didn't leave *them* to Linda Baker too, she thought bitterly.

The memory of yesterday's sudden revelations, and the sur- prise will, made Kate's eyes fill. As she impatiently brushed away a tear and glanced at Bessie's desk, the typewriter caught her eye. It seemed to her that there was something she should remember, but what was it?

She did not have time to think about what could have trig- gered her subconscious, however; having heard a sound be- hind her, she turned to find Vic and Linda standing in the doorway.

"Oh, Kate," Linda said sweetly. "I'm so glad you're clear- ing Bessie's things out of the room for us."

The downstairs bell rang. "I'll get it," Vic Baker an- nounced.

You're not taking over yet, Kate said to herself as she quickly followed him down the stairs.

A moment later, Kate saw the welcome sight of Alvirah on the front steps and heard her ask, "Is Kate Durkin, the lady of the house, on these pristine premises?"

10

Lenny had gotten back to the apartment at midnight and tiptoed to his bedroom—mostly cleared of the clothing Lilly was mending—and gone to bed right away.

When he woke up at nine the next morning, he was surprised to hear the sound of voices in the other bedroom, then realized it was Saturday and Star had no school.

It also meant that Aunt Lilly probably was still in bed if she wasn't at Mass. She never had been the same after a bad fall last summer. She tried to tell him she was fine, but he had overheard her telling a neighbor that the doctor thought a blackout had been caused by a small stroke. Whatever had caused it, he definitely had seen a big difference in Lilly since he last had been here in September.

He had told her that he'd been in Florida, working for a delivery company. She responded that she was happy to know he had a regular job, and that he shouldn't worry about Stellina. Sure, I shouldn't worry about Star, he thought. Aunt Lilly would be happy if I never showed up here again.

Well, part of what I told her was true, he thought as he reached for a cigarette. I *did* make deliveries. Deliveries of little packages that made people happy. But it was getting too risky down there, so he thought he would come back to New York, pick up some small-time action and get to know Star. I'm just a nice, concerned single father, living in a respectable building with an old aunt, he thought. And that's good, because this way when Lilly closes her eyes for good, Star and I will at least know each other real well. Who knows? I might even be able to put her to work for me.

He thought over the situation as he puffed his cigarette down to the stub, ground it out in a tray with sewing supplies, then decided to light another one to settle his nerves before he faced Aunt Lilly.

Even when Star had still been an infant, and he would take her for an outing in her carriage, Lilly had been suspicious every time. Lenny smiled at the memory of all the goods he had been able to deliver, while people smiled and cooed at his beautiful baby. But when he got home, Lilly always peppered him with questions. "Where did you walk? Where did you take her? Her blankets smell of smoke. I'll kill you if you took her to a bar." She was always after him.

He knew, though, that he would have to be careful and not get Lilly all worried about the little girl. All he needed was to have his aunt get some crazy idea, like trying to trace Star's mother, his supposed girlfriend who'd gone to California.

Through some of his connections he had managed to get a

forged birth certificate for Star. The letter pinned to her blanket had said she was of Irish and Italian descent, which worked out fine. So I'm Italian and her mother was Irish, Lenny had decided, and told his source to fill out the mother's name as Rose O'Grady. He had thought of the song about Rosie O'Grady, which he liked when he was younger. He remembered some Irish kid in his class used to sing it.

Lilly would have a hell of a job trying to trace a Rose O'Grady in California, Lenny thought—it's a common name and a very big state—but any kind of inquiry was potential trouble, and he wasn't going to let it happen. He would have to start looking more like the concerned parent if he hoped to calm Lilly down.

After yawning, stretching, scratching his shoulder blade and pushing back his lank, dark hair, Lenny got out of bed. He pulled on some jeans, stuffed his feet into sneakers, remembered to put on a T-shirt, then went down the hall to his aunt's bedroom.

The door was open, and he could see that, as he had expected, Lilly was propped up in bed. The room was neat but crowded, with Star's narrow cot wedged between the bed and the wall.

As he stood in the doorway, Star's back was to him, and Lilly was listening to her recite the lines from her part in the Christmas pageant. Lilly had not noticed him, so he stood back quietly while Star, sitting cross-legged on the bed, her back ramrod-straight, her curly, dark-blond hair escaping from the barrette, said, "Oh, Joseph, it does not matter that they would not accept us at the inn. The stable will give us shelter, and the child will wait no longer to come to us."

"*Bella, bella,* Madonna," Lilly said. "The Blessed Mother

will be very pleased that you are to portray her." She sighed
and grasped Stellina's hands. "And today I will begin to sew a
white tunic and a blue veil for you, to wear in the pageant,
Stellina *cara* . . ."

Lilly looks like she should be in the hospital, Lenny thought
with a twinge of alarm. Her skin was gray, and he could see
beads of perspiration on her forehead. He was about to ask
her how she was feeling, but stopped and frowned as he
glanced at the top of the dresser. It was covered with a display
of religious relics and statues of the Holy Family and Saint
Francis of Assisi. Those he was used to—she always had been
super-religious—but he still regretted that years ago Lilly had
found the silver cup from which he had pried the diamond.

There'd been such a stink in the papers about it at the time,
because the cup that had been stolen had been the chalice of a
famous bishop. He knew it wouldn't have been smart to try to
hock it at the time; it was too big a risk for the few bucks it
might bring. Instead, he had tossed it in the back of his closet,
figuring he'd get rid of it at some point, like when he was in
another city.

Then Lilly had gone on one of her cleaning rampages and
found it, said it looked like a chalice, so he had to quickly
come up with some dumb story about how it had belonged to
Star's mother, Rose. He told Lilly that her uncle, a priest, left it
to her when he died. So, of course, Lilly polished it so that the
silver gleamed like new and put it up with her statues.

Oh well, it made her happy, Lenny thought, and not being
able to hock it at the time probably kept him from getting in
trouble. It was a cinch nobody was looking for it now, though,
and he wondered how much it would bring. At least Lilly
hadn't found the note that had been pinned to Star's blanket.

He had held on to that just in case anybody ever questioned where she came from, and he had to prove he hadn't kidnapped her.

He had wedged the note into a crack between the top shelf and wall of his closet. Lilly could never reach it, even when she used a dust mop to get at the shelf.

With a shrug, Lenny turned and went into the kitchen to check the refrigerator and grocery cabinet for breakfast makings. Lean pickings, he thought. Lilly obviously hadn't been shopping lately. He jotted a list of things to buy, grabbed his jacket and went back to her room.

This time he entered the room with a big "Good morning, how are my girls?" Solicitously he asked Lilly how she felt, told Star to be sure to do her homework and announced that he was on his way to the store.

After he rattled off the list of items he intended to buy, Lilly looked at him suspiciously but then relented and added a couple of things.

Outside, the air was sharp, and he regretted not wearing his cap. He would go to the diner and get a decent breakfast first, he decided. While he was there he would make a phone call to let his local sources know he was available to do their errands again, which he was confident they'd be glad to hear.

And once dear Aunt Lilly is out of the picture, I'll be able to make little Star a part of my operation, Lenny thought. She'll be a great partner for me—who'd ever guess?

Yes, working hand in hand, Star and her daddy will have a good delivery business going, he promised himself.

11

Sondra felt the eyes of the monsignor following her when she fled from church. Trying to muffle her sobs, she jogged back to the hotel. Once there, she showered, ordered coffee, then pressed cold wet cloths against her swollen eyes. I've *got* to stop crying, she told herself fiercely. I've got to stop crying! The concert was so very important, and she had to be prepared.

At nine o'clock she was scheduled to go to her rented studio in Carnegie Hall and practice for five hours. She had to get herself together. She knew she had been off form yesterday, distracted, not playing nearly to her usual standard.

But how can I think about anything but the baby? Sondra kept asking herself. What happened to my little girl? For these past seven years she had been picturing her living with a wonderful couple who maybe hadn't had a child of their own and who loved and worshiped her. But now she had no idea who had found her—or even if she had been found at all.

She looked in the mirror. What a mess! she thought. Her face was blotchy and her eyes swollen. There was nothing more she could do about her eyes, she decided, but her long, delicate fingers moved deftly as she dabbed base makeup over her face to cover the evidence of her tears.

I'll walk past the rectory again this afternoon, she decided. That thought at least was calming. It was the last place where she had seen her baby, and she felt near to her when she was there. Also, when she prayed at the portrait of Bishop Santori, something of the same peace her grandfather had described feeling when he prayed there all those years ago seemed to come to her. Her prayer was not to have the baby back. I don't have the right to ask for that, she thought. Just give me a way to know she's safe, and *loved*. That's all I ask.

She had taken a parish bulletin from St. Clement's, and now she dug it out of the pocket of her jogging jacket. Yes, she saw there was a five o'clock Mass. She would attend it, but she would arrive a little late. That way the monsignor wouldn't have a chance to try to speak to her. Then she would slip out again before it was over.

As she twisted her dark-blond hair, gathering it up at the back of her head, she wondered if the baby had grown to look even a little bit like her.

12

Over a pot of tea and a generous slice of Kate Durkin's melt-in-your-mouth crumb cake, Alvirah began to form a plan of action aimed at saving the townhouse from the clutches of the Bakers.

"Isn't it awful to think that you have to keep your voice down in your own home?" Kate asked. "Those two are always pussyfooting around. Just before you arrived, my heart almost stopped when I turned around and saw the two of them watching me. That's why I closed the door just now." Then she glanced at the copy of her sister's will and sighed. "I guess I can't do anything about it, though. They seem to have everything in their favor."

"We'll see about that," Alvirah said firmly as she turned on the microphone in her sunburst pin. "I've got a whole bunch of questions for you, so let's get started. Now, Monsignor came over to see you on Friday the 27th. He said that there was no question in his mind that Bessie would be leaving the house to you, although he did know that she was unhappy at the prospect of having kids mess it up." Kate nodded. Her soft blue eyes—magnified by large, round glasses—were thoughtful. "You know Bessie," she said. "She was so set in her ways, and she complained about how nothing would be the same here with a bunch of kids running around. But I remember that then she sort of laughed and said, 'Well, at least by then I won't be here to clean up after them—that'll be *your* job, Kate.' "

"That was Friday the 27th, right?" Alvirah asked. "How was Bessie over the weekend?"

"Tired. Her heart was just giving out, and she knew it. She had me get out her blue print dress and have it pressed. Then she told me that when her time came I should put her pearls on her. She said they really weren't valuable, but they were the only jewelry the judge ever gave her, other than the wedding band, of course, and that neither one was worth leaving to anyone. Then she said, 'You know, Kate, Aloysius was really a good man. If I'd married him when I was young, I probably would have had a family of my own and wouldn't have had a chance to get so fussy about scratches and finger marks.' "

"That was Saturday?" Alvirah asked.

"Actually, Sunday."

"Then on Monday she supposedly had the new will witnessed. Didn't you hear her banging away on the typewriter before that? What did you think when the witnesses came in for the signing?"

"I never saw them," Kate replied, shaking her head. "You know how I always volunteer for a couple of hours at the hospital on Monday and Friday afternoons. Bessie would never hear of me not going. She seemed pretty good when I left—she was sitting downstairs in her chair in the parlor, watching television. I remember she said she'd be glad to be rid of me for a few hours. That she was feeling all right and getting sick of me looking worried."

"And where was she when you got home?"

"Why, still there, watching one of her soap operas."

"All right. Now, the next thing I want to do is talk to those two witnesses." Alvirah studied the last page of the will. "Do you have any idea who they are?"

"I've never heard of them," Kate replied.

"Well, I intend to call on them. Their address is here under their signatures. James and Eileen Gordon, on West Seventy-ninth." Alvirah looked up as Vic Baker pushed open the door to the dining room without knocking.

"Having a nice little cup of tea?" he asked with forced joviality.

"We *were,*" Alvirah said.

"I just wanted to let you know that we're going out for a bit, but when we come back we'll be glad to help you carry dear Bessie's clothing downstairs."

"We're going to take good care of Bessie's possessions," Alvirah told him. "You don't have to worry about a thing."

The cheery expression disappeared from Baker's face. "I happened to have overheard what you just said about speaking to the witnesses, Mrs. Meehan," he snapped. "I'll be happy to give you their phone number. You'll find them to be perfectly responsible people." He fished in his pocket. "As a matter of fact, I have their card."

Baker handed Alvirah the card, then turned and walked

out, pulling the door closed behind him with a bang. Both women turned and watched as the door slowly swung open again.

"It won't stay closed," Kate said. "He's one of those fixit guys who talks a good game, and obviously he impressed Bessie. The truth is he can use a paintbrush, but that's about it." She pointed to the door. "Did you notice he didn't turn the knob just now? He pushed the door open. It used to stick, so he shaved it down. Now it doesn't even catch. Same thing in the parlor—that's become a swinging door." She sniffed.

Alvirah was only half listening. She was studying the card Vic Baker had given her. "This is a business card," she said. "The Gordons have a real estate agency. Now how about *that?*"

"He may not be able to fix doors, but he sure can get a will done," Alvirah told Willy late that afternoon, when he arrived home and found her sitting dejectedly in the living room of their apartment. "Jim and Eileen Gordon seem like straight arrows to me."

"How did they happen to become witnesses to the will?"

"According to them, almost accidentally. It seems that Vic Baker has been looking at townhouses and condos ever since he moved here nearly a year ago. They say they've taken him out a number of times, to look at homes. He had an appointment with them at three o'clock on the 30th, to see some place on Eighty-first Street, and while they were there, Linda apparently called him on his cell phone. She told him Bessie wasn't feeling well and wanted to get her new will witnessed. Vic asked the Gordons if they would mind. So the Gordons went along, and—now this is the part that's so upsetting—they tell me Vic and Linda both nearly fell over in a faint when Bessie read the will to them before she signed it."

"If the Gordons have been taking Baker out looking at real estate they must have checked his credit," Willy said. "Did you ask about that?"

"They did. Believe it or not, the Bakers are well fixed." She attempted a smile. "Cordelia keep you busy today?"

"I never got up for air. A pipe broke at the thrift shop, and I couldn't fix it until I turned off all the water. Good thing it was Saturday and there were no kids upstairs."

"Well, that won't be a problem soon," Alvirah said with a sigh. "And unless my gray cells come up with something I'm missing, there won't be a place for them anywhere." She reached up and flipped on the microphone in her sunburst pin. Deftly she rewound the last bit of tape, then pressed the PLAY button.

Eileen Gordon's pleasant voice was clear and easy to understand. "The last thing Mrs. Maher said was that now she could die in peace, knowing her home would remain pristine."

"I swear that miserable word 'pristine' is the key," Alvirah said as the dejected look left her face. "What is that expression Monsignor always uses when he's suspicious about something?"

" 'Something is rotten in the state of Denmark,' " Willy replied. "Is that what you mean?"

"That's it. In this case, though, I think there's something rotten on the Upper West Side," Alvirah said. "And I'm going to keep dropping in on the Gordons and talking to them until I find out just what it is. I think they're good people, but still there's something fishy about them just happening to be witnesses. Maybe they're very good actors, and I'm falling for their baloney."

"Talking about baloney," Willy said, "let's have an early dinner. I'm starving."

They were going out the door at six-thirty when Monsignor Ferris phoned. "Kate was at Mass," he said. "She told me you went to see the witnesses. How did it go?"

Alvirah gave him a fast rundown, assuring him she wasn't giving up. Then, before saying good-bye, she added, "Has that young woman we saw yesterday been around again?"

"She was here twice today. This morning she came to Mass, then left during the sermon. She seemed to be in great distress over something. Then I spotted her at the five o'clock, but again I didn't have a chance to talk to her. Alvirah, you said you thought she looked familiar. Any idea who she is or where you might have seen her before? I'd really like to try to help her."

"I've been searching my mind, but so far I haven't come up with it," Alvirah replied regretfully. "But give me time. The thing is, I am sure I've seen her picture somewhere, but I just can't place it."

Two hours later, as she and Willy passed Carnegie Hall on their way home from dinner, she stopped in the middle of a sentence and pointed. "Willy, look. It's that girl."

A glass-covered poster for the Christmas concert included photographs of the artists who would be performing, including Plácido Domingo, Kathleen Battle, Yo-Yo Ma, Emanuel Ax and Sondra Lewis.

Alvirah and Willy went over to read the caption under Sondra Lewis's picture. Even in this photo she appeared sad-eyed and unsmiling. "Why would a girl about to make her Carnegie Hall debut be so unhappy?" Willy asked, clearly puzzled.

"Obviously it has something to do with St. Clement's," Alvirah told him. "And I intend to figure out what that one's all about too."

13

When she had been very little, Stellina had asked Nonna why she didn't have a mother like the other children. Nonna had said that Stellina's mother left her with her Daddy because when she was born her mother became very sick and had to go to California to try to get better. Nonna said that her mother had been very sad to leave her, that she had promised if she ever got better she would come to see her. But Nonna also told Stellina that she thought that might never happen, and that she personally believed that God had called Stellina's mother to heaven.

Then, just when Stellina was starting kindergarten, Nonna had showed her the silver chalice she had found in Daddy's closet and explained that her mother's uncle, a priest, had given it to Stellina's mother, and that she had left it for Stellina. Nonna explained that the cup had been used to celebrate Mass and was blessed in a very special way.

The cup became a talisman for Stellina, and sometimes when she was just going off to sleep and was thinking about her mother, wishing so much that she could see her, she would ask Nonna if she could hold it.

Nonna teased her about it at the time. "Babies give up their security blankets, Stellina. Now that you're a big girl and going to school, you decide you need one," she had said. But she always smiled and never refused to let Stellina hold the cup. Sometimes in English, sometimes in Italian, and frequently in a mixture of both, she would reassure this wonderful little girl, the only real gift her otherwise worthless nephew had given her. "Ah, *bambina*," Nonna would whisper, "I will always take care of you."

Stellina didn't tell Nonna that when she twined her fingers around the cup, it was as if she could feel her mother's hands still holding it.

On Sunday afternoon, as she watched Nonna sew the blue veil she was to wear in the pageant, Stellina had an idea. She would ask Nonna if she could take the cup to the pageant and pretend that as the Blessed Mother she was giving it to the Baby Jesus.

Nonna protested. "Oh, no, Stellina. It might get lost, and besides, the Blessed Mother had no silver to give to the Baby Jesus. It wouldn't be right."

Stellina didn't argue, but she knew she had to find a way to persuade Nonna to let her bring the cup to the stable. She knew exactly the prayer she would say when she brought it there: "If my mother is still sick, please make her well, and please, please ask her to visit me just one time."

. . .

At Manhattan's 24th Police Precinct, Detective Joe Tracy expressed keen interest in the fact that Lenny Centino had once again resurfaced. He remembered Lenny from an investigation he'd been involved with a few years back. He hadn't been able to tie him directly to the crime, which had involved the sale of drugs to minors, but he was certain that Lenny was one of the guilty parties.

Tracy's partner pointed out that the rap sheet on Lenny was minor league—just a few breaking and enterings, penny-ante stuff—but Tracy was convinced that it was only because Lenny had not been caught.

"Sure, he served a little time," Tracy argued, "juvenile detention twenty-five years ago, record expunged, but in my opinion he only learned new tricks of his trade. He was arrested a few times, but never indicted. We never could pin anything definite on him, but I always was sure he was distributing drugs to high school kids. I remember how I used to see him pushing his kid in her carriage all over the West Side. I heard later that the kid was just a cover-up—that he stashed his stuff in the carriage, right there with the baby."

Tracy tossed his slim folder on Lenny Centino back on the desk. "Well, now that he's back, I'm going to keep my eye on him. If I see him with that little girl, I may just bring him in. He'll make a mistake eventually, and when he does, I intend to be there."

14

On Monday morning, as she and Willy were eating breakfast, Alvirah answered the phone and was delighted to hear the welcome voice of her editor, Charley Evans, announce that, while they never had been convicted, Vic and Linda Baker were clearly world-class con artists.

"Wait a minute," she interrupted. "I want to record everything so I won't forget a word." She ran to the bedroom, for her sunburst pin, turned on the microphone and hurried back. "Okay, Charley, shoot," she said as she held the pin to the phone.

"The Bakers make a habit of preying on elderly people with property," Charley said. "The most recent case was in Charlestown last year, where they got friendly with an old man worth a couple of million bucks. He apparently was mad at his daughter at the time, angry about the guy she married, but he never indicated that he intended to disinherit her. According to witnesses, these two crooks kept filling his ears with stories about his daughter and how she couldn't wait to get her hands on his money. Guess what?"

"They came up with a new will," Alvirah suggested.

"You guessed it. The old guy left his daughter a few bucks and her mother's jewelry. Everything else went to the Bakers. You see, they were smart enough not to grab everything. That would have been easier to contest."

"What about witnesses to the will?" Alvirah asked.

"Solid citizens, all of them."

"That's about what I expected," she said with a sigh.

"I found two or three other similar cases in the last ten years, but you get the idea. The wills have all been contested, but each time the Bakers won hands down."

"They won't *this* time," Alvirah vowed.

"I hope not, for your friend's sake, but here's a little free advice: Tell her to go down to Surrogates Court at 31 Chambers Street and file a notice of intent to contest because of undue influence. Otherwise the will could be probated in anywhere from a couple of days to a couple of months, depending on the judge. If she files the notice, it will at least delay transfer of assets. Who's the executor?"

"Vic Baker."

"They thought of everything," Charley commented. "Okay, Alvirah, let me know if I can help, and don't forget—I want a column out of this."

"You bet you'll get one, and I've got the headline for it," Alvirah said. "Write it down: EXPOSING THE SKUNKS."

Charley chuckled. "Go for it, Alvirah. My money's on you."

. . .

Over her third cup of tea, Alvirah told Willy about the conversation. "Now, honey," Willy admonished, "your jaw is
sticking out six feet. I know you're going to do your best, but
you've got to promise me you won't get into any danger. I'm
getting too old to worry about your being pushed off terraces
or drowned in bathtubs."

"The Bakers aren't the type to do anything like that," Alvirah said dismissively. "They're not violent, just sneaky. What
has Cordelia got lined up for you today?"

"Home Base," Willy said, shaking his head. "You know,
honey, I have to agree with the inspectors. That place *is* falling
apart. You can do just so much in the way of repairs with bub-
blegum and Elmer's glue. After that you need to call in the
heavy machinery. But anyhow, I'm going to get in an hour's
practice on the piano too. Cordelia heard me banging out 'All
Through the Night' when I was over there to fix that leak yesterday, and now she's decided to make that the closing song of
the pageant and wants me to play it. She has some crazy idea
that having me take part will show the kids that you can learn
something new at any age."

"That's wonderful!" Alvirah said, her face beaming.

"Well, I think it's a lousy idea," Willy said, "but kids aren't
judgmental, and the parents will only be looking at their own
kids, so maybe nobody'll even notice me. . . . Anyhow, what
are *you* up to?"

"I'm going to stop in on Kate. You know how it is. When
someone dies, everyone comes around for a couple of days,
then after the funeral, the person who's been left behind
wakes up and it sinks in that she'll never see that face or hear
that voice again. That's when friends are really needed, and

doubly so in Kate's case, because she has to put up with those crooks as well as missing Bessie. Then after I see her, I'm going to see Monsignor Tom and tell him I know who the young woman is who's been hanging around St. Clement's."

With her usual efficiency, Alvirah tidied the kitchen, made the bed, showered and then dressed, choosing one of the simple but elegant pantsuits her friend Baroness Min von Schreiber had helped her to buy on Min's last trip East. As Min constantly pointed out, left on her own, Alvirah gravitated to wildly inappropriate styles and colors, an opinion Alvirah humbly accepted.

As she was about to go out, she paused long enough to listen to Willy at the piano, practicing "All Through the Night." Proudly she noted that he was playing with increasing skill. Her lips silently formed the words as he sang the verses. The line "I my loving vigil keeping," seemed to her almost like a prayer. Well, I'm keeping a vigil for you, Kate, she thought.

When she arrived at the townhouse, she was shocked to find a calm but resolute Kate, who announced that after much thought, she had decided to find some other place to live, even if it was only a furnished room. She said if Bessie wanted the Bakers to have her house, then so be it. Bessie's intentions had been clear, and she had left Kate the use of the apartment and an income. "But I can't live in the same house as these people, Alvirah," Kate said. "Every time I think of Bessie, sick as she was, sitting at her desk and typing that will, then making sure to get witnesses in when she knew I'd be out—well, I just get a pain like a knife through me."

"Kate, you just reminded me of something I hadn't thought of. The will was signed last Monday, November 30th, right? But it was dated November 28th."

"Exactly. That was the day after Bessie told Monsignor she didn't like the idea of turning the house into a children's center. So even when she was joking with me about it over the weekend, saying it was going to be my problem dealing with all those children, she was sitting at that typewriter while I was out."

"How often were you out last weekend?" Alvirah asked.

"Just to morning Mass both Saturday and Sunday. But Bessie was a fast typist. You know how proud she was of that. She could have typed that will in twenty minutes."

"Oh, Kate!" Alvirah said. Her heart ached as she looked at her old friend. All the fight seemed to have left Kate. Her shoulders were slumped in defeat, and the spark that gave wiry strength to her small frame seemed to have been extinguished. Alvirah knew it was no use arguing with her—she had made up her mind. The best she could do was stall for time.

"Kate," she said, "just do me one favor. I've been making some calls about the Bakers. Already I've found out that they are known to be con artists. They've just never been arrested—yet! Give me till Christmas to prove that Bessie didn't write that will, and even though it looks like she signed it, I bet if she did, she never knew what she was signing."

Kate's eyes widened. "Oh, Alvirah, there's no way to prove that."

"Yes, there is," Alvirah said with a hearty confidence she did not feel. "And I already know where to start. As soon as I see Monsignor Tom, I'm going to the James and Eileen Gordon Real Estate Agency and tell them I'm hunting for a co-op. Those two are going to see a lot of me in the next couple of weeks. Maybe they're part of the Bakers' scheme, or maybe they've just had the wool pulled over their eyes, but one way or another, I'm going to find out which it is."

15

 Lenny Centino had managed to stay out of prison by not being too greedy. The deliveries he made of drugs were small-time and infrequent, so except for having attracted the unwanted attention of Detective Joe Tracy, he was never high on the hit list of any police officer. Also he never actually *sold* drugs, he just delivered them, which, if he were caught, carried a lighter sentence. The drugs had been paid for in advance, so he never handled the money either. He had earned a reputation among both dealers and users of being dependable, and of never dipping into the goods, so he was in demand.

Still, because he liked to limit his involvement with the always dangerous drug trade, Lenny worked off and on for a reputable liquor store. Making deliveries for them, he was able to scope out people's apartments. He was a gifted burglar—he always made his hit when he was sure people were out, and he never bothered with anything but jewelry and money.

His earlier, very satisfactory career of robbing poor boxes and votive candle offering boxes had ended with his theft at St. Clement's. The church's silent alarm and his unwitting kidnapping of Star had made him realize that he was getting too close to the edge. Now even the smaller churches were getting smart enough to put in silent alarms.

That was why it was with confidence in his own ability to survive that he let his contacts know that he was back in the city and once again available. Over a couple of beers on Monday afternoon he had bragged about what he'd been doing since September, helping to run a scam for a fake computer company. What Lenny did not know was that an undercover cop had infiltrated the group he was boasting to, and when the cop had filed his report at the precinct, Detective Tracy had picked up on it and now had Lenny under surveillance, which included a wiretap. What the police did not know was that Lenny feared just such a situation and had an exit planned. He had a stash of money from the last job, along with a fake identity and a hideout all arranged in Mexico. But since his return to New York, Lenny had added another element to the exit scenario. It was obvious that Aunt Lilly was dying. He was genuinely fond of Star, and she always had been an asset to his operation. She was also his good-luck charm, so he had decided that if he ever had to get out of the country, he'd take her with him.

And as he often told himself, "I *am* her daddy, and it wouldn't be right to abandon her."

Unspoken, but perhaps even more pertinent, was Lenny's awareness that a man traveling with a little girl would be unlikely to appear to anyone to be a crook on the run.

16

Sondra had promised herself that she wouldn't go near St. Clement's again. If Granddad weren't coming in for the concert, I'd go to the police right now, she thought. I can't live like this any longer. If someone found the baby in those few minutes, and read the note and decided to keep her, and she's being raised in New York, then there *might* be a fake birth certificate. It would have been easy enough for someone to claim the baby was delivered at home. In that hotel, no one knew that I had given birth—I never had a single pain.

All the pain has come afterwards, she reflected as she lay awake Sunday night. As dawn was breaking, she finally drifted off. After having slept for only a few hours, she awoke with a blinding headache.

She got up and listlessly put on her jogging clothes. A run

might clear my head, she decided. I've got to be able to concentrate on practice today. I've done so many things wrong—I don't want to add ruining the concert for Granddad to the list.

She had promised herself that she would stay in Central Park today, but when she came near the northern end of the park, her feet turned west. Minutes later she was standing across the street from St. Clement's, remembering once again the moment when she had held her baby for the last time. It had warmed up a little, and the street was busier, so she knew she couldn't dawdle for fear of drawing attention to herself. The snow that had been arctic white on Thursday was now almost fully melted, and the remaining dregs covered with soot.

It was very cold that night, she remembered, *and the snow on the sides of the street was icy. That secondhand stroller had a stain on the side. I scrubbed the inside, but it was so terribly shabby that I hated to lay the baby in it even for a minute. Someone at the hotel had thrown out the shopping bag I used as extra protection. I remember it had a Sloan's logo on it. I bought the bottles and formula at a Duane Reade pharmacy.*

Sondra felt a tap on her shoulder. Startled, she turned to see the concerned face of a somewhat plump, redheaded woman of about sixty. "You need help, Sondra," Alvirah said gently. "And I'm the one to give it to you."

They took a cab back to Central Park South. Once in the apartment, Alvirah made a pot of tea and popped bread in the toaster.

"I'll bet you haven't had a bite to eat today," she said.

Once again close to tears, Sondra nodded in agreement. She felt a kind of unreality, coupled with a great sense of relief.

Now that she was in this strange apartment with this strange woman, she felt comfortable.

She knew she was going to tell Alvirah Meehan about the baby, and she sensed just from Alvirah's presence that Alvirah would somehow find a way to help her.

Twenty minutes later, Alvirah told her firmly, "Now listen, Sondra, the first thing you've got to do is to stop beating up on yourself. That was seven years ago; you were a kid. You didn't have a mother. You felt responsible to your grandfather. You had your baby all by yourself, but you planned for it and you planned well. You had clothes and formula and bottles all ready, and you saved every nickel so the baby would be born in New York because you knew you wanted to live here someday. You dressed the baby and put her, nice and warm and safe, in a stroller on the stoop of the church rectory. You had chosen the church that had saved your grandfather when he knew his arthritis was robbing him of the gift he had as a violinist. You phoned the rectory less than five minutes later, and you thought the baby had been found by someone there."

"Yes," Sondra said, "but suppose some kids just pushed the stroller away as a joke. Suppose the baby froze to death, and when someone found her, they didn't want to be blamed. . . . Suppose—"

"Suppose some good people found her and she's now the light of their lives," Alvirah said with a conviction she didn't feel. Good people would have called the police and *then* tried to adopt her, she thought. They wouldn't have kept quiet about it all these years.

"I can't ask more than that," Sondra said. "I don't deserve more than that, because I just don't know . . ."

"You deserve a lot more than you think you do. Give your-self credit," Alvirah told her briskly. "Now you've got to get on with your violin practice and give New York music lovers a treat. You leave the detecting to me." Then, sponta-neously, she added, "Sondra, do you know how beautiful you are when you smile? You've got to do more of that, hear me?"

Over yet another cup of tea, bit by bit, she drew Son-dra out.

"Can you imagine what it was like for my poor grandfather, living alone, a music critic and violin teacher, to be suddenly stuck with a ten-year-old child to raise?" Sondra asked, a smile playing around her lips. "He had a very nice four-room apart-ment in a good building on Lake Michigan in Chicago, but still it was tiny, and he couldn't afford more space."

"What did he do when you moved in?" Alvirah asked.

"He changed his whole life for me. He turned his study into a bedroom and gave me the big bedroom. Whenever he went out, he hired someone to come in and mind me and cook for me. I might add, Granddad loved to go out to dinner with his friends, and, of course, he went to many concerts. There were a lot of things he had loved to do that he gave up for me."

"You're putting yourself down again," Alvirah said, inter-rupting. "I bet he was lonely before you came. I bet he took great comfort in having you with him."

Sondra's smile got wider. "Maybe, but the trade-off in hav-ing me as company was his freedom to come and go, all the lit-tle luxuries he had enjoyed." The smile vanished. "I guess I did make it up to him in a way. I *am* a good musician, a good violinist."

"Bingo!" Alvirah said. "You're finally saying something good about yourself."

Sondra laughed. "You know, Alvirah, you do have a way with words."

"That's what my editor says," Alvirah agreed. "Okay, I get the picture. You felt the responsibility to succeed, you won the scholarship, you met someone attractive and gifted, you'd just turned eighteen and you fell for him. He probably told you how crazy he was about you, and, let's face it, you were vulnerable. You didn't have a mother and father, or brothers and sisters. Instead you had a grandfather who by then was starting to get sick. Have I got it straight?"

"Yes."

"We know the rest. Let's skip to the present. No one as pretty and talented as you are lives in a vacuum. Have you got a boyfriend?"

"No."

"Too quick an answer, Sondra, which means you *do* have one. Who is he?"

There was a long silence. "Gary Willis. He's on the board of the Chicago Symphony," Sondra said reluctantly. "He's thirty-four, eight years older than I am, very successful, very handsome, very nice, and he wants to marry me."

"So far, so good," Alvirah volunteered. "And you don't care about him?"

"I could. I'm just not ready for marriage. Right now I'm an emotional basket case. I'm afraid that if I *do* get married, I'll never be able to look at my newborn's face without knowing that I left its sibling in a shopping bag out in the cold. Gary has been very patient and understanding. You'll get to meet him. He's bringing my grandfather in for the concert."

"I like the sound of him already," Alvirah said. "And don't forget, ninety percent of women today juggle husbands or families and careers. I know I did."

Sondra looked around the tastefully furnished apartment and out over the spectacular view of Central Park. "What do you do, Alvirah?"

"Right now, my career is lottery winner, problem solver and contributing columnist to the *New York Globe*. Until three years ago I was a spectacular cleaning woman."

Sondra's chuckle indicated she wasn't sure whether to believe her or to take what she said as a joke, but Alvirah did not elaborate. Plenty of time later for the history of my life, she thought.

They got up together. "I must get to practice," Sondra said. "I've got a coach coming today who has a reputation that sends chills down the spines of performers like me."

"Well, you go and give it your all," Alvirah said. "I'm going to figure out a way to try to track down that baby of yours without anyone knowing who's doing it. I'll call you every day, I promise."

"Alvirah, Granddad and Gary will be coming in the week before the concert. I know Granddad will want to go to St. Clement's. He'll be so sad to hear that Bishop Santori's chalice is missing. But in case we should run into Monsignor Ferris when we're there, will you talk to him first and explain that you and I have talked, and ask him please not to let Granddad know I've been hanging around the church?"

"Absolutely," Alvirah said promptly.

When they walked through the living room, Sondra stopped at the piano, where *John Thompson's Book for Mature Beginners* was on the rack, open to "All Through the Night."

She stopped and played the melody with one hand. "I'd forgotten all about that song; it's lovely, isn't it?" Without waiting for an answer, she played it again and softly sang, "Sleep, my child, and peace attend thee, All through the night; Guardian angels God will send thee, All through the night."

She stopped. "Sort of appropriate, isn't it, Alvirah?" Her voice broke. "I hope my baby found a guardian angel that night." She looked suddenly as if she might cry.

"I'll call you," Alvirah promised as Sondra rushed out.

17

 "Are you all through with me, Cordelia?" Willy asked wearily. "Both toilets are working, but I would suggest you tell the kids not to throw wads of tissue in them. Think of those pipes as belonging in an old-age home. Which is where I feel I should be right now," he added with a sigh.

"Nonsense," Sister Cordelia said briskly. "You're still a young man, William. Just wait till you get to be *my* age." There was a ten-year difference between the siblings.

"Cordelia, the day you're a hundred, you'll still have more energy than a Rockette," Willy told her.

"Speaking of which, I'm supposed to watch a run-through of the pageant. Come on, let's get upstairs. The kids will be going home soon," Sister Cordelia said, grasping Willy by the arm and propelling him toward the staircase.

It was quarter of six, and the rehearsal for the pageant was in full swing. They had reached the final scene, in the stable. A solemn-faced Stellina was kneeling across from a merry-eyed Jerry Nuñez, over the folded blanket that was substituting for the crib of the Christ child.

The wise men, led by José Diaz, were approaching from the left and the shepherds were gathering from the right.

"Slow down, all of you," Sister Cordelia ordered. She raised, then lowered, her hands. "One step at a time, and don't push. Jerry, keep your eyes *down*. You're supposed to be looking at the baby, not at the shepherds."

"Willy, play the closing song," she said.

"I left the sheet music home, Cordelia. I didn't think I'd be here this long."

"Well, sing it then. God blessed you with a voice. Start to sing very low, the way you'll do when you're at the piano, then bring up the volume. The children will join in, starting with Stellina and Jerry, then the wise men and the shepherds, then finally the chorus."

Willy knew better than to argue with his sister. "Sleep, my child," he began.

"José, I'll hang you out to dry if you trip Denny," Sister Cordelia said, interrupting. "Go ahead, start again, Willy."

At "Guardian angels God will send thee," Stellina and Jerry joined in. Their young voices, sweet and true, combined with Willy's tenor as they sang the next two lines together.

What a beautiful voice that kid has, Willy thought as he listened to Stellina. I swear she has perfect pitch. He studied her solemn brown eyes. A seven-year-old shouldn't look so sad, he thought as the wise men and shepherds and then all the students joined in: "Soft the drowsy hours are creeping, Hill and vale in slumber steeping, I my loving vigil keeping, All through the night."

At the end, Willy, Sister Cordelia, Sister Maeve Marie and the assorted volunteer aides applauded vigorously. "Just be this good two weeks from now at the actual performance, and we'll all be happy," Cordelia told the children. "Now put on your coats and hats and don't get them mixed up. Your folks will be here to collect you, and they shouldn't be kept waiting. They've been working all day and they're tired." She turned to Willy. "And I might add, so am I," she said.

"It makes me feel good to know that even you have some limits," Willy said. "Okay, since I've been here this long, I may as well hang around and help you clean up."

Twenty minutes later, he and the two nuns were at the door, waiting for Mrs. Nuñez to pick up Stellina and Jerry. When she arrived breathless and contrite, they waved away her apologies.

Sister Cordelia pulled her aside. "How is Stellina's great-aunt doing?" she asked.

"Not good," Mrs. Nuñez whispered, shaking her head. "She'll be in the hospital before the week is out, is my guess." She crossed herself quickly. "Well, at least the father's back. That's something, I suppose." She sniffed, as if to make it clear just how little faith she put in Stellina's father.

When Mrs. Nuñez and the children had left, Sister Cordelia said, "That poor child. Her mother deserted her when she was an infant. She's going to lose the great-aunt who raised her, and the father doesn't seem to be around much. From what I gather, he isn't worth a hill of beans."

"He's worth less than that," Sister Maeve Marie interjected. "Friday evening, he tried to pick Stellina up after she was already gone. He looked a little unsavory to me, so I made some inquiries about him with the boys at the precinct."

"Keeping your hand in at your old job, Detective?" Willy asked.

"It doesn't hurt. From the rumors, it sounds like Mr. Centino could be headed for big trouble."

"Which means that lovely child could end up in a foster home, or a series of foster homes," Sister Cordelia said sadly. "And in a few weeks we won't be able even to watch out for her anymore." She sighed. "All right, enough. Go home, Willy. You've been great, and you can pick up your paycheck at the end of the week."

"Very funny." He smiled, acknowledging her customary joke. As they left the building, they stood together for a moment on the sidewalk. "Have a glass of wine and relax, you two," Willy said. "I would take you out to dinner, but I haven't spoken to Alvirah since she called at noon to say she was going condo hunting, so I don't know when we'll be eating."

Cordelia looked astonished. "You're kidding. I thought you loved the place you're in. Why, Alvirah always said she'd have to be carried out of that apartment. Don't tell me she's serious about buying a different one."

"Of course not," Willy assured her. "She's just trying to get a line on that real estate couple who witnessed Bessie signing the will. She's hoping that if she goes out enough with one or the other of them, she might find out there was something fishy about that witnessing. Anyhow, I'm on my way, but you girls have done a great job. That pageant is going to be terrific. You ought to invite the mayor—let him see what you're doing."

The compliment did nothing to put cheer in their worried faces, and when he got home, an equally troubled Alvirah was waiting for him. "I've walked my feet off looking at condos with Eileen Gordon," she said.

"Learn anything?" Willy asked.

"Yes, she's a lovely person, and I'd stake my life she wouldn't take a sip of water that didn't belong to her, even if she was choking."

"So that means the Bakers probably pulled the old one-two on her and her husband," Willy said practically.

"Yes, but I was so hoping they'd turn out to be phonies too. It's easier to trap crooks than to convince innocent bystanders that they've been duped," Alvirah said with a sigh.

18

Monsignor Thomas Ferris's association with St. Clement's had begun forty years earlier, when he was a newly ordained priest. After seven years, he had been transferred to a parish in the Bronx; following that, he was assigned to the cardinal's staff at the cathedral office. Ten years ago, he had returned to St. Clement's as pastor, and it was there that he hoped to spend the rest of his active life. He acknowledged to himself that St. Clement's was his heart's home; he took great pride in the church—its history and its important position in the community. The only incident that had marred his tenure, and one that still bothered him seven years later, was the theft of Bishop Santori's chalice.

"I blame myself because it happened on my watch," he would say to brother priests who knew how strongly he felt about the loss. "There had been warnings about a string of church break-ins, but we just hadn't paid sufficient heed. Sure, we'd had the windows and doors alarmed, but it wasn't enough. We should have installed a motion detector. I talked about it but just never got around to it."

And while the cabinet containing the bishop's chalice had been equipped with a silent alarm, it had proved useless in this situation. By the time the police had arrived, the thief and the chalice were gone.

The loss always hit Monsignor Tom especially hard at the Christmas season, because it was during Advent that the chalice had disappeared. And while he and the parishioners constantly prayed for its return, his prayers were especially fervent at this time of year.

Some saints are born and not made—Tom Ferris believed that. He always held that they are born with an inner goodness that makes its presence felt, no matter what the circumstance. He had met Bishop Santori near the end of the bishop's life, after he had retired from official duties. The bishop had lived at St. Clement's until his death.

The man had an aura of holiness about him, Ferris reflected; that same aura had surrounded Cardinal Cooke.

On Monday evening, as the monsignor began to lock up the church, he passed the confessional. The thief who stole the chalice *had* to have been hiding in there, he thought. If the diamond in the chalice had been what he was after, I can only pray that the cup itself wasn't tossed away into a garbage dump.

The monsignor actually didn't believe that the chalice had been destroyed. In fact, recently he had been struck with the fanciful notion that the theft had taken place because the chalice was needed elsewhere, that in exile from its home at St. Clement's, it was fulfilling a greater mission.

As he left the church and locked the door behind him, he found himself automatically looking across the street to see if the mysterious young woman was there again today. When he saw she wasn't, he experienced a moment of regret; he hoped she would be back. Many times he had had the experience of people hovering nearby, reluctant to unburden themselves to him, who then finally screwed up their courage and approached him. *"Monsignor, I need help,"* is how they usually began.

His housekeeper had left dinner for him in the oven. His curate was out for the evening, so Tom Ferris had the luxury of reading without interruption while he ate the simple meal and sipped a glass of wine. When he had finished, he dutifully rinsed the dishes and put them in the dishwasher, remembering with some amusement the old days when the pastor— usually known among his six or seven curates as "the boss"—reigned as absolute monarch, and when the rectory came with a housekeeper who could cook like a dream and happily provided, and served, delicious meals, three times a day.

It was over coffee that the tranquil part of his evening ended with a phone call from Alvirah. "Monsignor Tom," she said, "I have a friend with a problem, and while I think I may have figured out a solution, I need to talk with you about it. You see, I'm writing a column about a young girl who, seven years ago, gave birth and left her newborn on the stoop of a rectory." She paused. "And I'm telling you this because it was your rectory."

"Alvirah, that never happened!"

"Yes, it did, but you didn't know anything about it. I'm convinced that it really did happen. Anyway, the point is that my editor will feature the story on the first page, and since we've got to protect the identity of the mother, we want any calls to be directed to you, because, after all, it *was* your rectory. I'll offer a big reward for information about the baby. You just have to handle the calls that come in."

"Alvirah, slow down."

"I can't. This is the perfect time for this kind of story to come out. For one thing, people pay more attention to this kind of human-interest story at Christmas, and for another, the child just turned seven last week. I'm writing the piece right now, and I need to know if it's all right to use your name as intermediary."

"I'd want to see what you've written first," he said cautiously.

"Of course. We really appreciate your cooperation, and I'm sorry to have to impose this way, but through the article and the reward we're sure to get a lot of attention. We're really hoping to locate the little girl, and we're hoping that if we don't say who the mother is, some do-gooder won't try to make an example of her and have her arrested for abandonment or child abuse. The point is, is it better if *you* don't know who she is?"

"Let me think about that," he said.

"It's not a problem for me," Alvirah said. "I can claim journalistic privilege if I get questioned."

There is a way that I can't be forced to reveal her identity, Ferris thought, but the seal of the confessional is not to be used as a convenience.

"Wait a minute, Alvirah. You said this happened just about exactly seven years ago. Are you talking about the night the chalice was stolen? Was *that* when the baby was left?"

"Yes, apparently it was. When the mother phoned the rectory, an old priest answered. She asked to speak with you, and he told her that the police were there because of some great excitement and that you were outside with them. She thought you'd found the baby already."

He made up his mind. "Write your story, Alvirah. I'm with you."

Monsignor Ferris hung up the phone with a sense of wonderment. Was it possible that whoever took the baby might have seen the thief leaving the church and be able to provide at last a clue to his identity? By helping this unfortunate mother, the monsignor might be able to also put to rest the nagging question of what happened to the chalice.

19

Whenever she went into Bessie's room, there was no question in Kate Durkin's mind that something was slightly out of order, but just what it was still eluded her. Exasperated by the nagging sensation, she finally prayed to Saint Anthony for help in finding whatever it was whose whereabouts she couldn't recall. In the course of her prayer she did admit to him that usually she was asking him for help with something tangible, like her glasses or pocketbook or her one piece of "good" jewelry, the tiny solitaire diamond in a Tiffany setting that had been her mother's engagement ring.

That time it had taken Saint Anthony two weeks to help her remember that she had hidden it in an empty aspirin bottle when she and Bessie had gone on a senior citizens' bus trip to Williamsburg.

"You see, Saint Anthony," she explained as she placed

primly folded underwear in an open box on the bed, "I *do* think that Alvirah just may be right, and that there's a chance the Bakers managed to fool Bessie and cheat me out of this house. Of course, I'm not *sure* she's right, but I *am* worried, because every time I come in this room and look at that desk with Bessie's old typewriter, a warning bell goes off in my head."

Kate noticed a run in a pair of folded stockings. "Poor Bessie," she said aloud. "Her eyes were going, but she wouldn't let me take her for new glasses. She said it was a waste of money to buy them when she probably wouldn't last until Christmas."

Well, she was right, Kate thought with a sigh as she opened the next drawer and reached for the flannel nightgowns that had been Bessie's uniform sleepwear. "My stars," she murmured, "poor Bessie, she must have put this one back without noticing she'd worn it." She shook her head as she brushed at the streak of powder on the neckline of a pink flowered gown with lace at the collar. "I'll wash it before I pack it," she murmured. "Bessie would have liked that."

She shook her head. No, actually I'm not surprised she tried it, then took it off, she said to herself. She never liked the lace. She said it scratched her neck. What surprises me is that she put it on in the first place.

She still had the gown in her hand when a sound made her turn. Once again, Vic Baker was at the door, observing her. "I'm preparing my sister's clothing to be sent to charity," she said sharply. "Unless you and your wife also claim her night-dresses."

Without answering, Vic turned away. That man *frightens* me, Kate thought. There's something scary about him. I'll be glad to get out of here.

That evening she went to the washing machine and was surprised to see that Bessie's pink-flowered nightgown was missing from the small pile of laundry she had gathered and left there.

I must be losing my mind, Kate thought. I could have sworn I'd brought it down. Oh well, I must have packed it. Now I'll have to go through all those darn boxes looking for it.

20

 On Friday, December 11th, Alvirah's story about the baby left at the rectory door of St. Clement's seven years ago appeared on the front page of the *New York Globe*. Almost from the minute the paper hit the stands, the phone calls began to pour into the special number at the rectory that Monsignor Ferris had hastily had installed.

His longtime secretary answered the calls, announcing that she was recording every conversation, and passed on to Monsignor the ones that seemed most likely to warrant further consideration. When he called Alvirah on Monday morning, however, the monsignor sounded glum. "Of the more than two hundred calls we've received so far, not one has any merit," he said. "Unfortunately, a lot of them have been from indignant people saying that they have no sympathy for anyone who left a newborn out in the cold, even if only for a few minutes."

"Have the police been around?" Alvirah asked.

"The Administration for Children's Services came by, and the caseworker I talked to was none too happy, believe me. The one thing we can establish is that there's no record of an unknown infant girl being found dead or abandoned in New York City at that time."

"I guess that's something," Alvirah said with a sigh. "I'm so disappointed this hasn't led somewhere. And I thought it was such a good idea."

"So did I," Monsignor Ferris said in agreement. "How is the mother doing? Incidentally, I've already figured out that she must be that young woman who was around here so often last week."

"But you still can answer honestly that you don't know who she is, can't you?" Alvirah asked with some concern. As usual, she was recording their conversation, just in case Monsignor said something that escaped her at first hearing.

"You don't have to turn off your mike, Alvirah. I don't know who she is, and I don't *want* to know. By the way, what is this I hear about you hunting for a co-op?"

"My feet are walked down to stumps," Alvirah admitted. "The Gordons are both nice people, but Monsignor Tom, I've got to tell you that while they may be fine at selling real estate, they are *not* the brightest things God ever put on earth. I swear they can take you into a pokey little dungeon and then tell you it's charming, and, you know, the crazy part is that they *believe* it. Then they get all excited when they tell you that instead of the million-two the owner is asking, you can pick it up for only nine hundred thousand dollars."

"Real estate people have to be enthusiastic about the places they show, Alvirah," Monsignor Ferris said mildly. "It's known in some circles as optimism."

"In their case, try tunnel vision," Alvirah responded. "Anyhow, I'm off with Eileen to see a place that she says has a spectacular view of Central Park. I can hardly wait. After that I'm going to go visit Kate and try to cheer her up."

"I wish you would. She keeps reading her copy of Bessie's will and finding a new way to get her feelings hurt. The latest is that Bessie's signature was written with such force that the pen almost went through the paper. 'It's as if she couldn't *wait* to give her house to strangers,' she said."

After hanging up, Alvirah sat for twenty minutes, lost in thought. Finally she put on her coat and hat and walked out onto the terrace.

The wind blew against her face, and she shivered, even though she was warmly dressed. I'm a failure, she told herself. I thought I was doing Sondra a favor—now she's gotten her hopes up, and for nothing. She'll be even more heartbroken. Her grandfather and boyfriend will be arriving tomorrow, and she has to keep up appearances in front of them as well as practice for the concert on the 23rd.

And I also gave Kate a smidgen of hope that I'd find some way to break this new will, but after looking at just about every empty co-op on the West Side, the only sure thing I came up with is that Jim and Eileen are nice people who must just *luck* into sales, because they sure don't listen when you tell them what you want to see.

. . .

"Nothing so far," she admitted sadly to Kate, when she stopped by the townhouse. "But as I always say, it ain't over till it's over."

"Oh, Alvirah," Kate said. "I think it's over. What bothers me is that I feel as if I'm living on an emotional roller coaster. I keep thinking of Bessie on that last Monday when I left her sitting there, watching her shows—you know how much she enjoyed *One Life to Live* and *General Hospital*—and going on about them, talking a mile a minute, telling me all about each character, and how they were all the time doing these terrible things to each other. And all the time she was planning to do something terrible to me."

That night Alvirah had one of her crime-solving bouts of insomnia. At one in the morning she finally gave up, went out to the kitchen, made tea and rewound her tape from the beginning.

Hercule Poirot, she thought. *Think like him!*

At seven, when Willy came out of the bedroom rubbing his eyes, he found a triumphant sleuth. "Willy, I may have a handle on this," she announced with an excited smile. "It starts with Bessie's signature on the will. You can't tell much from a copy. This morning I'm going to march myself right down to probate court and get a good look at the original. You never know what I might find."

"If there's anything to find, you'll find it, honey," Willy said, his voice still sleepy. "My money's on you."

21

He had been offered something big—a bigger job than he had ever been in on before, bigger even than the one he had done for the fake computer company. It wasn't his usual style, but Lenny decided to take the risk—one big payoff, and he'd be set for years. Besides, he had decided it was time to take off for Mexico, especially now that Star's mother was in town and was on the hunt for her.

The story in the *New York Globe* had really rattled him. It described everything about the way Star was left on the rectory stoop; all the details were there. Suppose one of the nosy neighbors in his apartment building started counting on their fingers and remembered that it had been exactly seven years ago that he had arrived with his infant daughter—that thought really bothered Lenny. And who knew? Someone might even remember the shabby blue stroller with the stain on the side.

There even had been a lot of talk about the case on some of the radio shows. Don Imus in particular had zeroed in on it. He had the police commissioner on his program, and the commissioner had said that if the person or persons who had taken the baby were found, they might be charged with kidnapping and face the possibility of a long prison term.

"When you find any valuable object that isn't yours, even if you don't know who the owner is, you're supposed to turn it in," the commissioner said. "That's the law. And what could be more valuable than a human infant?"

He and Imus had talked about the note, which had been quoted word for word in the article. "The fact that the mother wanted a good home for her child doesn't mean just *any* home," the commissioner had said. "That child became a ward of the city when the mother gave it up, and speaking for the city, we want her back. I would hope if anyone has even a suspicion of who might have that child, he or she will call in *immediately*. I guarantee no one will know who made the call, and the reward will be given without publicity."

Something else dawned on Lenny that Tuesday morning as he stirred sugar and hot milk into a cup of strong coffee he was taking to Lilly. His aunt's health was worse—she hardly had gotten out of bed the last few days—and he knew that if she went to the hospital and talked about Star to anybody, social workers probably would come to the apartment to check on her.

When he reached Lilly's bedroom, her eyes were closed, but she opened them when she heard his footsteps. "Lenny, I don't feel good," she said, "but I know if I go to the doctor, they'll put me in the hospital. I want to be able to see Stellina be the Blessed Mother in the pageant, so I want to wait awhile to go. But when I *do* go in the hospital, I want you to let her stay with Gracie Nuñez till I get back. You promise?"

Lenny knew that the pageant was next Monday afternoon, the 21st; that was also the day of his big job. He also knew that there wasn't even a chance Lilly would be able to go to the pageant, but if she could hold off that long before going to the hospital, everything would be great for him. Once the job was done, he would *make* Lilly go to the hospital, and when she was securely out of the way, he and Star would be on the road, probably by midnight. *She's my lucky star,* Lenny thought, *and I've got to keep her with me.*

He placed the coffee cup carefully on the wobbly night table next to the bed. "I'm going to take good care of you, Aunt Lilly," he promised. "It'll break Stellina's heart if you're not there to at least see her in that nice outfit you sewed for her. And I agree that when you do go to the hospital, it would be a good idea if she stays with Mrs. Nuñez until you come back. I have to work, and I don't want her to be here all alone."

Lilly looked pathetically grateful. *"Grazie,* Lenny, *grazie,"* she murmured, patting his hand.

The white tunic and blue veil were on a hanger on the clothes tree next to the dresser. As Lenny looked over at them, a gust of wind from the slightly open window sent the veil fluttering, and he watched as it drifted to the right and touched the chalice on the bureau.

Another warning, Lenny thought. The fact that the police had been at St. Clement's seven years ago because of the theft from the church had been prominently mentioned in the *Globe* article. The history of the chalice, and even a picture of it, had been a featured story on another page of the paper.

Lenny would have liked to grab the chalice and get rid of it, but he knew he couldn't risk that. If it disappeared, then Lilly would cause a stink, and Star would tell all her friends.

No, the chalice had to be put on hold too. But only for now. When he and Star finally did take off, there was one thing he knew for sure: That chalice was going to end up at the bottom of the Rio Grande.

22

 Sondra could no longer bear to read a newspaper or turn on the television or listen to the radio. Alvirah's story about the baby had set off a media furor that made her cringe with shame.

On Monday night she had fished in her suitcase and found the unopened bottle of sleeping pills the doctor had prescribed, for when she had one of her occasional bouts of insomnia. She never had taken even one of them, preferring to tough it out rather than yield to the temptation to use something she considered a crutch. But by Monday, she knew she had no choice. She simply had to have some sleep.

When she awoke at eight on Tuesday morning, however, her cheeks were wet with tears, and she remembered that in her vague, troubled dreams she had been weeping. Groggy and disoriented, she finally managed to sit up and tentatively put her feet over the side of the bed.

For several seconds, the hotel room seemed to spin around her, the flowered draperies blending with the striped fabric on the couch in a kaleidoscope of color. I would have been better off either to have stayed awake all night—or to have swallowed every pill in the bottle, she thought fleetingly. But then she shook her head. I'm not that much of a coward, she told herself.

A long, hot shower, with the water pelting her face and soaking her hair, helped to restore some sense of focus. She pulled on a terry-cloth robe, wrapped her hair in a towel and forced herself to order scrambled eggs and toast with the usual juice and coffee.

Granddad and Gary are arriving tonight, she reminded herself. If they see me like this, they'll keep asking what's wrong until I break down and tell them the whole story. I've got to practice well today. And I've got to practice especially well tomorrow, when Granddad will be listening. I've got to give the kind of performance that makes him feel that all the years of teaching me and sacrificing for me were worth it.

Sondra got up and walked to the window. Today is Tuesday the 15th of December, she thought, as she looked down at the street, already bustling with midtown traffic and pedestrians rushing to work.

"The concert is next Wednesday," she said aloud. The day after that is Christmas Eve—that's when we're supposed to go back to Chicago, she thought. Only I'm not going. Instead, I'm going to ring the bell of St. Clement's rectory, something I should have done seven years ago instead of running two blocks to a phone. I'm going to tell Monsignor Ferris that I'm the baby's mother, and then I'll ask him to call the police. I can't live with this guilt for one day longer.

23

At ten o'clock on Tuesday morning, Henry Brown, a clerk at the Surrogates Court on Chambers Street in lower Manhattan, looked up and said, "Good morning," to a determined-looking woman of about sixty, with red hair and a somewhat prominent jaw. A keen judge of human nature, Henry noted the smile lines around the woman's mouth and the crinkles around her eyes. He knew that these hinted at a pleasant disposition, and that the irritation he saw in her face probably was just of the moment.

He thought he had her pegged: She'd be a disgruntled relative who would want to examine the will of a relative who had cut her off.

He quickly learned he was right about the desire to see a will, but the woman was not a relative.

"My name is Alvirah Meehan," Alvirah explained. "It's my

understanding that wills filed for probate are public documents and I have the right to examine a particular one if I choose."

"That's quite right," Henry said pleasantly. "But of course it must be in the presence of a member of the staff."

"I don't care if the whole city government is hanging over my shoulder," Alvirah said brusquely, but then softened. After all, it was not the fault of this helpful clerk that the closer she got to seeing Bessie's actual will, the more steamed up she felt herself becoming.

Fifteen minutes later, Henry Brown positioned beside her, she was studying the document. "That word again," she muttered.

"I beg your pardon?"

"It's just that the word 'pristine' sticks in my craw. You see, I would swear that the lady who wrote this will never used that word in her entire eighty-eight years."

"Oh, you'd be astonished how literary some people get when they write their wills," Henry said helpfully. "Of course, they do come up with some lulus, mistakes like 'irregardless' or 'to reiterate again.' " He paused, then added, "I must say, though, that 'pristine' is a new one. I've never seen that word used before."

Alvirah had tuned out when she heard the dismaying opinion that it might be considered customary to put some unfamiliar and perhaps highfalutin words into a will. "Now, what's this?" she asked. "I mean, look at this last page. The will is already signed."

"That's known as the attestation clause," Henry explained. "By the terms of New York State law, the witnesses must complete this page. It attests that they've witnessed the signing of the will, and the testatrix, in this case, Mrs. Bessie Durkin Maher, must also sign it. In essence it's a reconfirmation of the witnessing of the will. Without it, the witnesses would have to appear in court at the time of the probate, and, of course, when wills have been standing for years, the witnesses may have moved or died."

"Take a look at this," Alvirah ordered, holding up two pieces of paper. "Bessie's signature on the will and then on this—what did you call it?—attestation clause. See there? The ink is different. But they had to be signed at the same time, right?"

Henry Brown studied the two signatures. "Definitely these are two different shades of blue ink," he said. "But perhaps your friend Bessie decided her signature on the will, while totally legible, was written in rather light ink, so she simply changed pens. There's nothing illegal about that. The witnesses signed with the same pen," he pointed out.

"One of Bessie's signatures is firm, the other wavy. It's also possible that she signed these papers at two different times," Alvirah said.

"Oh, that would be illegal."

"I couldn't agree more!"

"Well, if you're quite finished, Mrs. Meehan . . ." Henry did not complete the sentence.

Alvirah smiled at him. "No, I'm not, I'm afraid. I can't tell you how grateful I am to you for giving me all this time, but I know you don't want there to be a miscarriage of justice."

Henry smiled politely. Anybody who gets cut out of a will screams miscarriage of justice, he thought philosophically.

"Look, Henry," Alvirah continued. "It's all right if I call you Henry, isn't it? You should just call me Alvirah." Without waiting to see if Henry accepted this elevation of their acquaintance, Alvirah said, "Bessie swears this was her last will. I swear this thing is a phony. Besides, where did Bessie get the know-how to type this attestation clause? Tell me that."

"Well, she may have asked someone to type it for her, or someone may have given her a copy of the form," Henry said patiently. "Now, Mrs. Meehan, I mean, Alvirah—" he began.

"All right," Alvirah said, interrupting him. "I know it's not proof, but these signatures look different, and I say Bessie didn't sign these papers at the same time." Briskly she gathered up her things. "Okay, Henry, thank you," she said, rushing out, a woman with a mission.

Alvirah went directly to the James and Eileen Gordon Real Estate Agency. She was scheduled to see yet another co-op, this one on Central Park West and described by Eileen Gordon as "a steal at two million."

In the course of pretending interest in the place and hearing Eileen once again exclaim about the beautiful view—even though the view was somewhat limited, since the apartment was on the second floor and looked directly into trees—Alvirah managed to turn the conversation to the signing of Bessie's will.

"Oh, yes, the dear sweet old girl signed both papers," Eileen said, her round eyes opening wide as she smiled reminiscently. "I'm sure of that. But she was obviously getting very tired. I think that's why the second signature was quite wavy on the line. If she changed pens, I didn't notice. The truth is I may have been just kind of looking around the room. That townhouse is in almost perfect condition. I mean, a few things, like the living room door, need fixing, but that's nothing. With the way prices are now, I could get three million for that house easily."

For once I think you're right, Alvirah thought, as, thoroughly disheartened, she turned off the microphone in her sunburst pin.

24

"That Lenny Centino is smarter than he looks," undercover detective Roberto Pagano told his boss, Joe Tracy, on Wednesday night when they got together at a prearranged meeting place. "Since that first time I met him, he hasn't once shot his mouth off about the deliveries he made for the so-called computer company—or anything else we could pin on him. If it hadn't been for a couple of beers loosening his tongue, I don't think he'd have said anything that first time."

"And at the least a smart lawyer could get any charges knocked down," Joe worried. "That's why I keep my fingers crossed he doesn't back out of the setup on Monday night."

"I don't think he will," Pagano said reassuringly. "If my hunch is right, Lenny is playing traveling music. I think he knows it's getting hot for dealers on the Upper West Side these days. He wants to make his killing Monday night, then I'll bet you he's long gone."

"Long gone, maybe, but not to where he *thinks* he's going, I hope," Tracy replied. "Sure, if Lenny goes through with the job, we have him hands down. But suppose he gets nervous and disappears on us?" Which brought something else to Tracy's mind. "He's been picking up his kid the last few afternoons at that Home Base center. How come he's becoming such a good daddy all of a sudden?"

"Maybe he just wants to make sure that she remembers him after he takes off," Pagano said with a shrug. "I can't imagine he would let himself get saddled with a seven-year-old."

"I guess we can count on that," Tracy agreed.

25

The final rehearsal for the pageant was scheduled for Friday afternoon, and Lenny had made it a point to attend, explaining to Sisters Cordelia and Maeve Marie that since he would be at work at four o'clock on Monday afternoon when the pageant would be performed, he didn't want to miss his only chance to see his daughter as the Blessed Mother.

With his best stab at an ingratiating smile, Lenny explained that Stellina's nonna was very, very sick, but that he would always be there to take care of his little girl. "It's you and me against the world, right, Star?" he asked, stroking the hair that was tumbling onto her shoulders. "I'll even have to learn how to brush that pretty mop of yours." He smiled again at the nuns. "Nonna can't clip the barrette so good anymore."

The women nodded, their expressions frosty. Then Sister

Cordelia turned from him and clapped her hands. "Okay, children, take your places for the final rehearsal. Oh, there you are, Willy. I was afraid you'd forgotten us."

Willy and Alvirah were coming up the stairs, Willy's face wreathed in a smile of resignation. "Cordelia, it's a week till Christmas. Believe it or not I had some shopping to do."

"And I have made my last outing with the Gordons," Alvirah said. "They practically threw me out today. They said they sensed that I wasn't ready to make a move right now, and they gave me the names of some of their competitors I could call in case I wanted to keep looking for a co-op for the rest of my life."

"Then we must accept that the good Lord doesn't want us to be in business after January first," Cordelia acknowledged. "And you mustn't blame yourself, Alvirah. You haven't left one stone unturned to try to prove Bessie's will was a fake." She turned briskly away. "Now let's get started with the rehearsal." Turning back to Alvirah, she lowered her voice and nodded her head almost imperceptibly toward Lenny. "That fellow there is Stellina's father. Sit next to him. He's trying to make a good impression on us, so I know he'll talk to you. See what you make of him. I think he's up to no good."

Sister Cordelia was right. Lenny *did* talk—straight through the rehearsal, only interrupting his tale of how he gave up a good job in the Midwest because he missed Star so much but couldn't take her away from his beloved aunt, to make noisy and oddly inappropriate exclamations on how cute the children were. In the course of his ramblings, he told Alvirah about the pretty Irish girl he had married who had been Star's mother.

"Her name was Rose O'Grady. We used to love to dance together. I'd get the band to play 'Sweet Rosie O'Grady' when we were out, and I'd sing it in her ear."

"What happened to her?" Alvirah asked.

"It's something I don't tell many people. She got postpartum depression so bad we had to have her hospitalized. Then . . ." Here Lenny's voice broke, fading off. "They didn't watch her carefully enough." The last words were delivered in a dramatic whisper.

Suicide, Alvirah thought. "Oh, I'm so sorry," she said sincerely.

"Nonna told Star her mama was sick and had to go far away, and that we probably wouldn't hear from her ever again. I think we should have maybe told her straight out that her mama was dead, but Nonna keeps saying not yet," Lenny explained, pleased to have gotten the scenario down so well.

There was one small glitch in the rehearsal when Rajid, the third wise man, dropped the jar that supposedly held the myrrh. "It's all right, Rajid," Sister Cordelia called as she saw tears gather in his eyes, and Sister Maeve Marie swooped in to pick up the pieces. "It was just a little accident. No real problem. Keep going, all of you."

Willy went to the piano. It was time for the closing scene in the pageant. "Sleep, my child, and peace attend thee." He played and sang softly.

Stellina and Jerry looked up from their kneeling position beside the cradle, which was now in place. "Guardian angels God will send thee," they sang, their voices young and sweet and true.

"That's a nice song," Lenny said. "It reminds me—"

"Sshh!" Dear God, can't he shut up long enough to listen to

his own child? Alvirah thought, now so irritated that if she had had duct tape handy she surely would have pasted it across his mouth. She noticed that Stellina's eyes had flickered over to him when he spoke, but then turned away, as though in embarrassment.

She's savvy enough to know her father's a creep, Alvirah thought. That poor child. She actually looks a little untidy today. Her hair is tangled; usually it's pulled back so neatly.

Untidy, but still beautiful, she thought: the curly dark-blond hair, almost waist length, the fair complexion and haunting brown eyes. Her expression is almost adult in its sadness, Alvirah thought. Why do some kids get such a bad break in life?

Lenny clapped loudly when the rehearsal was over. "Great!" he shouted. "Really great stuff! Star, your daddy's proud of you!"

Stellina blushed and turned away, averting her eyes. "Your daddy's proud of you," Jerry mimicked as he got to his feet. "You're such a good little Blessed Mother, ha, ha, ha."

"It's still not too late to get a new Saint Joseph," Sister Cordelia warned the boy, thumping him on the head. "Now remember to bring your costumes to school with you Monday, children. You'll get dressed here."

"I'm going to pick up Star at school and take her home to put on her costume," Lenny told Alvirah. "Her nonna can't make it to the pageant, but she wants to see her dressed up. Then I'll have to go to work."

Alvirah nodded, absentmindedly, her attention focused on Cordelia as she collected the gifts the wise men were to present. The foil-covered chocolates made a realistic offering of gold, she thought. The painted bowl Cordelia had brought from the convent for the frankincense made a pretty offering. I'll pick up another jar to replace the one Rajid dropped, she thought. Then she noticed Stellina take Cordelia's hand and lead the nun to the side.

"Telling secrets?" Lenny observed, a tone of alarm creeping into his voice.

"Oh, I doubt that," Alvirah said quickly. "I know Stellina has been asking Sister Cordelia and Sister Maeve Marie to pray for her nonna."

"Oh, yeah," Lenny said after a few moments. "I guess that must be what she's doing."

Gratified with the impression he thought he had made at the rehearsal, Lenny left with Stellina, explaining to everyone in earshot that he was taking her out for dinner. "Now that Nonna can't be worrying about meals, I guess I gotta get me a cookbook," was his parting comment.

On the way to McDonald's, he asked Star if she had been asking the sister to pray for Nonna when she took the nun aside.

"I ask Sister that every day," Stellina said quietly. Instinctively she knew that Daddy might not like what she had *really* asked Sister—that if Nonna allowed her to bring the silver chalice that had once belonged to her mother's uncle, could Rajid carry it to the stable, to replace the jar he broke?

To her delight, Sister had said that would be fine. Star was sure if she begged Nonna, she would give her permission to bring it. And when Rajid puts it down by the cradle, I will pray that if my mother hasn't gone to heaven yet, she will come to see me just once.

It was a wish and a hope that now had become almost a constant, urgent need. But a faith that was growing stronger and stronger seemed to promise Star that if the chalice could become a gift to the Christ child, her prayer would be answered.

Her mother really would come to her, at last.

26

Peter Lewis, Sondra's grandfather, arrived on Wednesday afternoon. It was both a relief and a disappointment to her that Gary did not accompany him. "He'll be here for the concert," her grandfather said, "but he's very busy and could not take the extra time. Besides, I think he is astute enough to know that in the days before an artist is performing in a major concert, she is better left alone with her music, and with as few distractions as possible."

Sondra knew what her grandfather was implying. Gary Willis loved music with a deep passion and understood the strains inherent in an artist's life.

"I'm glad he waited," she said, "but I'm thrilled that you're here. Granddad, you look spectacular." It was an unexpected delight to her that her grandfather looked so well. Even though the signs of the arthritis were always visible in his swollen wrists and fingers, the triple bypass had restored color to his face and vigor to his appearance—things she had feared he had lost with age and illness.

When she told him how healthy he looked for his years, he responded, "Thanks, Sondra, but seventy-five is considered to be only the dawn of aging today. An unobstructed blood supply to the heart does wonders, although I hope that's something you never need to find out for yourself."

At least, Sondra thought, in an effort to draw some comfort from the situation, Granddad looks strong enough to take it when I tell him about the baby and what I'm going to do after the concert. But just thinking about it, she grew paler.

"And you look thin and troubled," he told her crisply. "Is something wrong, or is it just the usual preperformance nerves? If so, I'm disappointed. I thought I had cured you of that."

She had turned aside the question. "Granddad, this *is* Carnegie Hall," she had told him. "It's different."

He had then spent Thursday and Friday renewing old friendships, while she practiced with her New York coach.

On Friday evening, at dinner, he talked about his visit to St. Clement's and having learned of the theft of Bishop Santori's chalice. "Apparently that same night a baby was abandoned there," he said as he studied the menu, absorbed as always in the task at hand. "It seems to have been the subject of a recent newspaper article." He paused. "Grilled Dover sole and a salad," he announced, then he looked across the table at her, his eyes probing. "When I take you to Le Cirque 2000, my dear, at least have the courtesy to look interested in the menu."

The next day, when he came to hear her practice, she could read the disappointment in his eyes. She was rehearsing a Beethoven sonata, and while she knew her playing was technically perfect, she was also aware that there was neither passion nor fire in her music. And she knew that her granddad was aware as well.

When she was finished, he shrugged. "Your technique is marvelous; it can't be faulted. But you have always withheld something of yourself from your music. Why, I don't know. Now you are withholding *everything.*" He looked at her sternly. "Sondra, keep it up, and you will appear and immediately disappear from the major concert stage, like *that!*" He snapped his fingers. "What is wrong? You withhold yourself from a man who loves you, and whom I believe you love in return. You resent me. I do not know why, but I have been aware of it for years. Does nothing touch you?"

With a shrug of dismay and resignation, he turned and began walking toward the studio exit.

"I am the mother of the baby who was abandoned at St. Clement's," she shouted at him, the words hanging in the air.

He stopped and turned, his expression incredulous, but with a look of deep concern in his eyes.

With little expression in either her face or her voice, Sondra told him everything, the words rushing out of her.

When she was finished, there was a long silence. Then he nodded. "So that is it. And I see that, in a way, you blame me because you let her go. Maybe you are right and maybe you are not. It is no matter. We will move heaven and earth to find her. We will tell Gary; he has enormous resources at his disposal. And if he does not understand, then he is not worthy of you. Now," he picked up Sondra's violin and thrust it into her hands. "Now play with all your heart to the child you are seeking."

Sondra tucked the violin under her chin and reached for her bow. In her mind she could see her child. But would she have blond hair like her own, or would it be like her father's—silky, dark? Her eyes—were they still brown or blue like hers, or dark hazel like his? He was a man she had known so briefly, and in the end cared not a whit about, but he had fathered her child. She will be like me, Sondra decided. She will look as I did at her age.

She's seven now; music must be in her soul, she reflected as she drew the bow across the strings. She still eludes me, but I see her in the distance. I hear her footsteps. I feel her presence. She senses that I want her. Forgetting her grandfather, Sondra began to play.

I never gave her a name, she thought. What would I have called her? What do I call her in my heart? She sought the answer as she played, but could not find it.

When the last notes faded into silence, after a long pause, her grandfather nodded. "Now you are becoming a true musician. You are still holding back, but that was an infinite improvement. You will be required to play an encore. What have you chosen?"

Sondra did not know what her answer would be until she heard herself say it: "A simple song of Christmas," she told him. " 'All Through the Night.' "

27

On Sunday morning Alvirah and Willy went to Mass at St. Clement's. Kate Durkin was in attendance as well, and, at her insistence, they went back to the townhouse for coffee.

When they arrived, the Bakers were just going out. "Linda and I are on our way to pick up the morning papers," Vic said jovially. "We always take a crack at the Sunday *Times* puzzle."

"I knew a guy who claimed to ace it every week, but when somebody checked him once, they found he was cheating, putting down gobbledygook to fill in the blanks," Willy said. "A friend of yours maybe?"

Baker's smile froze. Linda shrugged and tugged at his sleeve. "Come on, hon," she pleaded.

"I see he put away his black tie," Willy observed, as he watched them walk down the block arm in arm.

"It's a wonder she doesn't break her neck in those high heels," Alvirah observed. "There are patches of ice all over the sidewalk."

"Trust me, she won't fall," Kate said. "She's a pro in those things—wears them all the time." Kate turned the key in the lock and pushed open the door. "Come on in. That wind goes right through you."

"Let's have our coffee in the parlor," she said as they took off their coats. "I lit the fire in there this morning, and it feels cozy. Bessie loved to sit in the parlor and have coffee and my fresh-baked crumb cake after Mass on Sundays."

Kate refused to allow Alvirah to assist her in setting things out. "What's a few cups and plates! You've been running around on my behalf all week. Go in and sit down."

"I always liked this room," Willy observed as he settled into the deep leather chair that had been the treasured possession of Judge Aloysius Maher, whose portrait in judicial robes still looked down at them benignly from the wall over the mantel.

"It's a wonderful room," Alvirah agreed. "You don't get these high ceilings and carved mantels anymore. Just look at the details on the windows. That's workmanship. I can't stand it that poor Kate isn't going to get to enjoy all this for the rest of her life." She turned around, then sighed. "Well, I guess Bessie won't mind if I take her favorite chair. I can just see her sitting here, her feet on the hassock, watching her shows—and woe betide you if you interrupted her during *One Life to Live* or *General Hospital*. Then what does she do with her next-to-last breath? She sneaks upstairs when Kate's back is turned, and just to do her out of this house. Why, that means she missed at least one of her shows on her very last day on earth."

"Maybe they have *Soap Opera Digest* in heaven, and she's been able to catch up," Willy suggested.

Kate came in carrying a tray, which she placed on the coffee table. "Oh, Willy," she said, "would you mind closing the door. 'Hon' and 'Dearie' will be back with the papers any time now, and I don't want them to come in and bother us."

"My pleasure, Kate," Willy said with a grunt as he got up.

At the mention of the Bakers, the subject of the will came up. As a reflex gesture, Alvirah turned on the microphone in her sunburst pin.

"Bessie always wrote with the judge's pen, and she never used blue ink in it," Kate said when Alvirah talked about the differing shades of blue ink on the will and the attestation clause. "But then again, she did a lot of crazy things during those last few days."

"What about her typewriter?" Alvirah asked. "I thought she said something about it on Thanksgiving."

"I'm not sure," Kate murmured.

"All right. How bad was her eyesight?" Alvirah queried.

"She had bifocals; you know that. But the prescription for the reading lenses needed to be strengthened. If she didn't hold something up close to her face, she had trouble making it out. She may have signed those papers thinking she was signing for a delivery of paint or varnish or tools," Alvirah said. "I was here once when Baker brought her a receipt to sign for a delivery. He handed her his pen."

"All of which won't help you in court," Willy observed. "Kate, I'd walk a mile for a piece of that crumb cake."

Kate smiled. "No need to do that—there's plenty right here. Bessie loved it too. Told me that even after she was gone, I should fix a piece for her and set it out in this room on Sunday mornings. She said she'd haunt me if I forgot."

And then along came the Bakers, Alvirah thought. From the foyer she heard the click of the outside door. "The heirs are back," she murmured, and then watched in dismay as the door to the parlor swung open and Vic and Linda Baker smiled in on them.

"Elevensies," Vic said in his usual jovial tone. "That's what they call it in England, having a morning snack break like this. It's always around eleven o'clock." He took a step into the room. "My, that crumb cake looks spectacular, Kate."

"It is," Alvirah said flatly. "Didn't you adjust that door for Bessie, Mr. Baker?"

"As a matter of fact, I did, yes."

"Is that why it swings open so easily?"

"It needs a bit more adjusting." Clearly uncomfortable with the conversation, he turned to leave. "Well, I'm off to try my hand at the puzzle."

They waited until the sound of Vic's heavy footsteps and the bouncy staccato of Linda's heels could no longer be heard. "You can't insult that guy, can you?" Willy observed.

"It's more than that," Kate said. "He's curious about what we're saying. Thank God, I'm almost through clearing out Bessie's room. He always hangs around when I'm in there." She frowned. "You know, Alvirah, talking about the typewriter, the space bar has needed fixing too. Unless you type very slowly, it keeps skipping. That just dawned on me. I've been looking at the typewriter there in Bessie's room, trying to remember what Bessie *did* say on Thanksgiving."

Alvirah swallowed the last drop of coffee and regretfully

declined a second piece of crumb cake. "Let me take a look at that typewriter," she said.

There were a few sheets of plain paper in Bessie's desk. Alvirah inserted one into the typewriter carriage and began to type. The carriage skipped several spaces whenever she touched the space bar, forcing her to use the back key constantly. "How long has it been like this?"

"At least since Thanksgiving."

"Meaning either Bessie typed her will *before* Thanksgiving—which would have meant that she was lying in her teeth to Monsignor when he saw her the day after Thanksgiving—or she typed it over the weekend, literally one word at a time. Who's kidding who?"

"But it doesn't add up to proof, honey," Willy reminded her. He looked at the stack of boxes against the wall in Bessie's room. "Kate, can I help you with those?"

"Not yet. There's one more thing to pack up, and I can't find it. I put a pink-flowered flannel gown of Bessie's out to wash, and now it's disappeared. It had a streak of face powder on it, and I don't want to let it go out soiled." She lowered her voice and looked furtively over her shoulder. "You know, if Linda Baker didn't dress like a dime-a-dance girl, I'd swear Vic might have taken it for her. Now what do you make of *that?*"

That afternoon, while Willy watched the Giants play the Steelers, Alvirah sat at the dining room table and once again listened to all the taped conversations she had collected concerning Bessie's will and the townhouse. As she listened she made notes, her brow furrowing as certain remarks jumped out at her.

The score was tied, and the game was in the fourth quarter when she yelled, "I think I figured it out! Willy, Willy, listen to me. Would you have called Bessie a 'dear, sweet old girl'?"

Willy did not take his eyes off the screen. "No. Never. Not on the best day of her life."

"Of course not. Because she *wasn't* a dear, sweet old girl. She was a tough, stubborn, crusty old girl. But that's what it's all about. And after all that trooping around I did with the Gordons, I finally figure it out sitting right here at home."

Even though the Giants had made a first down and were on the Steelers' three-yard line, Willy gave Alvirah his full attention. "What did you figure out, honey?"

"The Gordons never laid eyes on Bessie," Alvirah said triumphantly. "They witnessed somebody else signing that will. Vic and Linda sneaked in a ringer while Bessie was watching her shows."

Two hours later, Alvirah and Willy arrived at Kate's townhouse with Jim and Eileen Gordon in tow. They already had alerted Monsignor Ferris and Sisters Cordelia and Maeve Marie to be there, and they found them sitting in the parlor with an equally bewildered Kate.

"Alvirah, what's all this about?" Cordelia demanded.

"You'll see. The heirs are joining us, aren't they?" Alvirah asked.

"The Bakers?" Kate replied. "Yes, I told them you were coming, and that you said you'd have a surprise for them."

"Wonderful. Kate, you haven't met these nice people have you? Jim and Eileen Gordon witnessed—or *thought* they witnessed—Bessie signing the will."

"*Thought* they witnessed?" the monsignor said.

"Exactly. Now, Eileen, you tell us what happened when you came in that day," Alvirah said.

Eileen Gordon, an earnest expression on her pleasant face, said, "Well, if you remember, we had been out with Mr. Baker, showing him a simply beautiful duplex on West Eighty-first, right across from the museum. It's in one of the finest buildings in the—"

"Eileen," Alvirah said, struggling to control her irritation, "tell us about witnessing the will."

"Oh, yes, well, Mrs. Baker had called, and when we arrived here with Mr. Baker, Mrs. Baker asked us to come in quietly. She said there was an elderly lady in the parlor who didn't like to be disturbed when she was watching her programs. The door was shut, so we tiptoed up the stairs to the bedroom, where Mrs. Maher was waiting for us."

"Elderly lady in the parlor!" Kate exploded. "That was Bessie!"

"Then who was in the bedroom?" Monsignor Ferris asked.

The Bakers were heard coming down the stairs. "Why don't we ask Vic?" Alvirah suggested as the couple entered the parlor. "Vic, who was the lady you dressed up in Bessie's pink-flowered nightgown? An actress? Another cheat who was in on the deal?" Baker opened his mouth to speak, but Alvirah didn't give him a chance. "I have pictures of Bessie that we took here just a few weeks ago, at Thanksgiving—nice, clear close-ups." She handed the photos to the Gordons. "Tell them what you told me."

"She is definitely not the lady who was in bed and who signed that will," Jim Gordon said, looking at the photos.

"Yes, there was a similarity, but no way is this the lady," Eileen Gordon agreed as she vigorously shook her head.

"Tell us the rest, Eileen," Alvirah suggested.

"When we came downstairs the door to the parlor had swung open, and we could see an old lady sitting in that chair." Eileen pointed to Bessie's chair. "She didn't turn her head, but I could see her profile—*she* was definitely the lady in Alvirah's Thanksgiving pictures."

"How much more do you need to hear, Vic, old boy?" Willy asked. "Tomorrow morning, Kate files to contest the will, the Gordons tell their story and I give it a few days before you frauds are indicted."

"I think it's time for us to move on," Vic Baker said pleasantly but quickly. "Kate, because of this misunderstanding, we'll be leaving immediately. Come, Linda. We'll pack right away."

"Good riddance to the two of you. I hope you go to jail," Alvirah called after them.

"You told me to bring champagne," Monsignor Ferris said to Alvirah a few minutes later as they stood in the dining room and he popped the cork on the bottle. "I see why."

Sister Cordelia and Kate were both just beginning to understand what all this meant. "Now I'll never have to leave my home," Kate gasped.

"And I won't have to abandon my kids," Sister Cordelia exulted. "Praise be to God."

"And to Alvirah," Sister Maeve Marie said, holding up her glass.

For a moment a shadow came across Monsignor Ferris's face. "Now if only you could set things right for that missing baby and retrieve the bishop's stolen chalice, Alvirah."

"As Alvirah always says, 'It ain't over till it's over,' " Willy said proudly. "And as I always say, my money's on her."

28

 As promised, on Monday afternoon, Lenny picked up Stellina at her school. "Star," he said hurriedly, "Nonna just had a weak spell, and the doctor came. They're sending for an ambulance. She may have to be in the hospital for a while, but she'll be fine. I promise you."

"Are you sure?" Stellina asked, looking searchingly into his eyes.

"You bet."

Stellina ran ahead, and as she turned the corner she saw a stretcher being wheeled from their apartment house along the sidewalk to a waiting ambulance. Her heart pounding, she raced to it.

"Nonna, Nonna," she cried, reaching for her beloved great-aunt.

Lilly Maldonado tried to smile. "Stellina, my heart is not so good, but they'll make it better, and then I'll be back. Now you must wash your hands and face, and brush your hair, and put on your Blessed Mother outfit. You can't be late for the pageant. Then tonight, after the pageant, Daddy will bring some of your clothes to Mrs. Nuñez's; you'll sleep at her house till I get back."

Stellina whispered, "Nonna, Rajid, who is one of the wise men, broke the jar that was supposed to hold the myrrh. May I please, please bring my mother's cup for him to carry in the pageant? It was a holy cup. You told me it belonged to her uncle, a priest. Please. I'll take such good care of it. I promise."

"We have to go, little girl," the ambulance attendant said, tugging at Stellina's arm, trying to get her away from the stretcher. "You can visit Nonna at St. Luke's Hospital. It's on 113th Street, not far from here."

Tears came to Stellina's eyes. "I have a prayer that I just know will come true if I bring my cup, Nonna. Please say it's okay."

"What is your prayer, *bambina?*" Lilly's voice was heavy as the sedation the emergency crew had administered began to take effect.

"That my mother will come back," the little girl said, tears starting to roll down her cheeks.

"Ah, Stellina, *bambina,* if only she would come before I die. Yes, yes, take the cup, but don't let Daddy see you. He might not let it go."

"Oh, Nonna, thank you. I'll come and see you tomorrow, I promise."

Moments later, the ambulance, its siren shrieking, was gone.

"Star, we've got to hurry," Lenny urged.

. . .

Home Base was festively decorated with a Christmas tree and beribboned ropes of pine. Over the weekend, some volunteers had built a platform at one end of the big upstairs room to give the effect of a stage. Another volunteer had hung ancient velvet portieres at both sides of the platform. Folding chairs had been set up for the audience, and the parents and siblings and friends of the children in the pageant were now happily pouring into the room.

Alvirah had arrived early to help Cordelia and Maeve get the children dressed for the pageant. By means of dire threats, Sister Cordelia was able to maintain reasonable order among the excited performers. At ten of four, just as they were all getting nervous about her, Stellina arrived.

Alvirah quickly took her in hand. "Did your nonna see you in your outfit?" she asked as she straightened the blue veil over Stellina's waterfall of dark-gold hair.

"No. They took her to the hospital in an ambulance," Stellina said quietly. "Daddy promised to take me to see her. Will she get better, Mrs. Meehan?"

"Oh, I hope so, dear. But we will help take care of you while she's away. You know how afraid we were that we would have to close Home Base? Well, now, because of a miracle, we can keep it open—and that means we'll see you every day after school."

Stellina's smile was wistful. "Oh, I'm very glad. I'm happy here."

"Now run over there and take your place with Saint Joseph. Can I hold that bag for you?" Alvirah reached to take the plastic grocery bag Stellina was clutching.

"No, thank you. I have to give my cup to Rajid to carry. Sister Cordelia said it was all right for me to bring it. Thank you, Mrs. Meehan."

As she scurried to where the other children were gathered, Alvirah stared after her. What is it about that child? She reminds me of someone—but who? she asked herself as she went to her seat.

The lights dimmed. It was time for the Christmas pageant to begin.

"Simply wonderful!" was the universal comment as the last notes of "All Through the Night" faded away and the applause began. Cameras flashed from all around the room as parents acted to preserve the moment. Alvirah suddenly tugged at Sister Maeve Marie's sleeve. "Maeve, I want you to get a close-up of Stellina," she said. "I mean *several* close-ups of her."

"Sure, Alvirah," Maeve agreed. "She was the perfect Blessed Mother. When she sang, she brought tears to my eyes. She put so much feeling into the words."

"Yes, she did. She has music in her soul."

A wild, crazy thought that was becoming certainty had crept into Alvirah's head, but she didn't want to admit it even to herself. We can try to check the birth records for a start, she thought, but oh, dear God, is it possible?

"I've got some good ones of her," Maeve said a few minutes later, gingerly holding out the Polaroid photos she had taken. "They'll be clearer once they finish developing. And I have a cute one of her and Rajid. He's handing her silver cup back to her."

Her silver cup? No! *Her chalice!* Alvirah thought. You may be wrong, she warned herself. You could be just getting carried away. But one thing at least can be proved immediately. "Maeve, if you've got more film, get some close-ups of that cup," she said. "Ask Stellina to hold it up for you."

"Alvirah, come on," Willy called. "You're supposed to hand me the presents to give the kids."

"Maeve, get those close-ups and hang on to them for me," Alvirah ordered. "Don't let them out of your hands."

She hurried to Willy's side. The presents were on a table behind her. "All right, Santa, this is for José," she announced heartily, as the young boy eagerly reached out his hands.

Willy put an arm around him. "Wait a minute, José. Sister Maeve will be right over to take a picture of us."

Alvirah was frantic to get away, to be off following up on her suspicions, but it was easier just to finish helping Willy with the presents than to get someone else to do it.

Meanwhile, Cordelia and her volunteers were busy passing out candy and soda, although some people had begun to leave. To Alvirah's dismay, she saw that Grace Nuñez was about to depart with José and Stellina in tow.

When she called out to her, Grace bustled over. "Where are you taking Stellina?" Alvirah asked.

"I'm gonna drop her off at home for now," Grace explained. "Her daddy will bring her to stay with me tonight. He says he wants to have dinner with her first, after he gets off work. I got to stop at my sister's for a while, but he told me he'll be home early. She knows to lock the door herself, don't you, Stellina?"

"Yes, I do. Oh, I hope he'll be able to tell me how Nonna is," Stellina said earnestly.

Ten minutes later all the presents had been dispensed and all the pictures taken. Alvirah ran to Sister Maeve

Marie and picked up the Polaroid shots. Then she grabbed her coat.

"What's up?" Willy asked, his voice muffled through his fuzzy Santa Claus beard.

"I've got to show Monsignor Tom some pictures," she said over her shoulder. "Meet me there."

The monsignor was out but was expected back soon, Alvirah was told. Willing the time to pass quickly, she waited in the rectory parlor, pacing back and forth. Willy and the monsignor arrived at the same time, half an hour later. The monsignor was smiling. "What a nice surprise, Alvirah," he said cheerfully.

Alvirah didn't waste words. She handed him the pictures. "Monsignor Tom, look at these."

He studied the picture of Stellina taking the cup from Rajid during the pageant, then he looked at the close-up Maeve Marie had made of the cup alone.

"Alvirah," he said quietly, "do you know what this is?"

"I think so. It's Bishop Santori's chalice. And do you know who I think that little girl is?"

He waited.

"I think she's the infant who was left at your rectory door the night the chalice was stolen."

29

 Grace Nuñez walked Stellina to the door of the apartment she shared with Nonna and her daddy. She watched like a mother hen while the little girl went in, then listened for her to turn the double lock. "I'll see you later, honey," she called from the hallway, then left, confident that Stellina would never open the door to anyone except her father.

Inside the apartment it was quiet and dark; Stellina noticed the difference immediately. Without Nonna, it seemed strange and lonely. She went around the apartment turning on lights, hoping to brighten the place. Going into Nonna's room, she started to take off her Blessed Mother costume, but then stopped. Nonna had wanted to see her wearing it, and she hoped that her daddy would take her to the hospital.

She took the silver cup out of the bag and sat on the edge of the bed. Holding the cup made her feel less alone. Nonna had never before been away when she came home, never once.

At seven o'clock, Stellina heard footsteps pounding up the stairs to the hallway. It couldn't be Daddy, she thought. He never runs.

But then he was banging on the door. "Star, open up! Open up!" he cried frantically.

As soon as he heard the click of the locks, Lenny turned the handle and threw himself into the apartment. It had been a setup! The whole thing had been a trap! He should have *known* it, he told himself, snarling. That lousy new guy in the crew was an undercover cop. Lenny had managed to get away by the skin of his teeth once he realized what was going on, but they were no doubt combing Fort Lee for him right now, and they would be checking this place in minutes. He had to risk stopping here, though—his fake identity papers and all his cash were in the bag he had packed and left here this afternoon.

He raced into his room and grabbed the bag from under his bed. Stellina followed him and stood in the doorway, watching. Lenny turned to glance at her and saw that she was holding the chalice. Well, that was good, he thought. He wanted it out of here, and the sooner the better.

"Come on, Star, let's go," he ordered. "We're getting outta here. Don't try to bring anything but your cup." He knew he probably was crazy to bring the kid now that the police were after him, but she was his good-luck charm—his lucky star.

"Will you take me to see Nonna, Daddy?"

"Later, maybe tomorrow. I told you, come on. We got to go." He grabbed her hand and headed back down the hall, pulling her behind him.

Stellina grasped her silver cup as she stumbled to keep up with his pace. Without locking the door behind them, they raced down the stairs—one flight, two flights, three flights, as she struggled not to fall.

At the last landing before the lobby, Lenny stopped abruptly and stood listening. Nothing so far, he thought, feeling a moment of relief. He only needed another minute and they would be in the car he had managed to steal, and then he was home free.

He was halfway across the foyer when the outer door suddenly burst open. Yanking Star in front of him, Lenny pretended to reach for a gun. "You shoot me and she gets it," he shouted, without conviction.

Joe Tracy was at the head of the squad. He wasn't about to risk a child's life, however hollow the threat. "Everybody back!" he ordered cautiously. "Let him go."

The car Lenny had was only a few feet from the front of the building. The police watched, helpless, as he dragged Star to the vehicle, opened the driver's door and threw in his bag. "Get in and crawl over to the other side," he told her urgently. He knew he would never hurt her, but hopefully the cops didn't.

Star obeyed, but when Lenny got in and slammed his door, he let go of her hand to turn on the ignition key. In a lightning moment, she opened the passenger door and jumped out of the car. Clutching the chalice, her veil flying behind her, she ran down the street as the police closed in on the car.

Ten minutes later, Alvirah, Willy and Monsignor Ferris arrived to find Lenny handcuffed and seated in a patrol car. They climbed the stairs to the apartment and learned that Stellina and the chalice were missing.

As they stood in the living room of the apartment where Stellina had lived these past seven years, they told Joe Tracy about the chalice, and about their suspicion that Stellina was the missing infant of St. Clement's.

One of the policemen came in from Lenny's bedroom. "Take a look at this, Joe. Found it wedged between the shelf and wall in the closet."

Joe read the crumpled note, then handed it to Alvirah. "She *is* the missing infant, Mrs. Meehan," he said. "This confirms it. It's the note the mother pinned to her blanket."

"I have a call to make," Alvirah said with a sigh of relief. "But I don't want to make it until Stellina is found . . ."

"We're combing the city for her," Tracy said as his cell phone rang. He listened for a moment, then broke into a broad smile. "You can go ahead and make your call," he told Alvirah. "The little Blessed Mother was just picked up attempting to walk all the way to St. Luke's Hospital to see her nonna." He spoke into his phone. "Take her over there," he ordered. "We'll meet you at the hospital." He turned to Alvirah, who had picked up the phone that sat on an end table. "I presume you're trying to get in touch with the child's mother."

"Yes, I am." Let Sondra be in the hotel, Alvirah prayed.

"Ms. Lewis left a message that she is having dinner in the restaurant with her grandfather," the desk clerk said. "Shall I page her?"

When Sondra came on the line, Alvirah said, "As fast as you can, grab a cab and get up to St. Luke's Hospital."

Detective Tracy took the phone from her. "Forget the cab. I'm sending a squad car for you, ma'am. There's a little girl I'm sure you'll want to see."

.   .   .

Forty minutes later, Alvirah, Willy, Monsignor Ferris and Joe Tracy met Sondra and her grandfather outside Lilly's room in the hospital's cardiac care unit.

"She's in there with the woman who has raised her," Alvirah whispered. "We haven't told her about anything. That's for you to do."

White faced and trembling, Sondra pushed open the door.

Stellina was standing at the foot of the bed, her profile to them. The soft light seemed to halo the shining gold hair that spilled from beneath the blue veil.

"Nonna, I'm glad you're awake now, and I'm so glad you feel better," she was saying. "A nice policeman brought me here. I wanted you to see me in my beautiful dress. And see, I took very good care of my mother's cup." She held up the silver chalice. "We used it in the pageant, and I made my prayer—that my mother would come back. Do you think that God will send her to me?"

With a sob, Sondra crossed to her daughter's side, knelt down and folded her in her arms.

In the hallway, Alvirah pulled the door closed. "There are some moments that aren't meant to be shared," she said firmly. "Sometimes it's enough just to know that if you believe hard enough and long enough, your wishes can come true."

Epilogue

 Two nights later, on December 23rd, a capacity audience gathered at Carnegie Hall for the gala concert that would feature luminaries of the musical world and would be the New York debut for the brilliant young violinist Sondra Lewis.

In a prime center box, Alvirah and Willy were seated with Stellina; Sondra's grandfather; her boyfriend, Gary Willis; Monsignor Ferris; Sister Cordelia; Sister Maeve Marie and Kate Durkin.

Stellina, the object of countless curious glances, was seated right in the front row, her brown eyes sparkling with delight, blissfully unaware of the stir she was causing.

For two days the city newspapers had featured the story of the reunited mother and child and the recovery of the beloved chalice. It was a wonderful human-interest story and especially appropriate for the Christmas season.

The articles had featured pictures of Sondra and Stellina, and as Alvirah said, "Even a blind man could see Stellina's a clone of her mother. I can't believe it didn't hit me sooner."

When questioned about indicting Sondra for abandonment, the district attorney had said, "It would take a bigger Scrooge than even my enemies think I am to press charges against that young woman. Did she make an error by not ringing the bell of the rectory instead of running to a phone? Yes, she did. Did she, an eighteen-year-old kid, do her best to find a home for her baby? You bet she did."

To which the mayor had responded, "If he *had* indicted her, I'd have made his life miserable."

A wave of applause began as the conductor came onto the podium. The houselights dimmed, and the evening of exquisite music began.

Alvirah, splendid in a dark-green velvet dinner gown, reached for Willy's hand.

An hour later, Sondra appeared onstage to tumultuous applause. Monsignor Ferris leaned over to whisper, "As Willy would say, you did it again, Alvirah—and I'll never forget that you're the reason we have the bishop's chalice back. Too bad the diamond was lost, but the important thing is the chalice."

"I think Willy deserves the credit," Alvirah whispered in return. "If his sheet music for 'All Through the Night' hadn't been open on the piano, Sondra wouldn't have picked out the melody and sung it. That started me thinking; then when Stellina sang it in the pageant, I was sure."

As Sondra raised her bow, they settled back to listen. "Look at that child," Alvirah whispered to Willy, pointing to Stellina.

Clearly the little girl was transfixed by her mother's playing. Stellina's face shone with wonderment.

When the encore came, and Sondra began to play "All Through the Night," she looked up toward the box in which her daughter was seated. Audible only to those seated right around her, Stellina began to sing. No one could doubt that mother and daughter were performing to and for each other. For them, there was no one else in the world.

When the last notes died away, there was a hush. Then Willy leaned over and whispered, "Alvirah, honey, it's too bad I didn't bring my sheet music. They could have used a little piano accompaniment. What do you think?"

About the Author

Mary Higgins Clark is the author of twenty-three novels and three short-story collections, all of which have been national bestsellers. She lives with her husband, John Conheeney, in New Jersey.